THE
DUKE
OF
SEDUCTION

◆ *The Untouchables* ◆

USA TODAY
BESTSELLING AUTHOR

DARCY
BURKE

Chapter One

✦❦✦

Oh heart, know thou conquering hand.
Lush maiden, walking o'er the land.
With a word, she captures your mind,
Leaving life's burdens far behind.

-From An Ode to Miss Anne Berwick
by The Duke of Seduction

London, February 1818

LADY LAVINIA GILLINGHAM slipped into Lord Evenrude's library and gently closed the door behind her, blocking out the not too distant sound of the ball she'd just escaped. Knowing her time was short, she hurried to the bookshelves, her gaze scouring the spines for the book she sought. Ah, there it was.

The Geologic History of Cornwall.

Her heart picked up a bit of speed as she plucked it from the shelf and settled herself on a nearby settee. A fire burned in the grate, offering light along with the sconces on the walls and a small lantern atop a table near where she sat.

The tome wasn't terribly lengthy, and yet she still wouldn't have time to read it all. She'd do her best and perhaps find another opportunity to make her way into Lord Evenrude's library. He was a member of the

Royal Society, and if her parents wouldn't be shocked and horrified, she'd simply ask to borrow it. Her parents *would*, however, be shocked and horrified. So she conducted her research and studies in relative secret.

She soon lost herself in the description of the rocks and dirt of Cornwall and might have believed herself to be there if not for the sudden jolt of awareness that accompanied the soft press of lips—lips?—against her neck.

Gasping, she snapped the book closed and dropped it to the settee as she jumped to her feet. She turned to face the man bold enough to do such a thing. Lord Northam, of course.

Her eyes immediately narrowed. "What on earth are you doing?"

He had the grace to appear contrite. "I beg your pardon. I thought you were someone else."

"Of course you did." Lavinia didn't bother keeping the sarcasm from her tone.

He bowed, his tall, athletic frame bending with grace and elegance. "My deepest apologies. I didn't mean to interrupt your reading." His gaze dipped to the book, and he leaned forward slightly over the back of the settee, as if he were trying to read the title on the spine.

"Well, you did. And now I suppose I must leave so that you can meet your…lover." The word felt strange on her tongue, or maybe that was because she was alone in a secluded place with one of London's most notorious rakehells.

His eyes widened for the briefest moment. "Er, yes." He gave his head a sharp shake. "I mean, no. I'll leave you to your book."

"How kind of you, now that you've already caused

considerable disruption. I suppose as soon as I sit back down, your paramour will interrupt me too. No, I should be the one to leave." She began to step around the settee.

"Well, that is very thoughtful of—"

The sound of the door clicking open cut off his speech. "Hide under the desk," he hissed. "Quickly!" He turned abruptly and hurried to the door.

Or at least Lavinia assumed that was where he meant to go since she didn't stand there and watch. She spun about and threw herself beneath Lord Evenrude's pedestal desk. It was large enough for her to hide under, but open in the center so that if Northam's lady friend looked toward the desk, she'd likely see Lavinia's blue dress against the dark mahogany of the wood.

It was, however, the best she could do. In hindsight, she should have dashed behind the curtains at the window. On the other hand, this allowed her to see what was happening in the library.

On the other *other* hand, she probably didn't want to do that.

"Oh, Northam!" The breathy exclamation floated across the library, and Lavinia watched the sweep of a dark pink, flounced skirt as the woman turned toward the marquess, her hands sliding up around his neck.

Lavinia tensed as the woman stood on her toes, presumably to kiss him. Except Northam clasped her upper arms and gently held her away from him.

"I'm afraid we'll need to postpone our assignation."

"Why?"

Lavinia heard the pout in the woman's voice and gritted her teeth.

"Have you changed your mind?" She turned from him, and Lavinia squinted at the woman, whom she instantly recognized as Lady Fairwell, a young viscountess perhaps a few years older than Lavinia's twenty-three years. "Beatrice said you would, that you would tire of me very soon."

"Nonsense," he soothed as he reached for her and turned her back around, which gave Lavinia a bit of relief. His gaze darted toward Lavinia, and they made brief but pointed eye contact. She'd no idea what he meant to communicate, if anything, but she rolled her eyes at him. "I'm afraid someone might have seen me come this way. I was just going to leave when you arrived."

Lady Fairwell gasped. "I can't be discovered with you!"

Then perhaps you ought not be carrying on with a man who isn't your husband, Lavinia thought. She shook her head as she huddled beneath the desk.

"Of course not. You go back to the ball, and we'll find another time to meet."

"Promise?" Lady Fairwell wheedled.

"I promise."

Lavinia tried not to gag, particularly when Lady Fairwell stood on her toes again and pressed her mouth to his. The kiss was over as quickly as it had begun as the marquess set the viscountess away from him and gestured toward the door.

"Go quickly now," he urged.

She swept from the room, and the marquess locked the door.

Lavinia scooted out from the desk as he rushed over to help her up. She didn't bother taking his hand as she scrambled to her feet. In her haste, she stepped on the hem of her gown, which tripped her forward. Directly into Northam's arms.

He caught her close against him. "I've got you." His embrace was strong and sure, and he smelled of clove and leather. If he were anyone else, she might consider lingering a moment.

"And now you can let me go." She made sure her heel was free of her hem as he righted her on her feet.

"I was only trying to help," he said a bit defensively, his dark blond brows gathering together on his wide forehead as he stepped back.

"I don't require your assistance, Lord Northam."

He smoothed his hand over his lapel, his gray-green eyes narrowing slightly in a manner that only made him more attractive. Which he needed no help with—he was already one of the best-looking men in Britain. He was one of those gentlemen who looked dangerously handsome one moment—when he wasn't smiling as now—and dizzyingly charming the next when he *was* smiling, as he did in the next breath. "You know who I am?" His lips curved up, and his straight white teeth showed briefly.

Lavinia snorted and didn't care what he thought of it. "Everyone knows who you are."

"Then you have me at a disadvantage, for I have no inkling of your identity." His tone carried a hint of flirtation, but she imagined he couldn't help doing so.

"Nor should you." Though a part of her flinched in disappointment. *Oh, why should he know you?* They had absolutely no reason to cross paths. In fact, she should escape this interlude as soon as possible.

He blinked at her, clearly expectant. "Are you going to enlighten me?"

"No. I'm going to leave."

"Come, you must tell me your name, at least."

She sent him a dubious look. "Must I? We haven't

been properly introduced."

"Something tells me that wouldn't normally bother you," he said wryly.

She scowled at him. "Do not flirt with me. I am not taking the place of Lady Fairwell."

He cocked his head to the side. "My apologies, *again*. I didn't mean to suggest you should."

She straightened, then abruptly recalled what he'd told Lady Fairwell. "Did someone really see you come in here?" A rush of panic spiked up her spine.

"No, I said that to get Matilda—Lady Fairwell—to leave."

Relief poured through Lavinia, but she didn't want to tempt chance. "I need to do the same." She stepped around him on her way toward the door.

"You aren't going to say anything about this, are you?"

She half turned to see he'd pivoted and was watching her warily. "No. I don't like gossip."

"Be careful to look before you leave—just make sure no one is outside." He nodded helpfully with a placid but encouraging smile.

Blast. Her heart picked up speed as she went to the door. She unlocked and opened it slowly and only the barest fraction, just wide enough to peer outside and check to see if anyone was hanging about.

Satisfied that there was no one present, she slid through the crack and snapped the door shut behind her without a backward glance. Taking a deep breath, she smoothed her hands over her waist as she hurried to the ballroom. Just before she got there, she turned and looked back at the library, recalling that she'd left the book on the settee. She didn't dare go back to replace it on the shelf. Well, there was no help for it.

Lord Evenrude would know someone had read his book about Cornish rock formations.

Spinning back around, she ran square into another person, a young woman she didn't know.

Lavinia kept them both from falling. "Oh my goodness, I beg your pardon!"

"It's quite all right. I'm afraid I stole up behind you. I thought you were someone else." The young woman was perhaps a couple of years younger than Lavinia with bright red-gold hair and sharp blue-green eyes. "I'm Frances Snowden."

"How do you do? I'm Lady Lavinia Gillingham."

"Pleased to meet you. This is only my second ball, so I don't know very many people."

"Indeed?" Lavinia linked her arm through the other woman's. "Well, come along, Miss Snowden, and I'll introduce you to my friend, Miss Colton. We were just saying earlier that we need a third."

"A third?"

They moved into the ballroom, and Lavinia squinted as she steered them toward Sarah, who stood alone in the corner. Lavinia winced. When she'd left for the library, Sarah had been in the company of her mother.

"We used to be a trio," Lavinia said. "Until our friend Diana married a duke in December. We've missed having a third person in our group." They'd arrived at Sarah's side, and Lavinia withdrew her arm from Miss Snowden's. "With a third, there's less likelihood of anyone being alone." She gave Sarah an apologetic look. "I wouldn't have gone if I'd known your mother was going to abandon you."

"Well, you were gone a long time," Sarah said with a touch of curiosity in her gaze.

"Allow me to present Miss Frances Snowden,"

Lavinia said, gesturing toward their new addition. "It's her first Season, so, naturally, she needs us."

Sarah's blue eyes sparkled as she grinned. "Splendid! Do we know her sponsor?"

Lavinia looked to Miss Snowden, who answered. "That would be my sister, Her Grace, the Duchess of Clare."

Lavinia exchanged a look with Sarah before wincing toward Miss Snowden. "Perhaps you'll prefer different friends. We, er, we tend to hug the wall."

"On purpose?" Miss Snowden asked.

"Somewhat," Lavinia said. "It's our fourth Season, and we aren't—well, we aren't related to an Untouchable, if you understand my meaning."

Miss Snowden nodded knowingly. "My brother-in-law. The Duke of Desire." She leaned toward them, lowering her voice. "Did you know my sister and her friends came up with those names in the beginning? They regret it a bit since it seems to have run amok. Now there's a Duke of Every Single Thing. Or so it seems. Take this Duke of Seduction fellow. I don't suppose either of you know who he is?"

Sarah shook her head. "We don't. What do you know of him, Miss Snowden?"

"First, you must call me Fanny, and I'm afraid I couldn't possibly find different friends. I've already decided to like you both, so you're stuck with me. As to the Duke of Seduction, I probably know as much as you. He writes those gorgeous poems in the *Morning Chronicle*, and so far, two of the four women he's written about have avoided spinsterhood and either been married or betrothed."

"I believe the number will be three," Sarah said. "My mother informed me this evening that Miss Lennox is on the verge of becoming betrothed as well."

"Well, three of four, then," Fanny said with a grin. "Lucky them."

"Provided they are happy." Lavinia shuddered. "There's nothing worse than having to marry when you don't wish to."

"It seems you two have avoided such a fate," Fanny said. "Has it been difficult?"

Lavinia gave her a grim look. "Progressively so. I'm afraid we both need to obtain husbands this Season or find ourselves pushed into unions we may not have chosen."

"Surely your parents wouldn't make you marry someone you didn't want to." Fanny held up her hand. "Forget I said that. I know nothing of how the Marriage Mart is supposed to work. I am only here by the grace of my sister, and there is no pressure for me to wed, save what I expect."

Sarah looked at her intently. "And what is that?"

"To fall in love like my sister. To find a man who will look at me the way West—His Grace—looks at her." There was a wistful quality to her voice that Lavinia recognized.

"I think we all want that," Lavinia said with a half smile. For some inexplicable reason, she thought of Lord Northam. He was such a terrible rake. Did he want that? Or was he content to carry on temporary love affairs that likely had nothing to do with falling in love?

Sarah pivoted toward Fanny. "If you're hoping to fall in love, you may need to choose different friends. We aren't often asked to dance or promenade. As, Lavinia said, we're wallflowers."

"Well, I shall say just two things on that subject,"

Fanny said authoritatively. "One, I said I didn't want different friends, and I meant it. If you turn me away, it will be very cruel of you." She flashed a smile to show that she didn't think they would actually do that, and of course, they wouldn't ever. "Second, as I am a *horrendous* dancer, it's perhaps best that I align myself with people who don't dance."

This sent them all into a burst of laughter until Lavinia's eye caught a swirl of dark pink skirt nearby. She lifted her gaze and squinted at Lady Fairwell strolling past with another woman, their heads bent together in conversation.

As Lavinia watched them, she realized she hadn't told Sarah—and now Fanny—about her encounter with Northam. They'd simply been talking about other things, she told herself. She could mention it now.

His words came back to her as well as her response that she didn't like gossip. She'd never considered sharing information with her confidantes to be gossip, but Northam had expressed his desire that she not say anything. And she was a woman of honor. Or at least she tried to be.

Besides, there really wasn't anything to tell. She'd watched him extricate himself from Lady Fairwell's embrace. Then Lavinia had traded barbs with him. More accurately, she'd tossed barbs and he'd flirted. And he'd caught her in his arms. He'd also kissed her neck. A flush crept over her skin as she recalled the touch of his lips upon her flesh. She'd been kissed by the alluring Marquess of Northam. And she wasn't going to tell a soul.

"What sort of man would write poems about young women?" Sarah was asking as Lavinia sought to reenter the conversation after falling down a rabbit hole in her mind. It was, unfortunately, a rather common hazard, and one she'd become good at compensating for.

"It should have been a scandal," Lavinia said, as if she hadn't just gathered enough wool to outfit an entire regiment.

Sarah nodded in agreement, a dark curl brushing her temple. "And yet it wasn't."

"I daresay because his words were so lovely."

"And while they are clearly specific to his subject, he doesn't seem to be an intimate," Sarah said. "All the women he's written of have indicated they don't know who he is either. And clearly, he didn't want them for himself; otherwise, he would have made himself known."

He appeared to want to cast a glow on those who'd been relegated to the shelf, or almost anyway. Lavinia had met Miss Berwick, his first subject. And while they weren't close friends, Lavinia knew she was twenty-six years old and that her parents had decided not to press her on the Marriage Mart this Season. Miss Berwick was not a great beauty, and she was bookish and quiet. She seemed destined to be a governess. Until the Duke of Seduction had made her the most popular woman in London last fall. While Lavinia and Sarah had been at a house party, Miss Berwick had vaulted into the realm of the Untouchables. In January, she'd wed a widowed earl and become an instant mother to his two small children. She was, as evidenced by the thank-you letter she'd addressed to the Duke of Seduction and had published in the *Morning Chronicle*, ecstatically happy.

And now Lavinia had gathered enough wool to clothe a second regiment. She forced herself back to the conversation.

"Well, he must be a kind-hearted soul, if nothing

else," Fanny said. "What do you think he is, Lavinia?"

"Do you mean who?"

Sarah let out a short laugh. "I'm afraid she drifted off, Fanny. She does that sometimes." She turned to Lavinia. "We were pondering what sort of man he must be. Is he married? We decided that was doubtful, and yet he seems to have experienced love. We suspect a widower. And perhaps older. I would guess forty at least. He seems to have a wisdom younger bucks don't."

"Your deduction is sound," Lavinia said. "If he's a widower who's loved before, one might think he'd try to find love again. Why not court one of these young women he's singled out?"

Fanny tapped her finger against her chin. "An excellent question. Perhaps he doesn't think he can find love a second time."

"Or perhaps he's still so in love with his deceased wife that he simply can't love another." Sarah looked between them with a glazed expression.

"The excessively romantic tone of his poems certainly supports that," Lavinia said.

Fanny's lips tipped into a smile. "Perhaps he'll write a poem about one of you."

Sarah laughed, but Lavinia cringed inwardly. "I think that level of scrutiny might be rather unsettling." If she were to garner the focus of Society, she'd rather it be about something worthwhile, such as a geologic discovery, rather than whom she might or might not marry. "It's not going to happen, in any case. No, I think we're on our own, Sarah."

"Probably," she agreed with a sigh. "By Season's end, we'll be wed—or on our way to the altar—or we'll officially be spinsters."

Right now, Lavinia wasn't sure which she preferred.

WILLIAM BECKETT, MARQUESS of Northam, stared at the closed door for a moment before turning to survey the library in the hope that Lord Evenrude kept a bottle of whisky. Seeing none, Beck's gaze fell on the book the mystery woman had discarded on the settee.

Circling around the piece of furniture, he plucked it up and read the spine. *The Geologic History of Cornwall.* What sort of young woman read such a thing?

He thumbed through the tome for a moment and shook his head before looking for where it might have been on the shelf. Finding a space, he tucked it between two other books.

Geology. She'd stolen into a viscount's library to read about geology. He was suddenly embarrassed about his assignation, which was odd since he'd never been before. But then he'd never been up against a haughty young woman who had sought to use a library for its intended purpose, whereas he'd planned to sully it. Yes, embarrassment fit the moment.

A haughty young woman with spectacular chocolate eyes and hair the color of cinnamon. Good Lord, was he hungry? Or was it that she'd just been pretty enough to eat? No, not pretty. That wasn't the right description. She was attractive, but her chin was perhaps a trifle too strong and her cheeks too severe. She was captivating, in possession of some unidentifiable quality that made you want to know more about her in the hope of naming it.

And right now, he didn't even know *her* name. He turned and left the library and went in search of his friend Felix, the Earl of Ware. Finding him in the gaming room, he waited until Felix extricated himself from the card game and joined him near the door.

"Ready to go?" Felix asked.

"Not quite. Let's repair to the ballroom for a bit." He didn't wait for Felix to respond before turning and leading him to the door that led to the ballroom.

Felix groaned. "Why? If you're going to dance, I'm leaving without you." They'd planned to go to Brooks's Club as soon as Beck had completed his assignation.

"I'm not going to dance. I'm merely trying to find a woman."

"Didn't you just meet a woman?" Felix snorted. "You're insatiable."

Beck rolled his eyes. "Our plans were interrupted."

"I see. How disappointing. Do you need me to create a diversion so you can try again?" Felix was quite adept at causing a disruption, usually for the purpose of general hilarity, but occasionally to allow for Beck or someone else of their acquaintance to accomplish some other act. At Oxford, Felix had been rather notorious for his abilities. Now, he tended to use his skills for organization. No one planned a game or activity better than Felix.

Because of this skill, Felix tended to know people Beck didn't, though identifying a young miss on the Marriage Mart might be beyond even him. Like Beck, Felix steered fairly clear of those looking for a husband.

"I don't need a diversion," Beck said. "I need you to tell me who someone is."

They stepped into the ballroom, and Beck instantly felt a prick of annoyance. The whole notion of young women putting themselves on display as if they were vegetables at the market disgusted him. Society put far too much stock in how a woman looked and on her standing in their rigid hierarchy.

"Why are we trolling the ballroom?" Felix asked.

"I met a young woman earlier and didn't get her name. I'm hoping you might know her."

Felix stopped and stared at him. "A young woman? You detest the Marriage Mart. What the devil are you doing?"

Beck scowled as he tugged Felix's sleeve. "Don't stop. People will want to approach us to converse."

"And we wouldn't want that," Felix muttered. "Where is this astounding young woman?"

Continuing his perusal of the ballroom, Beck scoured the far corners. At last he saw her, huddled with two other young women. "Ten o'clock, in the corner. Cinn—red-brown hair. Blue dress. Taller than the other two she's with."

"I don't immediately recognize her, but then I can't get a good look at her," Felix said. "I'd suggest we move closer, but I'm guessing you'll say no."

"Perhaps a little." Beck led him closer to the wall.

Felix looked at him sharply. "We're into the wilds now. Why is this woman so important? And if you met her, why didn't you learn her name?"

"Never mind any of that. I'm simply curious."

"I see her now. That's Lady Lavinia Gillingham. She's a close friend of Sarah's. And that's Sarah to her right."

Beck turned to Felix and stopped. "Colton?"

Felix nodded. "Anthony's sister, yes."

Anthony Colton was one of Felix's closest friends. They'd grown up together.

"Do you want me to arrange a formal introduction?" Felix asked.

"That won't be necessary. I was merely curious." Lady Lavinia…*Gillingham*. Her father was an earl. And Beck had been closeted alone with her. Hell, he'd kissed her bloody neck. Suddenly feeling overheated, he wanted to beat a hasty retreat from the ballroom.

"I believe she's Sarah's bluestocking friend. Anthony says she's terribly smart and likely would've bested him at school."

That would perhaps explain her interest in geology. What sort of young woman left a ball to read a book? The interesting sort.

"Sarah's a bit of a wallflower, isn't she?" Beck asked as they left the ballroom.

"Yes, though I don't understand why she and her friends aren't wed," Felix said. "They're attractive, and they hail from good families."

"That isn't always enough." Beck kept the darkness from overtaking his tone, but the statement still came out gruff. He couldn't help it. He knew too well what young women went through and how whether they were accepted or successful could affect them. The familiar tightening of his chest stole his breath for a moment.

"To the club, then?" Felix asked.

"No, I think I'm done for the evening." Beck's mood had darkened, and his muse was dancing a merry tune in his head.

An hour later, he leaned back in his chair behind his desk and scrubbed his hand over his face. His cravat hung untied around his neck, and his coat lay on the floor. He unbuttoned his waistcoat as he stared down at the words he'd written. It wasn't his typical work, but then she wasn't his typical subject. Lady Lavinia didn't appear to be flirting with the shelf, but what did he really know?

Not much, and he usually tried to glean as much information as he could before launching a campaign. However, Lady Lavinia was different.

For some reason, he felt bad about his encounter with her earlier. He'd kissed her and flirted with her and generally put her in an uncomfortable situation. None of the other women he'd written about had suffered his abuse. Lady Lavinia had handled the entire affair with aplomb, evidencing an ability to take care of herself. Why, then, did he want to help her?

Because she deserved notice. She was intelligent and beautiful, and she was a *wallflower*. She ought to have her pick of gentlemen. And Beck would see that she did.

Chapter Two

❈

Sweetly loving is she, and chaste,
A glory to her sex, with grace.
A tribute of bone, blood, and pride,
Her heart is center in the sky.

-*From* An Ode to Miss Rose Stewart
by The Duke of Seduction

LAVINIA NIBBLED HER roll as she perused the *Botanical Magazine*. Breakfasts with her parents were always spent reading newspapers and magazines and generally ignoring each other. Her father sat to her right, and her mother, as was the norm, was late to the table.

The countess swept into the sitting room where they took breakfast overlooking the patio and small garden. She dropped into her seat at the small round table with a murmured "Good morning," which was met with a response of similar brevity and volume.

A few minutes later as Lavinia finished her roll and was intently reading about violets, her mother's shriek filled the air. Lavinia snapped her head up.

"What the devil is wrong with you?" her father asked with alarm.

"He's written a poem to Lavinia." Mother thrust the paper toward her husband as she turned an ecstatic grin to Lavinia. "*An Ode to Lady Lavinia Gillingham.*"

"Who?" her father asked gruffly, taking the newspaper and eyeing the text.

"The Duke of Seduction." Her mother's tone carried pride and enthusiasm.

Lavinia suddenly wanted to toss up the roll she'd just eaten. She didn't want his stupid poem or the attention it would bring.

Father looked at Lavinia over the newspaper, his eyes narrowing. "What nonsense is this? Has someone been courting you without speaking to me? What manner of blackguard behaves in such a manner?"

Her mother let out an exasperated sigh. "It's not like that. The Duke of Seduction writes poems about young women who need a nudge on the Marriage Mart. He's already written about four young women, and two have become either wed or betrothed."

Father blew out an impatient breath. "That doesn't mean I want him writing about my daughter."

"Not even if it will see her married by Season's end? She'll be instantly popular, just as the other young ladies have been."

Father set the paper down, and his expression went from irritated to interested. "By Season's end, you say?"

Lavinia fought the urge to jump to her feet and run from the room—or from the house entirely. "Or not. This could have no impact." She could only hope.

"Nonsense," her mother said with a shake of her head. "You're pretty enough, your father's an earl, and you've a dowry. You'll just need to keep your mouth closed more often than not and stop prattling on about rocks. I'm confident you can do that." The pleading light in her brown-eyed gaze proved she wasn't as confident as she said.

"She'd better," Father said. "It's past time you're

wed. We've allowed you to search for a gentleman you want, but perhaps your expectations are too high." He set the newspaper down next to Mother.

Ah yes, shared interest, mutual respect, love... Those were ridiculous to hope for.

"Most definitely," Mother agreed. "But now she'll have a wider range of gentlemen to choose from. Perhaps one will stand out and suffice."

Suffice. "Do either of you care that I'd rather not be the latest on-dit?"

Mother blinked. "Of course I care. But I don't understand. Why wouldn't you want to be the most popular girl in London, if only for a short time?"

It wasn't the popularity but the reason for it. If she could be renowned for some sort of scientific discovery, she'd gladly accept the attention. But to carry the burden of others' curiosity and intrusiveness wasn't something she desired. And she had the bloody Duke of Seduction to blame for it. She wondered how his other subjects felt about the notoriety. Apparently, they didn't mind, since two—and likely three—of them were now betrothed. Who was the fourth? Perhaps Lavinia would seek her out...

The countess picked up the paper and handed it to Lavinia. "Don't you want to read your poem?"

"Not particularly." If it was like the others, it would be a mosaic of lovely words and charming phrases. It would be beautiful and complimentary without any hint of intimacy. She thought of the gentlemen she knew and tried to imagine which one could be this presumptuous duke. So presumptuous that he'd even given himself his own ducal nickname.

She and her friends had been silly to think of him as kindhearted. The man was a menace, and Lavinia meant to unmask him to put a stop to this madness.

Mother pouted. "It's a very nice poem. His finest yet, I think. He even extolls your intellect. Clearly, he knows you."

Lavinia tried to resist reading the poem, but if the man had written of her intelligence, she was curious. Without picking up the newspaper, she arched her neck to read the words. It wasn't terribly long, but then none of them were, if she recalled. Three or four stanzas. Hers was four.

"Perhaps there will be a second poem." Her mother's hopeful tone drew Lavinia to look up from the paper.

"I should hope not." Though Lavinia was fairly certain he'd written more than one poem about each of his subjects. Except, perhaps, his last one—Miss Jane Pemberton.

Father gave her a pointed stare, his dark brown eyes boring into hers. "This could be a boon for you, and you'll treat it as such. I'm weary of funding Seasons," he grumbled.

"Yes, do look at it as a boon," her mother cajoled. "We'll get to the park a bit early today and see what happens." She rose from the table. "We must select your finest walking ensemble! Come, let us prepare." She turned and started from the breakfast room.

Lavinia could feel what little freedom she possessed slipping away.

"Get up, then," her father said loudly, but not yelling.

Burying her frustration, Lavinia stood and followed her mother from the room. She cursed the Duke of Seduction with every step.

It was, thankfully, a temperate afternoon as they walked into the park at nearly a quarter past four. They were a trifle early, but still within the realm of fashion. Or so Lavinia's mother said. She'd also said that Lavinia was not to speak of rocks, dirt, or anything to do with science.

Still wishing the Duke of Seduction a series of misfortunes, Lavinia had managed to dash off notes to Sarah and Fanny earlier that afternoon asking them to meet her in the park.

They waited just inside the Grosvenor Gate, and Lavinia was eager to go to them. She expected her mother to chastise her for immediately joining her friends, but the countess was quite busy with her own group of women, who, given their frequent looks toward Lavinia, were assaulting her with questions about the Duke of Seduction.

It had already begun.

"Let us walk," Lavinia said, wanting to leave the vicinity as soon as possible. She was permitted to walk with her friends along the footpath to the Serpentine and back.

Sarah fell into step on Lavinia's left and Fanny on the right.

"So my prognostication came true," Fanny said, but without pride or excitement. "He did write about one of you." She looked at Lavinia with concern, her brow creased in straight, neat pleats. "Clearly you are not pleased."

Lavinia gritted her teeth. "I don't want to be interesting because some anonymous man says I am."

"But his motives seem pure," Fanny said, though her voice held a bit of question.

"How do we really know?" Lavinia asked as a cool breeze stirred the ribbons of her bonnet beneath her chin. "Perhaps if he made himself known, we could understand his true reasoning. This anonymity lends a rather sinister air, don't you think?"

"Sinister?" Sarah laughed. "Lavinia is being dramatic, Fanny. She does that sometimes. She can also be rather fearless, and I guarantee if she knew the identity of the Duke of Seduction, she'd call him out on his behavior posthaste."

"Indeed I would. Which is why I'd like to find out who he is."

"Of course you would," Sarah said. "We all would."

"But I have reason to, beyond curiosity. He is meddling in my affairs, my *life*."

"Yes, dramatic," Sarah murmured.

Lavinia scowled at her dearest friend. "How would you feel if he wrote a poem about *you*? You may be next, after all."

Sarah cocked her head to the side. "I'm not sure how I would feel, but if it meant I might dance more or perhaps meet the man of my dreams, I would appreciate the assistance." She turned toward Lavinia. "Maybe you'll meet the man you're destined to fall in love with."

"Or maybe I'll meet someone my parents will marry me off to who won't support my endeavors."

"Your geology, you mean," Fanny said.

Lavinia had shared her interests with Fanny yesterday when she and Sarah had called on her. They'd solidified the friendship they'd started the night before at the Evenrudes' ball.

Sarah exhaled. "You oughtn't be pessimistic. Why not see what happens?"

"My parents have forbidden me to speak of geology or anything else I find interesting. How am I to ascertain if a gentleman and I will suit?"

Wincing, Sarah ducked her head. "I see what you mean."

Lavinia linked her arm through Sarah's. "I know you're trying to find the bright side of this, and I love you for it. I *shall* try to do the same. I'd like to speak with Miss Pemberton."

"Why is that?" Fanny asked.

Lavinia took Fanny's arm so they were all linked as they moved toward the Serpentine. "I'm curious what this did for her marriageability, whether it's been a help or a hindrance."

"But we already know it's been a help to at least two of his subjects, if not three," Fanny said.

"So it seems. But do we know if they're all happy?" Lavinia planned to withhold judgment until she spoke to one or more of them.

"Well, that wouldn't necessarily be the Duke of Seduction's fault, would it?" Sarah asked. "He merely elevated their visibility. What happened next could be due to a number of influences."

"I'm beginning to agree with Lavinia," Fanny said. "It's a dangerous game the Duke of Seduction has started. Even if his motivation is charitable, who's to say a young lady wants to be managed in this way?"

Lavinia nodded sharply, smiling. "My point exactly!"

"This looks like trouble."

A loud masculine voice drew Lavinia to squint down the path at three men coming their way. Due to the setting sun and her myopia, she wasn't able to identify them right away.

Sarah, bless her, knew of Lavinia's nearsightedness and leapt to the rescue. "Trouble," she scoffed. "You're the trouble, Anthony."

Anthony was her brother, so Lavinia knew at least

one of them. The space between them lessened, and she recognized the one to his left—the bloody Marquess of Northam.

"Good afternoon, dear sister," Anthony said with a bow. "You know Felix, of course." He gestured to his right to the Earl of Ware. Lavinia had met him before too.

"Of course." Sarah gestured to Fanny, and Lavinia unlinked her arms from theirs. "Allow me to present our new friend, Miss Frances Snowden, sister to the Duchess of Clare."

Anthony's dark brows climbed up his forehead. "Auspicious company, sister."

"No more than you." Sarah inclined her head toward Northam.

"Have you not met Northam?" Anthony asked. "I presume he doesn't really require an introduction. This is the Marquess of Northam."

The marquess gave a sweeping bow directed at all three of them, but his gaze landed solely on Lavinia. "I'm so pleased to make your acquaintance."

Her name hadn't yet been mentioned, but she was certain he knew it already. How? Had he asked after her? Had Anthony told him as they'd approached along the path? Oh bother, did it really *matter*? She'd only withheld her identity from him the other night to be contrary. Because he'd kissed her neck thinking she was his paramour. A shiver danced along her spine. She blamed it on the decreasing temperature.

"This is my dear friend, Lady Lavinia Gillingham," Sarah offered.

"Lady Lavinia." Northam's eyes glinted, and though Lavinia couldn't see the color from the distance, she knew from their encounter in Lord Evenrude's library that they were a gray green. Like moss on a tree hidden deep in the forest. A secret-keeping tree.

A secret-keeping tree? Good heavens, she was the recipient of one flattering poem and suddenly she was waxing romantic.

"Where are you ladies headed?" Anthony asked.

"The Serpentine," Sarah said, glancing at the dimming sky. "Though I wonder if we ought to turn back." Clouds had moved in, and, coupled with the sun setting, twilight was coming quickly.

"May we escort you?" Northam asked politely. He'd thankfully directed his attention toward Sarah for the question. Lavinia took a moment to relax—and reflect upon why he set her on edge.

Sarah exchanged looks with both Lavinia and Fanny before agreeing to his offer.

They turned and started along the path. Somehow, Lavinia ended up in the rear with the marquess. She refused to let him rattle her. Or think about his lips on her flesh.

"May I apologize again for the other evening?" he asked.

"You can apologize every day for eternity if you like. You don't owe me any explanation or excuse. There was, thankfully, no harm done."

"Save the book you left on the settee," he murmured.

She turned her head toward him. "Why bring that up?"

"I was interested in your selection. *The Geologic History of Cornwall?*" He tipped his head. "I replaced it on the shelf for you."

"That was the least you could do after interrupting me."

His mouth split into a grin. "So it was."

Lavinia ignored the way her stomach tilted when he smiled like that. "Were you able to meet with Lady—I mean *your paramour* later?" She shook her head and fixed her gaze forward. She'd meant to tease him, but realized it was an inappropriate question. "Never mind." Why was she trying to tease him? To put herself at ease?

"I was not, alas. In fact, I haven't seen her since."

The urge to taunt him took over. "Careful, you're going to lose your rake status."

He laughed, too loud at first, drawing the attention of the others who turned their heads. Quickly stifling his mirth, he waved his hand. "I made a bad pun. Not worth repeating." He flashed a smile for good measure, which Lavinia suspected would distract just about anyone from pressing him.

They walked in silence for a moment as conversation flowed in front of them. At last, he whispered, "Are you teasing me, Lady Lavinia?"

He'd moved a bit closer. The timbre of his voice, and his proximity, sent another shiver along her flesh—this time across her shoulders. If she closed her eyes, she was certain she'd feel the touch of his mouth on her neck.

No, she wasn't going to think of that.

"Inappropriately." She kept her voice low. "My apologies."

"You must never apologize to me," he said. "Remember, I am to beg your forgiveness until the end of my days."

Now he was teasing her. Or flirting. Yes, flirting. That was what he'd done the other night. She peered sideways at him. "Are you capable of conversing with a woman without flirtation?"

"Yes, but I understood my rake status was in question, and I can't have that."

Oh, he was good. She'd give him that. Lavinia allowed a smile while she quashed a giggle.

"I've done it," he said, rejoicing rather quietly, presumably not to draw the others' attention again. "I've made you smile."

"It's not hard," she said with more than a bit of sarcasm. "I am generally regarded as a jovial sort." She narrowed her eyes at him. "Why do you want to make me smile?"

"I'm merely being friendly."

"Are we to be friends?" She gave him a wry look. "Do you have many young, unmarried female friends?"

He laughed again, but softly this time. "No. You would be my first."

"I'm afraid I don't count any marquesses among my close acquaintance. And given your…reputation, I'm afraid a friendship between us wouldn't be acceptable."

"Because Society would frown on that." The flat tone of his response surprised her.

"And you frown on Society's rules?"

"When they don't make sense, yes. Why can't unmarried men and women be friends?"

He'd spoken that question too loudly, and it was far too provocative to ignore.

"Because something inappropriate will happen," the Earl of Ware said. He stared at the marquess and shook his head. "Have you gone daft, Beck?"

Everyone laughed at this, except Lavinia, who stole a look at the man beside her. Beck. The name suited him. Strong, succinct, with an edge and also somehow charming. He was a dangerous man because of his reputation, and yet she couldn't help find him engaging.

And it wasn't because of the way his kiss had made her tingle.

Well, maybe a little.

The conversation continued as the Grosvenor Gate came into view, albeit fuzzily for Lavinia.

"Unmarried men and women can be friends," Sarah said, shooting a haughty look toward Ware. "I've known you for years, Felix. Doesn't that make us friends?"

Anthony scoffed. "No, that makes Felix *my* friend and you my sister."

"I have to side with Miss Colton on this," the marquess said. "If she's known Ware for years and Ware is a good friend of her brother's, doesn't it follow that they are also friends?"

The earl glowered at Northam. "Shh! Don't let anyone hear you. Just suggesting such a thing will see us married off before spring." He sent an apologetic wince at Sarah. "Not that marriage to you would be horrible, but I think we can both agree that we wouldn't suit."

"God, no," Anthony said. "Perish the thought."

Sarah pursed her lips at them. "Lucky for both of you I agree. Otherwise, I might be gravely offended."

"I'm beginning to think London is mad," Fanny said quietly, her gaze moving over everyone.

Northam grinned. "Then you've got the right of it."

"There you are!" Lavinia's mother swooped in like a bird of prey. And Lavinia certainly felt trapped. "There are people who want to meet you." She flicked a glance toward Sarah and her brother, whom they had, of course, known for years. It was clear Mother preferred Lavinia capitalize on her newfound celebrity than squander time with her friends.

"I was meeting new people, Mother," she said sweetly. "Do you know the Marquess of Northam?"

It seemed the countess hadn't even noticed him, for her eyes widened briefly. She quickly recovered and offered a curtsey. "I am not certain if we've been introduced. It's a pleasure, my lord."

He bowed in response. "The pleasure is mine." He extended his bow to Lavinia. "Thank you for the promenade, Lady Lavinia."

They exchanged farewells, and the trio of gentlemen departed, while Sarah retreated to her mother and Fanny joined her sister and some other ladies.

"You promenaded with the marquess?" her mother asked. "He must have read the poem." She clasped her hands together and smiled widely. "It's already working!"

"I don't know if he read it or not, Mother. He was simply with Anthony when we encountered them on the path. It would have been rude for us not to be introduced. He also met Fanny."

Mother pressed her lips together. "She *is* the sister-in-law of a duke. But it's only her first Season." Her tone turned cross. "It's your turn, not hers."

"It doesn't work that way, Mother," Lavinia said with a sigh.

Shaking her head and, seemingly, the irritation away, the countess forced a bright smile. "Come, there are some people who wanted to meet you and others who wanted to say hello. You are in demand now, my dear. And it's about time."

As Lavinia turned to walk with her, she could only hope that time would be short-lived. The sooner she could return to blessed anonymity, the better.

TWO DAYS LATER, Beck stood from his breakfast table feeling pleased. The third woman he'd written about, Miss Lennox, had just become engaged to Mr. Laurence Sainsbury. That made three women he'd helped secure matrimonial success. He could only hope Miss Pemberton and Lady Lavinia would enjoy the same outcome.

Beck went into his study, where his gaze immediately fell on the small portrait of his half sister that sat on his desk. With her dark hair and petite frame, Helen took after her mother, Beck's father's first wife. Helen's solemnity was evident in the likeness, her green eyes dark and serious, her mouth set into a slightly sad tilt. Or maybe he attributed his own sadness to the image. Every time he looked at her, he felt a pang of sorrow and regret. If he'd been older, he could have helped her. He would have done anything to keep her safe and happy. But at thirteen, he'd been far too young to do anything but watch helplessly as she'd fallen prey to the cruelties of Society.

All he could do now was try, somehow, to help those who needed it. He didn't want any young woman to endure what she had. And it seemed he was making a difference.

He missed those of his family who were gone—Helen, his father, his mother. He still had his oldest half sister, with whom he wasn't terribly close, and her family, as well as his stepmother, Rachel, and his half brother. George was only eleven, but his education as the next Marquess of Northam was already well underway.

Bypassing the desk, Beck went to the corner where

he kept his guitars—three of them. Picking up his favorite, he strummed his fingers over the strings, mindlessly at first and then plucking a tune. It was, in some ways, easier than words, whether verbal or written. With music, he could let loose of everything trapped inside him until he was empty.

He lost himself for a few minutes, or maybe it was an hour, playing whatever leapt to his mind, following a path of emotion and discovery. He felt much better when he finished, not that he'd felt bad to begin with. Music just made everything better.

A light rap on the door, which he'd left ajar, drew his attention. "Come."

His butler, the exceedingly efficient and supportive Gage, stepped inside. "I'm not disturbing you, am I, my lord?" Gage was always careful to wait until there was a lull in the music.

"Not at all. You have today's post there?" Beck met him near the door.

"Yes." He handed Beck the stack of missives, and Beck continued to his desk.

Gage followed him, his tall, muscular frame moving with a grace that belied his fifty or so years. "I liked what you were playing at the end there."

Beck moved behind the desk and looked up from sifting through his correspondence. "Thank you. A work in progress."

"One of your finer pieces, in my opinion."

Recognizing his solicitor's hand, Beck opened that missive and found what he was expecting—another letter from the editor of the *Morning Chronicle*. He skimmed the missive and provided a summary for Gage. "He wants more poems. Apparently, circulation is up." He dropped the letters on his desk and gave his butler a wry look.

"Unsurprising. The Duke of Seduction is quite popular, even among the servants." Gage shook his head, which still sported a thick mane of dark hair shot with silver. "No, none of them realize you are him."

For a moment, Beck had tensed. Now he blew out a breath in relief. Gage was the only person who knew of his secret identity, and Beck trusted him completely. "I can't write them too quickly," Beck said. "Each of them needs time to reap the benefits and hopefully make a match." He'd worried that he hadn't let enough time lapse before writing the poem about Lady Lavinia, but he'd been too eager to help her.

"You don't have to write a poem about a young lady in need of attention," Gage offered. "In fact, you needn't write anything new at all. Your catalog of work is extensive."

Gage had been his valet when he'd left Oxford, and Beck had promoted him after the former butler had retired following Beck's father's death. Because he'd been with Beck for so long, he knew more about Beck's life than anyone. That included his music, his poetry, and his masquerade as the Duke of Seduction. In fact, the nickname had been Gage's idea.

"I don't want to publish any of that," Beck said, repeating something he'd said on many occasions. The truth was that Gage was wearing him down. Maybe in another ten years, he'd be ready.

"I know you say it's too dark, but it's honest and beautiful. And some of it is quite romantic."

"If you mean in the way that Romeo and Juliet is romantic, then yes." Beck managed not to roll his eyes.

Gage chuckled. "All right, some of it leans to the tragic, but not all of it."

Beck arched a brow at him. "You think you've read even half?"

"Of course I wouldn't know. You are rather prolific, and I know there are things you don't share. Even with me."

That much was true. Beck kept his gaze from falling to the portrait of Helen.

"I understand Miss Lennox is engaged to be married," Gage said.

Beck nodded. "To Sainsbury. It's a good match. I think. What do I know?"

"Any hint of success with the others? Though I suppose it's too soon to tell with the last."

Yes, it was, but from everything Beck had observed and heard over the past two days, Lady Lavinia's popularity had risen dramatically. He still couldn't believe it had taken his intervention. She was exceptionally witty. He'd quite enjoyed their banter at the park the other day.

"I am optimistic on both counts," Beck said. "And I think I know who the next one will be." He felt he owed it to Lady Lavinia's friend Miss Colton to provide the same assistance. Her brother Anthony would likely appreciate it.

Gage's dark blue eyes flashed with surprise. "Already?"

"She's a friend of Lady Lavinia's. And the sister of a friend."

"You have a kind and generous soul," Gage said softly. "Sometimes I wonder, however, if you help others because you really want to help yourself."

The words hit Beck in the gut, making him flinch inwardly. "You think I need help?"

"That's not what I said. Forgive me if I'm speaking

out of turn."

Beck made a noise that was part grunt and part scoff. "You know that's impossible."

Gage was a father and a friend and an irreplaceable helper all in one. He was the one constant Beck allowed himself to rely on. His stepmother's focus was on her young son, as it should be. As Beck's parents' had been on him when he'd been young. Until Helen had died. And then it had all fallen apart.

"I don't know about *that*." Gage's tone was light, but there was truth in what he said. Beck kept some things close to himself, and once in a while, Gage tread too close. In those few instances, Beck had told him to back away. And one time in particular, Beck may have lost his temper. He didn't do it often, but when he did, there were usually casualties.

Beck turned his mind back to what Gage had said— that he helped others in an effort to help himself. That made sense, he supposed. And now he wanted to write about that. But first his correspondence beckoned.

A sound from outside drew them both to rush to the window facing the street. A coach was tilted, its wheel having fallen off. Without a word, Beck hurried from the study to the hall, Gage fast on his heels.

The late morning was cool, with a thick cloud cover. Beck glanced up, thinking it could rain. The sooner they cleaned up the mess on the street, the better.

He dashed to the coach as the coachman was opening the door and asking the occupant if she was all right.

"Are you injured, my lady?" The poor coachman sounded severely distraught.

Beck turned to Gage. "Fetch Cartwright."

Gage took himself off to the mews to get the head

groom.

Beck pivoted back to the coach just as the occupant emerged. "Lady Fairwell." He didn't bother hiding his surprise.

Her cheeks flushed a dark pink. It could have been due to the cold or the excitement of the accident, but Beck wasn't sure it was either. "Lord Northam, what a surprise to see you here. Do you live nearby?"

Though she'd never been to his house, of course, he suspected she knew where he lived. "Yes, right there." He turned his head and pointed to his house.

"Oh, I didn't realize." She smiled prettily as the coachman went to investigate what had happened with the wheel.

Beck wasn't sure he believed her, not that it mattered. "My head groom is coming to help. Hopefully, we can get this repaired and see you on your way before it rains."

"Perhaps you could take her ladyship home?" the coachman asked, his gaze tinged with concern. "Or keep her inside if the rain starts?"

"I'm happy to wait inside."

Beck turned his head to see Matilda smiling, a glint of anticipation lighting her eyes.

Beck considered the situation. It wouldn't necessarily be a scandal to invite her inside under the circumstances, but he didn't want to. He went to her side and spoke in a near whisper. "It's probably best if you don't come in."

She fluttered her lashes in open flirtation. "Why not? My coach is wrecked, and it's going to rain. In fact, I think I just felt a drop."

Where? The wide brim of her bonnet shielded her face, and the rest of her was covered with gloves, gown, and pelisse. Furthermore, he hadn't felt a thing.

Beck looked into the street to see if he could see any drops falling. But what he saw were neighbors who'd come outside to investigate what had happened. Mrs. Law, a notorious gossip, lived across the street. She came toward them, and Beck knew there wouldn't be an assignation between him and Matilda, not that he wanted one. In fact, there wouldn't be an assignation ever again. Their affair was effectively over due to this scene.

He was surprisingly relieved. "I can't invite you inside, Tilly," he said quietly, eyeing Mrs. Law's approach. "Not now, not ever."

She sucked in a breath. "So you *were* trying to end things the other night when you shoved me out of Lord Evenrude's library. You're a beast."

Gage had returned with Cartwright, and Beck was fairly certain the butler had heard her comment.

Then Mrs. Law was upon them. Her gaze fell on Beck and narrowed. "My goodness, Lord Northam, couldn't you see fit to even don a *coat*? Let alone a hat or gloves?"

"I was in a rush to make sure the occupants of this damaged coach were all right. I see you made sure to dress yourself for an excursion before you bothered to come outside." He kept his tone light and cheery but knew she'd feel the sting of his words. Gossipy, obnoxious women like her deserved them.

"As it happens, I do have an excursion," she said with considerable hauteur. She turned to Lady Fairwell. "May I offer you a ride home, Lady Fairwell?"

"Yes, thank you." She turned a perturbed stare on Beck. "Thank you for your *assistance* with my coach."

Beck offered a bow. "It's our pleasure, my lady. I'll

see that your repaired vehicle is delivered home. Your husband can rest assured it will be returned to him in excellent, if slightly worn, condition."

He hadn't meant to make a double entendre or deliver an insult, but realized he had. As a writer, his brain sometimes made connections it shouldn't. And as a man, sometimes those connections formed words that were perhaps better left unsaid. Ah well, it was too late now.

Matilda's eyes widened the barest fraction, and her lips parted briefly before she pressed them closed. Without another word, she turned and left with Mrs. Law.

"Have a good afternoon," Beck called after them. He went to where Cartwright leaned over the broken carriage with Matilda's coachman. No, not Matilda any longer, *Lady Fairwell*. "Can it be repaired?"

Cartwright looked up from where he knelt on the street. "I think so, my lord. We'll do our best to get it fixed posthaste. Philip and Fred are on their way with tools."

Beck knew the situation was in good hands with his grooms. "Excellent. Let me know if you need anything." He turned and walked back to the house. Gage beat him there, opening the door for him.

Once inside, Gage closed the door behind them. "Your latest paramour, I presume? Lady Fairwell, I mean, not Mrs. Law. The latter would be quite a shock."

"Why? I'm confident Mrs. Law has amusements outside her marriage. Have you noticed the way she looks at you?" Beck sent Gage a sideways glance tinged with humor. His butler, a widower, was quite good-looking. He drew stares from all classes wherever he went.

Gage rolled his eyes. "I meant because you wouldn't give her the time of day. She is not the sort of woman you pass time with."

No, she wasn't. He detested the gossips and the purveyors of opinion and judgment. "Yes, Lady Fairwell was my latest paramour."

"Was, my lord? I take it you weren't writing songs about her this morning? Or poems about her last night?"

"Yes, past tense. It was a short-lived affair, which suits me fine." In fact, he hadn't written a thing about Matilda. Last night's subject matter, as it so often was, had been a concoction of his imagination—a bluestocking whose attributes were ignored to everyone else's detriment.

He suddenly realized she was perhaps not entirely a fabrication.

Shaking thoughts of Lady Lavinia from his head, he turned. "Back to my correspondence."

As Beck entered his study, he felt a pull to the guitar once more. A ballad began to fill his mind, but it wasn't yet formed. He'd let it compose and cure, and later, he'd write it down. Unless it flitted away, as so many ideas did.

Not every notion was worthy of words. But the best of them could create…magic.

Chapter Three
❧3❧

She walks soft, her steps kiss the sand.
Her copper hair glows in each strand.
She speaks sure, with wisdom and wit,
To her charm, I wholly submit.

-From An Ode to Lady Lavinia Gillingham
by The Duke of Seduction

HOPEFULLY TONIGHT'S MUSICAL *performance will be entertaining.*

Lavinia determined that was the only way the evening would be saved. After a second poem, *A Song for Lady Lavinia Gillingham*, addressing her attributes had appeared in that morning's paper, she'd wanted to bury her head in a book and stay in her room for a week. Her parents, however, had differing ideas.

Mother was ecstatic and had even insisted on dragging Lavinia—and Sarah, since she loved shopping, and Lavinia would *never* turn down an opportunity to have her best friend at her side—to Bond Street that afternoon for something new for Lavinia to wear this evening.

They'd actually found a ready-made gown that required only minor alterations, and so now Lavinia found herself outfitted in the most recent evening fashion. The gown was ivory with a small repeating pattern of pink flowers with green leaves. The hem bore a wide flounce with a ruffled edge and was topped with rosettes of pink silk. The short sleeves and bodice were worked with more of the pink silk and another ruffled edge. A matching wrap completed the ensemble along with a pair of ivory gloves, ivory slippers, and a bandeau for her head with another trio of pink rosettes. With the floral pattern and the profusion of rosettes and pink, she felt like a bloody garden.

Sarah had assured her she would look lovely and would be the envy of every woman at the musical performance. Upon arriving, Lavinia squinted over the attendees in an attempt to find Sarah, but couldn't locate her. Instead, she noticed Miss Pemberton, who'd received the Duke of Seduction's attentions before Lavinia.

Without pause, Lavinia marched over to the young woman who stood with a couple who were probably her parents. Miss Pemberton's eyes lit with recognition as Lavinia approached.

"Good evening, Lady Lavinia."

"Good evening, Miss Pemberton. Might we take a turn?"

"Yes, let's." Miss Pemberton turned to her mother and excused herself, then linked her arm with Lavinia. They started off on a circuit of the Fortescues' large drawing room. "I'm so glad you came to speak with me."

"I thought it prudent that we join forces," Lavinia said.

Miss Pemberton's pale blonde head tipped forward. "Because of this Duke of Seduction nonsense."

Lavinia blinked at her, thrilled to hear she thought it was nonsense. "I'm so glad we agree. It's ludicrous.

The attention, I mean. No one cared who I was or what I did until he wrote a poem."

"A poem that isn't based on anything," Miss Pemberton scoffed. "I don't know a single gentleman who could—or should—write such things about me."

"Me neither. It should be a scandal, but since it's worked for three young ladies, it's suddenly acceptable."

"Enviable even," Miss Pemberton said with distaste. "My mother thinks it's the best thing that could have happened to me."

"Mine too!" It felt so good to have an ally. Sarah and Fanny had, of course, been incredibly supportive, but they hadn't endured it. Miss Pemberton had.

"The attention might not be such a bother if the men were genuine." Miss Pemberton peered at her with pale-lashed, light brown eyes.

Lavinia wasn't sure she agreed with the former sentiment, but the latter was certainly true. "They're just too fulsome with their praise, aren't they?"

"What an excellent word," Miss Pemberton said. "Yes, that's it exactly." She pursed her lips. "And yet three women have found happiness."

"Or so it seems," Lavinia noted darkly.

"Actually, I can attest to Miss Stewart's contentment. She is quite thrilled to be marrying Mr. Allardyce in a few days. Theirs seems a love match."

Lavinia felt a slight pang of jealousy, as she always did when she learned of a couple who had married for love—like her friend Diana, who'd wed the Duke of Romsey two months ago. In fact, Diana and Romsey had arrived in town just yesterday, and Lavinia was eager to see her.

"I'm delighted to hear of Miss Stewart's success,"

Lavinia said.

"If you call marriage success." There was an unmistakable edge of disdain to Miss Pemberton's tone.

"You aren't in favor of marriage?"

Miss Pemberton shrugged. "I hate that we judge a woman's 'success' by her ability to wed."

Lavinia stopped short and angled herself toward Miss Pemberton. "It's as if we were separated at birth."

Miss Pemberton laughed. "Except your hair is much darker and you are much taller than me."

"Only a few inches," Lavinia said, smiling. She turned, and they started walking once more. "I really am glad Miss Stewart is happy. That's really all that matters. What other people think doesn't matter."

With a nod, Miss Pemberton tugged at the necklace adorning her throat. "I agree. I do hope Miss Lennox is happy too."

"We should find out." Lavinia frowned. "Not that it matters if she isn't. Since she's betrothed, she's as good as married."

"That's certainly true." Miss Pemberton exhaled. "Society's rules are terrible, aren't they? Just look at the Duke of Kilve and the Duchess of Romsey. Their betrothal crumbled, and it didn't seem to bother either one of them—or their new spouses. Yet, they've been the center of all manner of speculative gossip." She was speaking of Lavinia's friend Diana.

"Actually, I know all the parties involved," Lavinia said. "They are as happy as anyone could be."

Miss Pemberton's fair brows climbed with interest. "You know them? I'm so delighted to hear things ended up as they should have done."

"Yes, though that won't stop a certain portion of

Society from being malicious about it." At least that was what Lavinia expected. Already, she'd heard mumblings about Diana and her husband—and Kilve and his wife, who was a lovely woman Lavinia had met last fall.

"They love fresh gossip—the more salacious, the better. I'm sorry to say your friend may be in for a rough patch." Miss Pemberton let out a soft chuckle. "On the other hand, it will take some of the focus off us."

Lavinia would never wish her friend to suffer in her place, but recognized that Miss Pemberton could be right.

"Actually, I should thank you," Miss Pemberton said. "When your poem appeared last week, things relaxed a bit for me. My mother wasn't happy about it, however." Her tone said she cared not one whit.

Lavinia laughed. "Glad I could help." She squinted across the drawing room as they neared their starting point. "Who do you suppose he is?"

"The Duke of Seduction?" Miss Pemberton joined her in searching the throng. "I've tried to work it out, but I can't imagine who would write like that. Unless Lord Byron has stolen back into London without anyone noticing."

Lavinia laughed again. "*That* would not go unnoticed."

"Certainly not," Miss Pemberton said with a grin. "I will let you know if I discern any clues. I *have* looked."

"I find myself listening intently to gentlemen, trying to determine if they speak in a similar cadence."

Miss Pemberton nodded enthusiastically. "I do the same. Unfortunately, the gentlemen think I'm terribly interested, which is usually not the case." She flashed another smile that made Lavinia laugh.

"I wonder why we haven't become friends before now," Lavinia said. "You must call me Lavinia. You are welcome to join me and my friends Miss Sarah Colton and Miss Frances Snowden anytime."

Miss Pemberton appeared genuinely surprised and pleased. "Thank you. My mother tends to keep me on a rather short tether, but since the poems, she's begun to let me loose. She reasons that I need to be accessible to suitors. Whatever that means."

"Good heavens, she isn't trying to see you compromised?"

"No." Miss Pemberton cocked her head to the side. "At least I couldn't imagine her doing such a thing. She's a terrible prude. Honestly, I've long since given up on trying to understand her. We couldn't be more dissimilar."

Lavinia thought of her own mother and how she'd never even tried to understand Lavinia's interests. Occasionally, her father talked to her about scientific matters, but such conversations always stopped when her mother entered the room. "Yes, we were definitely separated at birth."

Miss Pemberton's light laughter floated around them as she withdrew her arm from Lavinia's. "Then, dear sister, you must call me Jane. And now I see my mother is giving me an eye that bodes disaster. Until next time." She waggled her brows, then took herself off.

Lavinia's mother approached at that moment and immediately swept her in the other direction. "There you are, dear. I've someone to introduce you to." They reached the opposite side of the drawing room, where a man of middling height with a wide face dominated by a pair of thick, dark brows stood with her father.

"There you are," Father said with a smile. "Sir Martin Riddock, allow me to present my daughter, Lady Lavinia."

Lavinia curtsied to the gentleman, who was perhaps nearing his middle thirties. "Pleased to meet you, Sir Martin."

He bowed, but only slightly. It was as if he couldn't quite be bothered. Or, she thought more charitably, perhaps he had a sore back.

"The pleasure is mine, Lady Lavinia. Would you care to take a turn?"

Lavinia knew there wasn't really a choice, so she accepted his offer with a smile. Curling her hand around his elbow, she asked if he enjoyed musical performances.

Sir Martin led her around the edge of the drawing room in the opposite direction she'd gone with Miss Pemberton. Indeed, it was opposite of everyone given the flow of traffic, but Sir Martin seemed oblivious.

"I'm not particularly fond of music in general, but occasionally, I am taken with a piece. The Fortescues are friends of my mother's.

"I see." No music. She didn't dare ask if he liked rocks or dirt.

"I prefer horses and astronomy."

Lavinia's attention piqued. "Astronomy?"

"The stars and sky." His tone was condescending. He'd clearly thought she didn't know what the word meant.

"I'm quite familiar with astronomy," she informed him politely. Perhaps *too* politely. She wanted to say, *Caroline Herschel is a particular hero of mine*, but instead followed her mother's directive of not discussing science. It burned her tongue, however, since he had brought it up.

Sir Martin glanced down at her from where he stood at least six inches above her. "Indeed? I expect to be named a fellow to the Royal Society within the next few years."

Lavinia nearly tripped. To meet an eligible bachelor who was potentially interested in courting her—and why else would he ask her to promenade?—who was a scientist? She was momentarily speechless, a rare occurrence indeed. And helpful since she really wanted to tell him she was an amateur geologist but shouldn't.

"I shan't bore you with the details. If the sky were clearer, I would take you out on the balcony and show you Orion. Perhaps we'll meet again on a more visible evening."

"I should like that, thank you."

"I imagine horses might be of more interest to you. Do you ride?"

"I do." But horses weren't even remotely as interesting as stars and planets and comets.

"Let me tell you about my favorite mount." He smiled, briefly revealing teeth that weren't particularly even. Then he launched into a description of his horse, both in looks and temperament, and by the time they'd returned to her mother, she wondered why he wasn't courting the beast instead.

Thankfully, Sarah and Fanny were nearby, and after Sir Martin took his leave, Lavinia was able to go and speak with them, particularly since the performance was about to begin.

"Do you like your ensemble a bit more than you did this afternoon?" Sarah asked as they found three seats halfway back from the dais. "It's very smart."

Fanny eyed her as they sat down. "Don't you like it?"

"I feel rather…floral," Lavinia said, glancing down at herself.

"I think it's fetching," Fanny said. "I adore the bandeau in your hair."

Lavinia's hand went instinctively to her head. Her maid had carefully curled her thick, slightly wavy locks and fashioned the coiffure. "Thank you. It's just not what I'm used to."

"Who were you promenading with?" Fanny asked, lowering her voice as others sat down around them.

Lavinia, seated between Fanny and Sarah, glanced around and, squinting as usual, saw Sir Martin sitting a few rows behind her. A familiar figure at the back of the room pushed her to narrow her eyes even more. Lord Northam leaned against the doorframe, his arms crossed. He seemed to be surveying the room, his head moving—damn, she wished she had her spectacles— then suddenly, he stopped. And stared right at her. Her eyesight might not be entirely reliable, but she *felt* his perusal down to her bones.

"I think that was Sir Marvin or something or other," Sarah said, while Lavinia sought to find her tongue.

"Sir Martin," Lavinia corrected. "Riddock. Sir Martin Riddock."

Sarah peered at her expectantly. "How was he?"

"A bit dull, but he has potential." If she could get him to stop talking about horses and focus on the sky. "He's an astronomer and expects to be a fellow of the Royal Society."

Sarah's eyes lit. "How wonderful! See, the Duke of Seduction might have helped after all."

Stifling a groan, Lavinia tried to ignore the stares of too many people eager to detect why the Duke of

Seduction had chosen her to write about. She wanted to know that too.

She situated herself and stared straight ahead, ignoring all the intrusive eyes, as the musicians took the dais. She didn't want the Duke of Seduction's assistance. He needed to stop his meddling before it caused trouble. She'd do whatever she could to discover his identity and ensure he ceased his ill-conceived scheme.

THE MUSICAL PERFORMANCE was to be a quintet of strings. Rarely was there a guitar, but tonight, Beck was in for a treat. At least he hoped he was. The young Miss Fortescue was making her debut on the instrument, and he was eager to hear her play.

Guitar or not, he rarely missed a musical performance. Typically, he arrived just as it was about to begin, then stole away during the applause. On a few occasions, he endeavored to speak with the musicians, but he kept the conversation relatively oblique. It wasn't that he hid his interest in music. He was simply private about that aspect of his life, and no one needed to know how deeply it affected him.

Or how much he needed it.

He'd heard the Fortescues play before, and while they were accomplished, they lacked a certain flourish. By the middle of the first piece, Beck could see the young guitarist suffered from the same inadequacy. Beck wished he could take the girl aside and show her how to relinquish herself to the music. Perhaps she was just nervous. Beck probably would be, not that he'd ever played before an audience outside of his friends at school. So in that regard, the Fortescues had one up on him.

As his interest in the music waned, he found his attention kept drifting to the middle of the seating area, where Lady Lavinia sat between her friends. The more he watched her, the more he realized she squinted. Almost constantly. At least when she tried to focus on the dais. Every so often, her features would soften and she'd simply close her eyes and listen, her lips curved up in a slight smile. It seemed she enjoyed the music.

This made him unaccountably pleased. He reasoned that he was always pleased when someone appeared to like music. And not just for dancing, but for the sheer joy of being transported by a melody or simple notes that struck a chord.

His gaze moved over the spectators, and for the most part, they were less interested than Lady Lavinia. More and more, he looked only at her.

Then the Fortescues launched into a piece that stole his breath. The young guitarist played a solo, and it seemed that yes, she'd perhaps been nervous. Beck closed his eyes momentarily and found himself urging her on, as if she could hear his encouraging thoughts. She seemed to, as her notes climbed and cascaded and took him to another place.

He opened his eyes when the others started playing once more. And once more, his gaze found its way to Lady Lavinia. Only this time, her head was turned and her narrowed, myopic eyes were directed at him.

Had she been watching him as he'd listened to the guitarist? He felt suddenly exposed. And he wasn't sure he liked the sensation.

She returned her attention to the dais, but Beck's pulse took a moment—or four—to slow. The remainder of the performance passed somewhat quickly, with just two more pieces, both of which weren't as good as the guitarist's solo.

When everyone stood to applaud the musicians, Beck considered leaving. However, he wanted to compliment the young guitarist and tell her to keep playing, no matter what.

Except people crowded the musicians, and Beck didn't want to push his way to the front. Instead, he somehow found himself facing Lady Lavinia. "Good evening, Lady Lavinia. Did you enjoy the performance?"

"I did, thank you. Did you?"

"Yes, the guitarist was quite good."

"I thought so too. I haven't heard many guitarists. I like the sound of the instrument. I wonder if it's difficult to play."

"It depends," he said before he could censor himself.

Her dark auburn brows lifted slightly. "Do you play?"

"A bit." He was desperate to change the subject. His music was the most private part of himself, next to his lyrics and poems. But since he'd begun to share some of those—for the benefit of the young women he sought to help—that left him with just the music really. "I notice you were squinting at the dais."

A faint pink bloomed in her cheeks. "I was trying to see what she was doing with her fingers on the strings."

"I've seen you squint across the room and at the park. Do you have spectacles?"

"Yes."

"You should wear them." He lowered his voice and inched closer to her. "They wouldn't detract from your beauty."

Her flush deepened. "I'm not allowed."

He blinked, thinking he couldn't have heard her right. "Not…allowed?"

"Your opinion notwithstanding, my mother says they're unflattering to my face." She tipped her head to the side and seemed to overcome a bit of her embarrassment.

He felt horrid at causing her disquiet. "My apologies. I didn't mean to make you uncomfortable. You shouldn't have to squint to see."

"I have tried to argue that the squinting will give me early wrinkles," she said wryly, provoking him to laugh. He really did enjoy her wit. "My mother, however, thinks that's just an excuse."

"What would she do if you wore them anyway?"

The corner of her mouth crept up in a half smile. "Are you encouraging me to rebel, Lord Northam?"

"Perhaps," he murmured, thinking a rebellious Lady Lavinia would be a formidable and rather arousing thing.

Arousing?

"Last fall, I participated in an archery contest. I was quite pleased when I was able to hit the bottom of the target, if only for a moment. The arrow fell out," she explained. "Perhaps I should have sent the arrow somewhere dangerous. Maybe that would have persuaded my parents that I should wear my spectacles."

"Dangerous? Do you mean you should have hit someone?"

She shrugged. "Or maybe just come close."

"Except you possibly can't see well enough to make that distinction."

She narrowed her eyes slightly. "If only my parents

were as astute as you."

He laughed again, enjoying her company. "It's rather unfair, isn't it? Young ladies are held to ridiculously rigid rules in Society. I must say, sometimes I'm glad I'm not one."

She blinked at him, her eyes intense, and he had the sense that at this distance, she missed nothing. "I wonder if I ought to be insulted."

He was really botching things. First he'd made her uncomfortable, and now he was insulting her. "Not at all. I was trying to commiserate and failing miserably."

"It's all right. I believe I understand what you meant. I was teasing a bit—that's what happens when you have an older brother and you've been teased, as I was. Do you have siblings, Lord Northam?"

A pang of sorrow pierced his chest, but he firmly closed the door on the past and clung to this moment instead. "A younger half brother."

"I'm sure you tease him."

"No, he's quite a bit younger, just eleven," Beck said. "I really am sorry for your plight—with regard to the spectacles."

"It's all right. I've had to learn to accept annoyances. Such as all this attention directed toward me thanks to that Duke of Seduction."

Her scornful tone set him on edge. "What has he done?"

Her rich, spice-laden brown eyes widened. "Don't you know about him? He writes poems about ladies he seems to think require assistance on the Marriage Mart. It's incredibly presumptuous. And pompous. And many other words that end in 'ous,' I'm sure."

"Ah, yes." His cravat felt suddenly tight. "Presumptuous how?"

"In multiple ways. First, how can he possibly know a young lady's situation? Perhaps she has a perfectly good reason not to be married yet."

His discomfort took root and started to grow. "Is that the case with you?"

"I have reasons," she said vaguely. "Anyway, it's certainly not his affair. He doesn't even know me."

"You know who he is, then?" She didn't, of course.

"No, but I'd like to so I could tell him precisely what I think of his scheme."

Little did she know... "How do you know he doesn't know you? He must at least know *of* you."

"Yes, he seems to, but I haven't a clue who he is. I do plan to find out. As does Miss Pemberton, another of the poor young women he set his witless sights on."

Beck felt a bit ill. "So your complaint is that he's helping where no help is needed."

"Yes, and he's encouraging all manner of men to slither from the periphery and try to strike a match."

"Have you been bothered?" He braced himself for an answer he wouldn't like.

"Not precisely." Her response gave him a modicum of solace. "My parents are rather good at deterring the fortune hunters and the social climbers. But it's put me on display and made me into a commodity."

"Isn't that what the Marriage Mart does in the first place?" He might despise it, but he acknowledged it was the only way many young women in their class would gain a husband.

"Precisely why I prefer my wallflower status. The right man will find me—or I'll find him—or I'll gladly take my place upon the shelf. I'd much rather be unwed than unhappy. Rather, I should clarify: un*loved.*"

He was completely drawn in by her argument. "Love

is important?"

"Love is the most important, I think. And compatibility. I suppose I could forgo the former if I could be certain of the latter." She straightened, and her features tightened. "Oh dear, my mother is coming, and she's bringing another gentleman. Can't she see I'm talking to a marquess? Perhaps you should stay at my side indefinitely this Season, so as to drive off this nonsense the Duke of Seduction has created."

"If I thought it would help, I would." Beck was madly trying to think what he could do to rectify the situation entirely. What the hell had he done?

Furious with himself and generally disillusioned, he decided he couldn't face her mother and whomever she had in tow. "Forgive me if I take my leave for now," he said, offering her a bow.

"You're leaving me? Where are you going?"

"To do…rakish things." He winked at her for good measure and saw the flicker of something in her eyes.

Arousal?

There was that word again.

"Good evening, Lady Lavinia. Until next time when I shall act as your stalwart defender against the encroaching masses." He took himself from the drawing room as quickly as possible and didn't dare a backward glance.

Chapter Four

No countenance can be fairer,
No demeanor is merrier.
Her words heal the weak and weary,
Her presence uplifts the dreary.

-From An Ode to Miss Phoebe Lennox
by The Duke of Seduction

THE FOLLOWING AFTERNOON, Lavinia walked beside her mother to the park. It was a sunny afternoon, though a bit brisk. At least it wouldn't rain.

"Do you expect to see the Marquess of Northam today?" Mother asked as they neared the Grosvenor Gate.

"No." After their rather enjoyable conversation last night at the musical performance, he'd said he had to go do rakish things. She could only imagine what those things would be. Sudden heat swept up her spine, and she could feel the press of his lips on her neck as if he stood beside her.

"Why not?" Her mother sounded put out. "Your father and I hoped he was perhaps considering courtship."

"He's not. Have you forgotten he's a rake?"

"No, but even rakes have to marry when they've a title. Perhaps you'll be the one to tame him." She turned an expectant smile on Lavinia.

They passed through the gate as Lavinia said, "Are those kind of men redeemable?"

Mother blinked at her. "Does it matter when they're a marquess?"

Disgust roiled in Lavinia's gut. Eager to leave her mother's side, she squinted across the park until she spotted Sarah. But before she could go, Mother placed her hand on Lavinia's forearm. "You can't just walk off with your friends today. You need to linger here so that a gentleman may ask you to promenade."

"And if one doesn't?" Lavinia asked sweetly.

"One will. Things are in motion, my dear. You're an earl's daughter with a pleasing face and a dowry. All you needed was a bit of notoriety to bring you to the fore, and thanks to the Duke of Seduction, you have that now. You'll be wed in short order."

"Thanks to the Duke of Seduction." She gritted her teeth in an effort to keep the sarcasm from her tone, but judging from her mother's narrowed eyes, she was less than successful.

"You should learn to be grateful."

"I'm quite grateful for many things—a home, a family"—even if they did drive her to frustration—"the ability to read and learn, and so much more. You must forgive me if I don't feel the urgency to marry as you do. It will happen in its own time. You know that love is important to me."

"Yes, we know that, but it's been three years and there hasn't been a hint of it. If you dawdle much longer, your chances will be gone. You don't want to be alone, do you?"

Before she could answer, a gentleman approached. He was on the shorter side, with light blue eyes and a rather slight frame. Lavinia struggled to recall his name. She'd met so many new people in the last several days.

Her mother came to the rescue. "Lord Fielding, how do you do?"

"Very well, thank you." He bowed to the countess and then to Lavinia. "Good afternoon, Lady Lavinia. I hoped we could take a turn."

Lavinia cursed herself for spending too much time with her mother. Now she wouldn't be able to speak with Sarah. At least not for maybe a quarter hour. "Certainly." She forced a smile and took Lord Fielding's proffered arm.

"It's a lovely day," he said. "I daresay spring is in the air."

"It will likely be quite cold this evening, however."

He nodded. "Perhaps. Tonight is Lady Abercrombie's ball. Are you going?"

"Yes. Are you?"

"I am. You must save me a dance."

She must? It wasn't as if she could refuse. Unless… Would he believe she already had enough partners? Too bad she didn't. She prompted herself to say, "I should be delighted."

Irritation burned across her shoulders. She strained her eyes to see Fanny arrive and join Sarah, feeling a sharp pang of jealousy. They looked in her direction, and Sarah gave a small, obscure wave. Though Lavinia couldn't discern their precise expressions, she imagined they were empathetic.

"Do you have a favorite dance?" Lord Fielding asked.

She barely had a chance to reply, "Not particularly," before he began a lengthy comparison of country dances and which parts were better than others. By the time they turned to go back to her mother, Lavinia found she'd increased their pace in an effort to end the promenade as quickly as possible.

They passed another couple on the path, and Lavinia realized a moment too late that the young lady was Miss Lennox. Lavinia turned her head, slowing.

"Is something the matter?" Lord Fielding asked.

"No, I was just—"

He didn't seem to hear anything beyond "no" and continued his monologue about dances, telling her that his favorite was the minuet. Blast, she'd really wanted to speak with Miss Lennox.

At last, Lord Fielding returned her to the countess, but Lavinia was to be disappointed again because she was instantly set upon by another gentleman for another promenade. She sent a longing stare toward her friends, then squinted hard enough to see they gazed at her with something akin to pity.

Inwardly groaning, Lavinia accepted Mr. Barkby's arm, and they followed the same path she'd just taken with Fielding. "Did I see you at the Fortescues' last night?" he asked.

"I was there, yes." She hadn't seen him, but she wouldn't say so.

"I didn't particularly enjoy it, did you?"

"I did, actually."

"Indeed?" He sounded quite surprised. "What did you like about it?"

"They were all very accomplished. The guitarist displayed amazing skill."

He made a clicking sound with his tongue. "I didn't care for it. But then I prefer listening to a soprano if I must attend a musical performance."

She turned her head toward him. "Why attend last

night's, then?"

His gaze met hers without a touch of irony. "Because that's what one does during the Season."

Mr. Barkby spent the remainder of their promenade telling her about his favorite sopranos. By the time they returned to her mother, Lavinia felt like a wilting flower desperate for water and sunlight and considered weeping with frustration.

Already there was another gentleman waiting to walk with her. Lavinia wanted to scream, but just then, her gaze caught Lord Northam nearby. Near enough that she could see him without straining her eyesight overmuch. She sent him a pleading look—if there was ever a time to play the role of defender, it was right now.

He seemed to understand, because he strode toward her. She exhaled with relief as her mother drew her focus to the gentleman who was already there. "Lavinia, this is Lord Devaney. Lord Devaney, allow me to present my daughter Lady Lavinia."

He bowed as she curtsied just as Northam arrived.

"Good afternoon," Northam said with a smile.

Devaney was a few inches shorter than Northam, who had to be an inch or two over six feet, but was perhaps five years older. Devaney's nose was a trifle long and his lips on the thin side. He turned and greeted the marquess. "Afternoon, Northam."

Lord Northam hesitated, and Lavinia recognized his affliction, for it was the same one she'd suffered earlier—not recalling someone's name. "Lord Devaney, are you enjoying the park today?" Lavinia said, not because she was trying to be polite, but because she wanted to say his name so the marquess would know it.

"Afternoon, Devaney," Northam said. His left eye,

which was closer to her, sent her a quick, grateful glance.

Devaney sniffed as he directed his attention to Lavinia. "The park is quite fine today, Lady Lavinia. It will be even finer if you walk with me."

"Actually, she already planned to walk with me—we arranged it last night at the Fortescues'." He offered a bland smile as he edged closer to Lavinia.

Oh dear, that was a fib her mother would certainly ask about. Lavinia could hear her now, "Why did you tell me you didn't have plans to see the marquess today when clearly you did?" Hopefully, Lavinia could believably plead forgetfulness.

"Ah well, since I arrived here first, I suppose you'll have to wait until we're finished," Devaney said. His tone was mostly pleasant but carried a bit of an edge. He glanced toward the horizon. "Although, if we take too long, you may not have enough light." He speared Northam with a sharp, taunting look. "That would be a shame."

"It would, and because of that and our prior arrangement, she should walk with me." Northam smiled again, but it didn't reach his eyes. He moved even closer to Lavinia.

Her mother lifted her hands, palms out toward them. "Now, gentlemen, you mustn't quarrel over my daughter." She laughed, and Lavinia could practically feel her glee.

"There's no quarrel," Devaney said, looking down his long nose—or trying to anyway—at Northam. "She'll walk with me now, and if there's time, Northam can take her for a quick spin."

Lavinia couldn't quite believe this was happening. It was, in a word, absurd. How she'd love to choke the

Duke of Seduction.

"Faint."

The slight whisper reached her, and she flicked a glance toward Northam, who barely inclined his head to indicate she should fall down. Was he mad?

No, he was trying to solve this dilemma. Or, she could just walk with Devaney.

In the end, it wasn't a choice at all. She bent her knees, fluttered her eyelids, and dropped to the ground.

Only she didn't reach the path, because the warm, strong arms of the Marquess of Northam, notorious rake, caught her first.

⋅ξ⋅3⋅

Beck swept her into his arms. It was not an easy feat, for she was taller than the average miss. It was also not very well thought-out as far as a stratagem for helping her avoid attention. This escapade would likely ensure she would be the most talked-about female in London for the next few days at least.

It was too late to alter course, however, and so he looked to her mother. "Where is your vehicle?"

Her eyes were wide as she shook her head. "We didn't take one."

"I have my curricle." He inclined his head toward Grosvenor Gate, where his vehicle sat with one of his grooms. He'd brought Philip with him to sit with the curricle. "I can see her home. What's your address?"

"Twenty-five Park Street," the countess replied, looking concerned. "I'll meet you there."

Beck gave her a nod before pivoting and carrying Lady Lavinia to his curricle. Everyone turned and stared as they passed. Her lids began to flutter.

"Keep your eyes closed," he murmured.

Her two friends, Miss Colton and Miss Snowden, approached him. Their faces were also creased with concern, perhaps even more than the countess's had been.

"What happened?" Miss Colton asked.

"I'm fine," Lady Lavinia said quietly but with considerable force, keeping her eyes shut. "Lord Northam is rescuing me from an untenable situation. I'll tell you about it later at the ball."

The two young women visibly relaxed, and Beck continued on to his curricle. He set her inside, propping her against the cushion. "Keep your eyes closed until we're moving." He turned to his groom. "Philip, I need to drive Lady Lavinia to her house. Please meet me at home."

"Yes, my lord." He waited to leave until Beck had climbed inside and started the vehicle on the path.

"Can I open my eyes now?" she asked.

"Yes." He glanced over at her as she blinked her eyes open and peered out the side of the vehicle.

"Well, that was one way to extricate me from that situation, I suppose." She sat up in the seat as they left the park. "I want to choke that bloody Duke of Seduction more than ever."

He winced and darted a look toward her to see if she'd noticed. She didn't seem to—she was adjusting her hat, which he'd knocked askew as he'd carried her to the curricle. "I did try to help," he said.

"Which I appreciate. It's not your fault Lord Devaney was behaving like a pompous jackanapes. Nor is it your fault the Duke of Seduction has caused this mess."

But it was, of course. "I wonder if he doesn't realize

you don't care for his assistance."

"I suppose that's possible. Perhaps I should write a letter to him and have it published in the *Morning Chronicle*." She tipped her head to the side, her eyes narrowing, but she wasn't squinting. She was thinking. "Yes, that's a splendid idea."

Rather than focus on his regret or discomfort, he tried for some humor to lighten her mood. "Do you plan to employ poetry?"

"Goodness, no. That's a rather unique skill, I think. At least to be good at it—and the duke most certainly is. For all his faults—and I'm prepared to say he must have *many*—he knows how to wield a quill."

That gave Beck an absurd measure of delight. He shoved it aside. "I apologize for resorting to a drastic measure. I couldn't think of another way to avoid you having to promenade with Devaney or, and this may have been more likely, fisticuffs."

She turned her body toward him. "Do you think he would have hit you?"

Beck shrugged. "*I* might have hit him." He slid her a glance and saw that her eyes widened briefly.

"Have you fought before?"

"At Oxford. Felix—that is, the Earl of Ware—and I got into plenty of trouble. Ware used to arrange amateur boxing matches. They typically devolved into a drunken brawl with less and less fighting and more drinking as the evening wore on." He winced again, and this time, he knew she saw. "My apologies. This isn't a terribly appropriate topic of conversation for a young lady."

"Perhaps not, but it's far more interesting than Lord Fielding's favorite dances or Mr. Barkby's penchant for sopranos."

"What's that?"

She waved her hand. "Nothing. Just the topics I was forced to listen to in the park. I'm certain you saved me from abject boredom with Lord Devaney. I feel confident he would have found a line of conversation that entertained only him and would be oblivious to my indifference. Why couldn't Sir Martin have been here today? At least he has the potential to be engaging."

"Why is that?"

"He's interested in science, astronomy in particular."

"And of course that would be far more appealing to you." For some odd reason, he was glad Sir Martin hadn't been there.

"Far more." She gestured to the right side of the street as they approached the intersection with Mount Street. "My house is just there."

He located the number twenty-five. "While we have another moment alone, let me apologize again for what happened in the park."

"I don't blame you at all."

"You might when this only serves to make you more popular."

"Blast, you may be right. No, you *are* right." She tipped her head back and blew out a frustrated breath.

He drew the curricle to a halt and stepped down. After walking around the back of the vehicle, he helped her to the street. "I regret the annoyance this will cause you."

"It's not your fault. It's entirely due to the meddlesome Duke of Seduction. If not for him, your interference wouldn't even have been necessary. If not for him, I would have enjoyed a pleasant walk in the park with my friends."

Beck's brain was working hard to come up with a

way to make things right for her. If he could. He certainly didn't want to make matters worse, as he'd probably done today. He offered her his arm and led her to the door.

The butler opened the door as they reached the top of the front steps. She let go of his arm and turned to him. "Thank you for seeing me home. Don't be concerned about me or my dilemma. I believe I've come up with a solution."

"The letter to the *Chronicle?*" At her nod, he made an offer that was perhaps ill-advised, but he did so anyway. "I'd be happy to deliver it for you." That way, he could ensure the editor would print it—Beck's solicitor would hand-deliver it and obtain the man's assurance.

Her gaze flickered with surprise. "That's rather helpful, thank you, but I don't know that it's necessary."

They were out of time for further discussion. Unless he accompanied her inside, and he hadn't been invited. Not that he wanted to be. Good Lord, he was treading far too close to a line he had no interest in crossing. Hell, he'd been so caught up in thinking of her situation, he'd failed to consider his own. People would think he was courting her. Or wanted to. Or was at least interested in her. She was unmarried, and he was a rake. An *Untouchable* rake, if one listened to Society's labels.

He scoffed inwardly. He didn't give a fig if they decided he planned to marry. He knew he didn't, and that was none of their concern. He bowed to Lady Lavinia and returned to his curricle, eager to be on his way before her mother showed up.

It was one thing for Society at large to think he

wished to wed, and another entirely for the Countess of Balcombe to believe he wanted to marry her daughter. He ought to keep his distance, which wouldn't allow him to protect Lady Lavinia from unwanted suitors. Nevertheless, it would be necessary.

Something else was necessary: it was time for the Duke of Seduction to disappear.

Chapter Five

❦

Descend you angels! Bring your light.
Give silence, meaning, patience, sight.
Grant leave for her splendor and grace,
Souls charmed by the song of her face.

-From Further Thoughts on Miss Rose Stewart
by The Duke of Seduction

AFTER BEING FORCED to stay home the evening after her "fainting" incident at the park, Lavinia was eager to visit Sarah. Both she and Fanny had sent short notes to Lavinia that morning asking what had happened. They'd sounded quite concerned. She'd sent notes back asking Fanny to join them at Sarah's house that afternoon.

The Coltons' butler showed Lavinia to the sitting room where she and Sarah always met. Sarah jumped up from the settee and rushed to greet her as the butler departed. "I'm so glad you're all right. I was so concerned after what happened in the park yesterday."

Lavinia took a chair angled near the settee and pulled her bonnet off. "I told you I was fine."

"Yes, but when you didn't come to the ball, and neither did your mother, Fanny and I were worried that you weren't. Fine, that is."

"It was all an act." Lavinia tugged her gloves from

her hands and set them on the arm of the chair. "Lord Northam was saving me from yet another promenade with a boring suitor."

Fanny arrived and joined them, removing her gloves. "I'm so pleased to see you're all right, Lavinia." A pin fell from her coppery hair as she took her bonnet from her head. "Bother," she muttered, bending to pick up the pin. A curl slipped free and fell against her cheek. She tucked it behind her ear with a soft grunt.

Things like this happened to Fanny with regularity—earrings fell out of her ears, stitching came loose on her gown, ratafia dribbled onto her lap. She'd said she was clumsy, but it wasn't always something she did. Rather, clumsy things just seemed to happen in her orbit.

"Is Northam a suitor, then?" Fanny asked.

"Goodness, no. Northam is a rake," Lavinia said.

"Rakes can be suitors, I think." Fanny looked at Sarah. "Can't they?"

"I suppose, though it's not typical. My mother says they have to settle down sooner or later."

Lavinia nodded. "My mother says the same thing. She has it in her mind that Northam is a suitor—he and Devaney did almost come to blows over who would promenade with me next."

Both Fanny and Sarah gasped. "Did that really happen?" Fanny asked. "That was the rumor at the ball last night, but we weren't sure if it was true." She exchanged a look with Sarah.

"It's true," Lavinia said darkly. "My lowest moment to date. And I'm so sorry you didn't hear it from me first. I was rather upset when Mother insisted I stay home and rest. I suppose I should be pleased she cared enough to make me do that instead of taking advantage of the extra notoriety and parading me around the ball."

Sarah's brow furrowed. "Let me see if I understand. Northam was trying to rescue you from the other gentleman?"

"From Lord Devaney, yes. But Devaney wasn't having any of it. He insisted he should get to walk with me first because he was there first. Northam argued that we'd prearranged to walk at the Fortescues' the night before."

As predicted, Lavinia's mother had queried her about that. Lavinia had managed to successfully convince her that she'd forgotten—she'd blamed the inundation of male interest and her inability to keep them all straight. The irony was that it wasn't entirely untrue. Except that Lavinia would never confuse Northam with anyone else. He was a singular male, likely because of the way they'd met. Her neck tingled, as it always did when she thought of that night.

"What a debacle," Sarah said, shaking her head.

Lavinia nodded. "Though it could have been far worse."

"It sounds like Lord Northam has become your champion," Fanny said with a small smile. "I know I don't have your experience with such matters, but it seems his suit can't be far off—rake or not."

Lavinia couldn't imagine such a thing. They'd become friendly, but there'd been no indication of attraction—the fleeting shivers along her neck notwithstanding. Those didn't mean she wanted his attention in that way. Still, she couldn't deny he'd become quite helpful. Which reminded her of the man who was the opposite.

Lavinia straightened and pinned both of her friends with a direct stare. "I need to put an end to this nonsense with the Duke of Seduction. I'm going to write a letter to him and send it to the *Morning Chronicle*."

Fanny, her gaze eager, leaned forward. "What will you say?"

"I will ask him to cease his poetry campaign. While he may have enjoyed some success with the first few young women, not all of us appreciate his interference."

Sarah pursed her lips. "I don't think you should."

Both Fanny and Lavinia stared at her, but it was Lavinia who spoke. "Why not?"

"Yesterday's event at the park already diverted more attention to you—everyone was talking about you fainting last night. You've become a bit of a hero to young women who would dearly love to have a marquess and an earl arguing over them. If you decry the Duke of Seduction, you might become a pariah."

Lavinia groaned and flung herself back against the chair. "This is a disaster." While becoming a pariah would certainly alleviate her current stress, it would potentially ensure she didn't marry at all this Season, and her parents would be furious. In fact, regardless of the impact, her mother would be incensed if Lavinia wrote a letter at all. Lavinia narrowed her eyes. "I shall have to write it anonymously, then. Just as he does."

Sarah's lips curved into a smile. "Brilliant. You must call yourself the Duchess of Independence."

"Perfect." Lavinia grinned.

"How do you plan to ensure the editor of the *Morning Chronicle* prints it?" Fanny asked.

Lavinia shrugged. "I would think he'd be eager. The duke's poems are quite popular." She recalled Northam's suggestion from the day before. "Lord

Northam offered to deliver the letter to the *Morning Chronicle*. To remain anonymous, perhaps I should accept his assistance."

"For a nonsuitor, the marquess is rather intent on helping you," Sarah said with a heavy dollop of irony and more than a bit of curiosity.

It was a trifle odd, but Lavinia knew he felt bad about the way they'd met and his inappropriate behavior. Still, most rakes—probably all rakes—would simply have laughed it off and perhaps even tried to seduce her after dispatching Lady Fairwell. Northam, it appeared, was not the average rake. And that intrigued her.

Which she had no time for. She wanted her boring life back where she could enjoy her time hugging the wall with her friends and talking at length about subjects that interested her. She wasn't able to take short jaunts to look at geologically interesting locations with so much attention directed at her. In fact, she despaired of being able to do that at all this Season, much to her disappointment.

"Unlike the Duke of Seduction, the marquess's help is actually *helpful*. For that reason alone, I'll accept it. Sarah, can your brother ensure Northam is at the park later so I can give him this letter for the *Morning Chronicle*?"

"Certainly." Sarah peered at her. "Perhaps I should have him ask Northam why he's helping you."

"No, don't do that," Lavinia said. "Hopefully, I won't require his assistance at all after this. Do you have foolscap here?"

Sarah rose. "Of course. I'll just run up to my chamber to fetch it along with the other writing implements." The moment she left, Lavinia began verbally drafting the letter with Fanny's help.

An hour later, they were finished, and the sealed letter was tucked into Lavinia's pocket as she left Sarah's house. Unfortunately, they were not able to go to the park because the sky decided to unleash a rainstorm that would have soaked them to the bone.

It was so wet, in fact, that Lavinia's mother considered not going to the Compton rout that evening. Lavinia had insistently talked her into it—not that her mother had needed much persuasion—and then tried to come up with a scheme in which she could get the note to Northam. Assuming he was even at the rout. This nonsense of men and women not being allowed to be friends was becoming increasingly bothersome.

As soon as she arrived at the Comptons', Sarah joined her with an excited air. "I spoke to Anthony and arranged things for Lord Northam to pick up your letter. I said you would leave it on the mantelpiece in the library."

Lavinia grinned. "Brilliant! You must thank Anthony for me. He really is a wonderful brother."

"Sometimes," Sarah said. "Sometimes, he's a... Never mind." She winked at Lavinia.

As soon as Fanny arrived, Lavinia stole away to His Grace's library. She'd never been in the room before, and it took a bit of searching to find it. She closed the door behind her and went to the hearth. Withdrawing the letter from her reticule, she set it on the mantelpiece next to a small figurine of a dog.

Then, because she couldn't help herself, she went to the bookshelf and perused the spines for anything of interest, pulling out unmarked spines here and there. One of them, a rather slim volume, was called *The*

Peculiar Rocks of the Outer Hebrides. Feeling as though she'd discovered a very special treasure, she slipped the book from the shelf.

Just a few moments later, the door clicked, and she pressed the book closed. She stared guiltily as Lord Northam entered. His gaze dipped to her hands. "Reading again, I see."

"I'm afraid I couldn't resist."

"Of course not." He moved closer. "What is it tonight, then?"

"The most delightful little book about the peculiar rocks in the Outer Hebrides. They sound astonishing, with a variety of colors and strata. I'd dearly love to see them someday." She replaced the book on the shelf with a sigh. Turning, she inclined her head toward the fireplace. "The letter is there."

His gloved fingers plucked it from the mantel. He glanced down at the name she'd written on the front. "I'll see that he gets it."

"Thank you." She took a step toward him so that only a couple of feet separated them. "My friends asked me why you are so keen to help me."

"Can't a gentleman simply perform a kindness?"

"Of course, but we don't have a connection. Some would find your assistance inappropriate. Especially given your reputation."

"As a rake."

She gave a little shrug. "You don't deny it. Indeed, you've told me you were going to engage in rakish activities. What's more, I've personal knowledge of your rakish activities." Heat rushed up her neck and flooded her face. "That is, because you met with Lady Fairwell." She averted her gaze from his because she wasn't sure she could stand another moment of the amused glint in his eyes.

"I daresay your knowledge isn't all that personal, but I understand your meaning."

"Why are you helping me?"

Now he looked away. "I felt poorly about the way we met, and I'm sorry the Duke of Seduction has caused you so much disquiet."

"Yes, well, I eviscerated him in the letter." She narrowed her eyes. "How I'd love to see his expression when he reads it."

He looked at her in surprise. "Eviscerated him? He was trying to do good, and he did actually help a few young ladies."

"I suppose, but I find the entire situation odd. Who is he to play matchmaker anonymously?" She cocked her head to the side. "Indeed, *who* is he? He has to be in Society to be aware of me and the others. And he's obviously well-educated, given his skill with words."

Northam lifted a shoulder. "An uneducated man could write as well."

"Perhaps, but he wouldn't be in Society." She thought back to their other conversations and his steadfast defense of the man. She took another step toward him so she could see his expression quite clearly. "Do you know him?"

Northam's dark blond brows arched for the briefest moment. "Why would you think so?"

"Because you're eager to defend him, and I recall you saying it had to be someone who knew me." She watched his reaction, but his gaze didn't even flicker.

"I was merely trying to help you determine his identity."

"Let us do that, then." She turned and paced a few steps before pivoting back to face him. "Who do you think has the skill to write poetry like that?"

"Perhaps Byron has returned."

She smirked. "Miss Pemberton suggested the same thing. I think we'd all know if he was back."

Northam shrugged. "Not if he is well hidden."

"I will concede that this duke is very well hidden, but it isn't Byron. I daresay he'd publish under his own name. This man is secretive. Who in Society is intelligent and secretive?"

He exhaled, his gaze tilting to the ceiling briefly. "That could be any number of gentlemen. Or maybe it's a woman. Have you considered that?"

"I had not. What an intriguing idea." She narrowed her eyes at him. "Are you trying to deflect my attention so I don't discover his identity? I find it odd that you are so keen to help me. It's almost as if you feel personally bad that this has caused trouble for me."

"I do feel bad. I'm sure it was never his intent to cause harm. Which is why I'm wondering if you maybe shouldn't send this letter."

She froze, wondering if she'd heard him right. "Wait, I thought you offered to deliver it for me."

"I did, but after you used the word *eviscerate*, I wonder if you should consider not sending it. Or, perhaps you could ask the editor to forward this to the duke so that he can hear your quarrel with his endeavors."

Anger began to bubble in her chest. "So the Duke of Seduction can write about me in a public manner, but I shouldn't do the same to him?"

The marquess had the grace to wince. "Er, no. I was simply offering another path to the same objective."

"My objective is to get him to stop, and publicly calling him out will be far more effective than sending him a note asking him to cease." She shook her head, then froze again, widening her eyes as she stared at this man she had to admit she didn't know very well. "Were you even going to deliver my letter?" She held her hand out. "Give it back."

"I'd rather not."

"Why not?"

"Because you don't need to send it." He exhaled, his gaze settling firmly—and apologetically on hers. "I'm the Duke of Seduction."

BECK WATCHED AS her eyes widened, then narrowed. Her jaw clenched, and she folded her arms over her chest, which rose and fell quite rapidly with her agitation.

"Explain yourself."

He handed the letter back to her, and she snapped it from his fingers, recrossing her arms over her bodice. The position pressed her breasts up so the creamy swell of flesh was more prominent above her neckline. He tried very hard not to look at it. "I really was just trying to help. The Marriage Mart is often unkind to young women, especially those who are the most deserving of attention."

"Like me?"

"Exactly like you. I'm so very sorry you found the attention I drew to you a burden. It didn't occur to me that you—or anyone else—would take it as such. I was quite mistaken, obviously."

"Obviously." The word dripped with disgust. "Why would you do such a thing? If you want to lend support to a young lady, dance with her or promenade with her in the park."

"I can't very well do that to a series of young, unmarried women."

"Why not? You're already a rake. I should think it would suit your reputation perfectly." She blew out a breath and lowered her hands to her sides, the letter still clutched in her fingers. "Never mind, I can see why that would be ill-advised. Your reputation could stain that of the young lady if you consistently failed to legitimately pursue any of them. However, I would argue that it wouldn't, not if you kept the association brief."

"I shall take that under advisement. In the meantime, I would like to continue my poetry campaign, as you called it."

"You still haven't told me why. Why would you do this in the first place?"

He'd hoped to avoid answering that question and thought he just might in the face of her ire. She'd launched the question and then forged on, but apparently she hadn't forgotten it. He considered a fabrication of some kind, but he simply couldn't come up with one. The truth, then. Or at least a half-truth.

"My sister was devastated by the Marriage Mart. She died lonely and utterly defeated."

Lady Lavinia stared at him for a long moment. "That's awful. I didn't realize you had a sister. When was this?"

"Sixteen years ago. She was my half sister. My father had three wives, and she was from his first. I have another half sister who is married."

"She found success, then."

"Not on the Marriage Mart. She fell in love with the local curate in Devon. He's a vicar in Cornwall now." Beck thought of his half sister, Margaret, and his nieces and nephews. They were a happy, close-knit family, and Beck knew Helen had been jealous of her sister's joy. She'd hoped to find the same things for herself—a husband, family, love.

But she hadn't. Instead, she'd found coldness and alienation. After four years on the Marriage Mart... He shook the thoughts away before Lady Lavinia detected there was more to the story. She was wickedly astute.

Beck straightened, shrugging off the ghosts of the past. "I wanted to save other young women from the same disappointment and loneliness."

She moved closer to him, and her anger seemed to have dissipated. "I'm so sorry about your sister. However, I am neither disappointed nor lonely. If I find a husband on the Marriage Mart—a man I can respect and love—then I shall count myself fortunate. However, if I am not so lucky and end up a spinster, there are worse things."

Yes, there were. He admired her outlook so much. And realized he'd made a terrible error. "I'm sorry I caused you trouble. I've tried to help fix things."

She smiled. "I know that now, and I appreciate it. May I suggest that you ascertain whether someone wants your help before you blindly offer it?"

"Yes. I shall endeavor to do that from now on."

"You want to continue being the Duke of Seduction?"

"The successful marriages of Miss Berwick and Miss Stewart seem to indicate I haven't been a complete failure," he said wryly. "The problem now is how I can continue to do that for women who truly want the assistance. Perhaps I can find a way to communicate with the subject first."

"That takes a bit of the romance out of it, doesn't it?

Instead of the excitement of seeing their name in the paper with a gorgeous poem, it will be transacted in advance. If people know that is happening, women will clamor to be the next subject. Already, young ladies and their mothers are trying to find a way to be the next object of your—the Duke's—attention."

Hell, this had become far more complicated than he'd ever imagined.

"You could still help, I think." She cocked her head to the side and turned to do another short pace before coming back to stand before him. "I could perhaps identify some young women who require a bit of assistance to elevate their visibility."

He wasn't quite sure he was hearing her correctly. "You'd help me?"

"Why not? You were so *very* eager to help me. Even if it wasn't well thought out."

"That's quite magnanimous of you." He purposely used a sardonic tone. "Perhaps I can return the favor by helping you in a way that would actually *help* you. What if I encouraged the right gentlemen in your direction?"

"What do you mean, the 'right' gentlemen?"

"Men you might find interesting. I can think of at least one fellow I was at school with who you may like. He possesses a scientific mind and was always digging in the dirt. He's a botanist and now lectures at Oxford."

The click of the door drew Beck to snap his head around. Someone was coming—there was no time. He clasped her hand and looked about wildly for somewhere to hide. The long, velvet drapes hanging at the window were their only option for concealment.

She thought so too, apparently, as she started in that

direction the second he made the connection. The curtains were drawn closed, so they tucked themselves behind the deep russet velvet. The air was cool against the window, but he was warm as his heart beat a steady pace in his chest.

It was also quite dark in their hiding spot, which was just as well. He wasn't sure he wanted to see her face. Was she afraid? Angry? Something else?

Muffled voices carried across the room. It was a man and a woman, and from the sounds of her moans, they'd come to the library for precisely what Beck feared. There was no help for it. They'd have to stand there and wait until the couple was finished. To do anything else would compromise Lady Lavinia, and that simply wouldn't do—and not just because he had no desire to marry. He'd already complicated things for her. Sullying her reputation would be unforgiveable.

Beck realized he was still holding her hand. He should let go. But it was dark, and perhaps he was an anchor for her. Or maybe that was just what he was telling himself. Maybe the truth was he *liked* holding her hand.

He released her and silently urged the couple to hurry.

"What the devil?" The man's exclamation was clearly intelligible.

The response—also masculine—was not loud enough to be heard. Beck strained to hear what they were saying, for the conversation continued.

Finally, one of them spoke with enough volume. "We were here first!"

Oh, good God, was it a second couple?

Warmth seeped into his side as Lady Lavinia pressed into him. "What's going on?" she whispered with quiet urgency.

"I'm not entirely certain."

"Are they arguing over who was here first?" she hissed. "That sounds awfully familiar."

Beck had to bite the inside of his cheek to keep from laughing.

The dispute continued for a bit longer, and then came the sound of an exaggerated exhalation. This was followed by the clear sound of the door snapping closed. Had one couple left?

Beck found the edge of the curtain in the middle of the window and slid his hand up to eye level. Moving the fabric the barest fraction, he peeked into the room.

The man was patting the woman's back, and when he lifted his head, Beck nearly shouted with laughter. It was the bloody Earl of Devaney. Apparently, he was having a bad week when it came to women and getting somewhere first.

Grinning broadly, he closed the curtain and listened for what would happen next. He prayed their mood had been dampened enough to encourage a retreat. A moment later, he heard the door close again. He waited a few beats and then peered around the edge of the drape once more. Seeing that the room was now empty, he let his shoulders relax and the air fully leave his lungs.

"Are they gone?" she whispered.

"Yes." He pulled open the drape and gestured for her to precede him from their hiding place.

She turned to him, her dark gaze sharp and curious. "Were they—?"

"Seeking an assignation, yes. Two couples with precisely the same idea. One of them included Lord Devaney."

Bright laughter spilled from her mouth, and he couldn't keep himself from joining in her rmirth. "Poor Devaney. Thwarted again." She shook her head. "I'd no idea library assignations were so popular. I've stolen into many libraries during social events, and I hadn't ever encountered such activity." Her gaze narrowed in on his. "Until you."

"This is my fault, then?"

She shrugged, her mouth hinting at a smile. "Why not? It seems you're to shoulder the blame for everything this evening."

He let out the laughter he'd been holding. "Lady Lavinia, you are the drollest woman I've ever met."

She flashed a smile and dipped a brief curtsey. "Thank you, my lord. And now I must away before someone else decides this is an excellent location for a rendezvous—which it clearly is. Perhaps I'll see you in the park tomorrow so we may further discuss our mutually beneficial association. I'm afraid we're going to have to stop meeting in libraries."

He couldn't keep from smiling in return. "Yes, quite." Sobering, he wanted to convey one important thing before she left. "I trust you to keep my secret. I ask that you not tell your friends about me."

She blanched but nodded. "I'm glad you told me. Your secret is yours and not mine to tell."

He inclined his head in appreciation. "Have a good evening, Lady Lavinia."

She picked up her hem and swept from the room. Suddenly, the space seemed darker, or at least far less alive.

Alive?

He had to acknowledge that Lady Lavinia carried a certain vibrancy that electrified every room she entered.

Her eyes moved, despite the fact that she couldn't see very well, or maybe because of it. She was constantly seeking and learning and storing information. He suspected she was collecting data, as a scientific mind might. He, on the other hand, obtained thoughts and feelings, emotions he might bend and transform into words or music. They were, in some way, rather alike.

And now they would help each other. He'd been loath to tell her the truth, both because he'd wronged her as the Duke of Seduction and because he hadn't wanted anyone to know his secret. Now she was the only other person besides Gage who did. That put her in a very specific and small class of people—those he trusted.

It was an alarming realization along with the way he'd enjoyed holding her hand. Those were not things a rake with no interest in marriage should think about.

Then he simply wouldn't.

Chapter Six

Mist fades fast, banished by her light,
She glows with warmth and joy so bright.
No storm, nor hurricane can stand
To resist her love; close at hand.

-From An Ode to Miss Jane Pemberton
by The Duke of Seduction

DUE TO ANOTHER storm the day before, Lavinia did not walk in the park, which meant she did not see Lord Northam. She had, however, spent a great deal of time thinking about him. About how he'd lied to her. About why he'd done so. About how much she liked him.

She'd never had a male friend before. It seemed odd for that to be the case—Lavinia tried to make friends wherever she went—but given Society's rules, it was deuced hard to cultivate a friendship with a member of the opposite sex. God forbid they spend time together without thinking sexual thoughts.

Which wasn't to say Lavinia hadn't entertained a few inappropriate ideas. All of them springing from that first moment of their acquaintance.

His mouth. Her neck.

Sensation danced along her spine, and she shivered.

"Are you cold?" her mother asked, looking up at the flinty sky as they approached Hyde Park. "Perhaps we should return home." She'd been vacillating all afternoon as to whether they should go. It was quite chilly, and yesterday's storm would ensure the park was muddier than usual. They always stuck to the paths, of course, but on a crowded day, that wasn't always possible. However, Lavinia doubted this would be one of those occasions.

"I'm not cold," Lavinia said, glad she'd brought her muff. "I'd like to continue. If the weather turns, we could be stuck inside for days. Best to take advantage while we can."

"True. We needn't stay long either. I can't imagine there will be many people in attendance."

Lavinia slid her an exasperated glance. "Sometimes it's just nice to go for a walk, Mother."

"Yes, of course. But we needn't do it in the sodden park if we don't care to be seen."

Biting her tongue, Lavinia strolled through Grosvenor Gate and immediately saw Miss Lennox with her mother. "Excuse me, Mother. I want to offer my congratulations to Miss Lennox. I haven't seen her since her engagement."

"I'll go with you," the countess said, dampening Lavinia's enthusiasm. "The first banns were read on Sunday, I believe.

They approached Miss Lennox and her mother. Both women were pale with dark hair, but whereas the older woman's eyes were brown, the younger's were a vivid green.

"Good afternoon, Mrs. Lennox, Miss Lennox," Lavinia's mother said.

Mrs. Lennox smiled warmly. "Good afternoon, Lady Balcombe." She shifted her gaze to Lavinia. "Lady Lavinia."

"We wished to offer our best wishes for Miss Lennox's upcoming nuptials. Mr. Sainsbury is quite a catch!"

Lavinia wasn't sure that was true. The man was heir to a barony, but he'd always struck Lavinia as one of Society's Insincere—those people who behaved one way in polite conversation and another when you weren't watching. Except Lavinia was always watching. Her position along the wall made that rather easy to do.

"He's quite charming, yes." Mrs. Lennox sent a smile toward her daughter, who looked as though she were rather bored. Was she? "Phoebe is so fortunate. The wedding is in just over a fortnight. There is much to do, of course."

"I can imagine. My eldest son is married, but it's different when it's your daughter."

"Yes, I would think so. Phoebe is my first and only."

Lavinia moved closer to Miss Lennox. "Are you enjoying the preparations?"

"Yes. As Mother said, there's plenty to do," Miss Lennox said without even a touch of zeal. Perhaps she didn't enjoy planning a wedding. "And yet here we are at the park."

Mrs. Lennox laughed softly. "So you can see Mr. Sainsbury." She turned to Lavinia. "How does it feel to be the latest beneficiary of the Duke of Seduction's prose?" Her guileless expression seemed to indicate she expected a favorable response.

Lavinia's mother rushed to answer, likely before Lavinia could say anything derogatory. "It's certainly elevated her profile!"

"I imagine she has plenty of suitors." Mrs. Lennox gave the countess a knowing look. "You'll be planning a wedding soon, I'll wager."

"Well, that would be splendid," the countess said with a nod. "I don't mind telling you I'd begun to wonder. Decent, eligible men are certainly in short supply."

"Don't forget interesting," Lavinia put in sweetly.

"I would add intelligent," Miss Lennox offered.

Lavinia nodded. "Most definitely."

Miss Lennox turned her head toward Lavinia. "Do you suppose the Duke of Seduction is intelligent?" There was an edge to her tone that spoke volumes to Lavinia.

"Probably," Lavinia said carefully. "He's at least interesting?" She flashed a smile and, when it wasn't reciprocated, let it slide from her mouth. "He's certainly good at interfering."

"Oh, I'd say he's *helping*," Mrs. Lennox said. "Phoebe agrees. If not for his poetry illuminating Phoebe's grace, she might still be on the Marriage Mart." Her gaze moved past her daughter. "Mr. Sainsbury is coming."

"I wasn't unhappy," Miss Lennox muttered.

Lavinia seized the moment to edge closer to Miss Lennox while their mothers conversed. "Are you unhappy now?" she whispered.

Miss Lennox's eyelids fluttered with surprise. "No. Sainsbury is pleasant and charming."

"And yet you don't sound very enthusiastic." Lavinia's anger toward the Duke of Seduction kindled anew. No, her anger toward Northam. She would tell him that he may have ruined Miss Lennox's life with his meddling. Except he *had* been trying to help. His sister's failure obviously weighed heavy on him and had driven him to action.

"This has all just happened so quickly," Miss Lennox

said. "It could be far worse. I'll be content with Mr. Sainsbury. It's certainly preferable to spinsterhood."

"Is it?" Lavinia couldn't say anything more, as Miss Lennox's betrothed arrived.

They exchanged pleasantries, and Lavinia concluded that Mr. Sainsbury was indeed charming and seemed besotted with Miss Lennox. His eyes lit up when he saw her, and he was effusive in his greeting. In fact, Miss Lennox perked up a bit in his presence, her features softening as he complimented her walking costume.

Lavinia hoped they would be happy. Unfortunately, Miss Lennox was stuck with her groom. To cry off after a betrothal caused considerable scandal, as it had for Lavinia's friend Diana.

As if conjured from her mind, Diana strolled into the park with another party to their "scandal," Violet, the Duchess of Kilve, whom Lavinia had met and befriended at a house party last fall.

Before Lavinia could excuse herself from her mother, Sarah seemed to appear out of nowhere. "Lavinia, may we walk for a moment?"

"Go ahead," the countess said resignedly. "There aren't many people here, so we won't stay long."

Lavinia linked arms with Sarah. "Did you see who just arrived?"

"Yes, that's why I came to get you," Sarah said.

They walked together, their pace quick, and met Diana and Violet on the path. Diana smiled warmly and they all ended up embracing and launching into a babble of excitement at seeing each other again.

Diana beamed at them. "I'm so glad to see you both."

"You look so happy," Sarah said. "It can't be from

encountering us."

"Why not?"

"Because your happiness jumps off every single letter you've written. It isn't us, it's your husband."

Diana blushed. "I can't deny it.

Violet nodded in agreement. "It's true."

Throwing her a sidelong glance, Diana laughed. "You are every bit as happy.

"Also true." Violet grinned. "But let us walk and discuss Lavinia and this Duke of Seduction business." Her eyes sparkled with mirth as she looked toward Lavinia. "Are you about to become betrothed?"

As they started along the path, Lavinia gave her head a light shake. "Heavens, no."

"You aren't being courted?" Diana asked.

"I have far more masculine attention than I used to, most of it not worth mentioning."

"Most of it?" Violet asked. "Does that mean there is *something* worth mentioning?"

Sarah blinked at Lavinia. "Is there? I didn't think anyone had caught your eye."

Why had she said most? Because the Season wasn't completely unremarkable. Because of Lord Northam. And yet what could she say about him to them?

Nothing without revealing the way they'd met and the way their friendship had developed and the direction their association was now headed as they worked to help each other. She felt a flash of remorse for keeping it all from Sarah, her dearest friend, but she'd promised Northam she wouldn't tell anyone he was the Duke of Seduction. And she wasn't sure how to relate the story now without disclosing that piece. What a *tangle*.

"You're right, Sarah. There isn't anything worth

mentioning. It's been a parade of suitors, and I'm weary of it already." She glanced back toward her mother, who was now talking with a few other ladies. Their gazes strayed toward Lavinia and her group, and Lavinia turned her head around. "My mother wishes I were more enthusiastic. She is confident I'll be wed by Season's end."

Violet's brow furrowed. "Don't you want that? I seem to recall you wanting to marry."

"The *right* gentleman. When—and if—he presents himself. It's not too much to ask, is it?"

"No," Violet agreed. "Take it from me. I was wed to a man I didn't choose and didn't love. Now that I am married to a man I do love—madly—I can say with utmost certainty that you should wait for the right man." She smiled, adding, "If you can."

"That's the real issue," Sarah said. "I'm not sure your mother will let you put it off any longer. My mother prays every day that the Duke of Seduction writes about me next."

Diana tipped her head to the side and regarded Sarah with curiosity. "Would you want him to?"

Sarah shrugged, surprising Lavinia. "Maybe." She flicked an apologetic look toward Lavinia. "I know you haven't liked the attention, but I think I might." Her shoulders lifted again. "Or not. I suppose I'd just appreciate the opportunity."

"Careful what you wish for," Lavinia said, her mind whirring. She could very easily ensure the Duke of Seduction wrote about Sarah. But Lavinia knew her friend. She might like the attention, but falling in love was even more important to Sarah than it was to Lavinia. The insincerity and triviality would wear on her just as it did Lavinia.

Sarah exhaled, her mouth sliding into a brief, slight frown. "I'm sure you're right."

Lavinia hoped her friend wasn't sad or, worse, jealous of Lavinia's current notoriety. "Would you really want the Duke of Seduction to write about you?"

"I don't know. Maybe I just want to be as popular as you." She flashed a smile at Lavinia.

She was jealous. Lavinia's chest ached, and she wove her arm through Sarah's. "I'm not *really* popular, but you know that. This will pass, and then we can go back to the way things were."

Sarah looked at Diana and Violet before sliding her gaze back to Lavinia. "Do we really want to? Marriage seems to agree with them."

"They're aberrations." Lavinia laughed. "I'm joking. But they're in love. If we find—*when* we find that," she amended, "we'll look as disgusting as they do now."

"And you're right, Lavinia," Sarah said, inclining her head toward a group of women gathered on an adjacent path. "Popularity isn't all that grand, especially when it's for the wrong reasons." The women were openly staring at the four of them, and Lavinia was about to apologize for being a nuisance when the words stuck in her throat. She squinted at the group and, even with her myopia, realized there was something different about their demeanor.

Violet let out a breath. "Well, that was to be expected. We knew our arrival would arouse a flurry of gossip and judgment."

"Yes." Diana looked at Lavinia and Sarah apologetically. "We're sorry if this causes you trouble."

Both Lavinia and Sarah scoffed. "We don't care," Lavinia said. "You're our friends."

"It's nonsense anyway," Sarah said with a surprising

burst of vehemence. "You're both happy. No one was ruined or hurt by what happened. If Diana had married Kilve, there'd be four unhappy people instead of four people who deserve the very best and will have it. If that's not acceptable to Society, well, I don't want to be a part of it."

They turned and walked back toward the gate. "I'm going to host a dinner party soon," Violet said. "I want to show people Nick isn't really the Duke of Ice."

"Isn't he?" Lavinia gave her a teasing smile.

Violet winked in return. "Not anymore. You'll find him quite changed, I think. Diana and I have transformed our dukes—fie on anyone who says it can't be done."

Lavinia recalled the conversation she had with her mother about reforming rakes. "Neither of them were rakehells, however. I can't imagine those can be changed."

"I think it depends on the man," Violet said. "If a woman is lucky, she can perhaps divert his rakish behavior so that he spends it all on her." She exchanged a knowing look with Diana, and their mouths curved into rather satisfied smiles.

"I do believe they're talking about sex," Sarah stage-whispered to Lavinia, who burst out laughing.

Violet and Diana joined in, and by the time they reached the gate, they were dabbing their eyes and making plans to go shopping in the very near future.

Just before they parted, Lavinia leaned over to Violet and quietly said, "When you send invitations to your dinner party, invite the Marquess of Northam." That would be one event where she could be assured of seeing him—so they could discuss their mutual assistance scheme.

Violet's eyes widened with curiosity, but before she could ask why, Lavinia added, "He's a friend of Sarah's brother's. And he isn't terribly fond of Society events. I think he might enjoy the company we keep."

"I'll be sure to add him to the list."

They said their good-byes, and Lavinia squinted down the path. "My mother is coming." She turned to Sarah. "She didn't really want to come today, but I dragged her along. And I'm so glad I did."

"I am too. How splendid to see Diana and Violet."

"Yes." Lavinia clasped Sarah's hands. "I hope you aren't upset with me and everything that's been happening. I would much rather trade places with you. You're far better suited to this than I am. I just want to talk about rocks and dirt and the age of the Earth. No one cares about those things."

"Yes, fashion and popular literature are far more interesting." Sarah rolled her eyes, then laughed softly. "You are my dearest friend, and I love you beyond measure. I am not upset with you. I am happy for you and sincerely hope this chaos draws forth the man of your dreams."

Sarah squeezed Lavinia's hands. "Now I must go before your mother arrives." She mouthed, *sorry* as she departed.

The countess slowed but didn't stop as she reached Lavinia. "I'm ready to go."

Lavinia fell into step beside her. "Then I suppose I am too."

Her mother sent her a perturbed look, and Lavinia feared she was in for a lecture. She was right.

"Why were you conversing with those women?"

Those women. "They're *duchesses*, Mother. They're also my friends. You like Diana."

"I did when she was respectable. Now she's a pariah. But I suppose that's just as well since she married one."

Lavinia stopped short on the pavement just outside the gate. "Mother. She's my friend. And a duchess. Have some respect, if not kindness."

"She eloped with the Duke of Ruin! You can't maintain a friendship with her, not in your precarious situation."

"Now my situation is precarious?" Lavinia narrowed her eyes as anger coursed through her. "I thought it was glorious."

"For now. Thanks to the Duke of Seduction, but my dear, you are not encouraging matters." She clasped Lavinia's elbow and guided her across the street. "You could have your pick of any gentleman, and you can barely be bothered to be civil."

"That's not fair. I'm quite civil, pleasant even. Yes, my enthusiasm is lacking from time to time, but so many of these gentlemen are boring and self-important." She slid an exasperated look at her mother. "I'll also argue that I don't have my pick of *any* gentleman."

The Marquess of Northam came inexplicably to mind. She didn't want to pick him. He was a rake and a poet, which was about as far from science as one could get without falling off the Earth, which one couldn't do, of course, because it was a sphere.

"Lavinia, pay attention!"

"Yes, Mother."

"I don't want you to spend time with the *duchesses* right now. Not at this important time—your entire future is hanging by a thread."

Lavinia gritted her teeth and swallowed a sarcastic suggestion that her mother should have been on the stage. Her flair for the dramatic was unparalleled. She thought of Violet's dinner party and vowed to find a way to attend. Father would be amenable to the idea. He was far more concerned with aligning himself with dukes than paying attention to gossip and nastiness.

They completed the walk home in silence, and upon their arrival, Lavinia went directly to her room. To hell with Society and its stupid rules. She had half a mind to ask Lord Northam to find her a husband as far outside London as possible.

An academic in Oxford could be perfect, and she began to see how love could play a secondary role. If she could have security and contentment without the drama of the ton watching her every move—and judging them—that might be enough.

Sarah's words came back to her. Perhaps she would be lucky enough to find the man of her dreams amidst the chaos. With Northam's help.

Why was it that when she thought about finding a husband, Northam had begun to spring to mind?

⁂

THE FOLLOWING DAY, Beck walked to the park. He should have gone yesterday, but it was cold and damp, and he suspected Lady Lavinia wouldn't go out in such conditions.

Or perhaps he'd just wanted an excuse to avoid her for a day. Which was silly since he'd agreed to help her find a husband. And she was going to help him find a new young lady to write about. Just as they couldn't keep meeting in libraries, they probably shouldn't keep meeting at the park. Their promenades had likely already been noted, which was the primary reason he'd refrained from going yesterday.

As soon as he passed through Grosvenor Gate, he saw her. She stood with her mother, and they were surrounded by a variety of people. Thankfully, Devaney was nowhere to be seen.

Beck considered whether he should bother. To intrude could result in a scene like the other day. He'd already decided he didn't want to be linked to her in that way. Hell, in any way.

Except he *was* linked to her. At least privately. From the minute he'd brushed his lips against her neck, they'd become intertwined somehow.

Intertwined? Dear God, that summoned thoughts better left unthought. Hadn't he already vowed to not think them?

As he stood there dithering, Lady Lavinia squinted in his direction. Dammit, the woman needed glasses. He'd like to see her in them. Perhaps he could convince her to wear them. Only it wasn't her decision, apparently. He didn't know her mother at all and had scarcely spoken to her father, but was inclined to dislike the woman.

Lady Lavinia continued to look his way, and his decision was made. Against his better judgment, he leapt into the fray.

"Why, it's the Marquess of Northam," her mother said, grinning. "Again."

Beck stifled the urge to roll his eyes as he bowed to her. "Lady Balcombe, a pleasure to see you this fine afternoon."

"And you, Lord Northam. I daresay you're here to see Lavinia. Why don't you take a promenade?"

That was precisely why he hadn't wanted to come over. Not because he didn't want to promenade with her, of course—and he needed to so they could exchange information—but because of the attention it would draw. He managed to lift one side of his mouth in a semblance of a smile at the countess. "I'd be delighted. If Lady Lavinia is amenable?" He turned to her, and she practically snatched his arm in her haste.

"Yes, thank you."

They walked away from the group, and with each step, he felt her relax more and more. "You're quite tense," he observed.

"You saw that gaggle." She peered up at him with a dry stare. "Haven't I reason to be?"

"Every single one."

"Every reason ever?"

"Yes."

She laughed. "Thank you. Now I must castigate you. Where were you yesterday?"

He looked down at her in surprise. "Were you here?"

"I was."

"You're rather hardy to brave the chill."

"It wasn't *that* cold. Besides, I had to get out. Too much time indoors makes me a bit mad." She flashed him an endearing smile. "That's why I like rocks and dirt so much. I was constantly digging in it as a child, much to my mother's displeasure." She shrugged. "I just liked being outside."

"I did too." He recalled growing up in Devon near the sea. "I liked to walk to the beach and watch the ocean. The sight and sound of the waves is what spawned my love of music, I think."

"How so?" She watched him intently, and he realized he'd never shared this with anyone. Not because it was a secret but because it had simply never come up.

"The rhythm. I found it soothing, like a song. My

nurse used to sing to me. She was Irish. She had a beautiful, lilting voice." He closed his eyes briefly and could almost hear her croon on the wind.

"That's lovely. I never thought of it that way before. To me, the ocean is harsh and relentless, carving away at the earth and yet gentle and creative, taking what it breaks away and building it anew."

The way she described it moved him, and he suddenly wanted to write down her words for a song. He worked to commit them to memory. "You speak with a poet's tongue," he said softly.

"I hardly think so, but thank you for the compliment." She stared at him a moment. "On second thought, you're the expert. If you say I am capable of poetry, who am I to quarrel with you?"

"A saucy vixen with a sharp tongue, that's who." He was teasing her, but also maybe flirting. As he'd done the night he'd met her. Only this time, she didn't seem offended. No, she appeared—maybe—to be flattered.

"First I have a poet's tongue, then I have a sharp tongue? Which is it?" She sent him a playfully demanding stare, but all he could think about was her tongue. *Damn it all.*

He cleared his throat. "We should focus on what we need to discuss. I received a letter from my friend at Oxford, Horace Jeffries. He's coming to town, and I'll arrange for you to meet him."

"How will you do that?" she asked.

"I haven't quite worked that out yet. I suppose I could bring him to the park?"

She nodded. "That would suffice. Might he be invited anywhere? Or perhaps he could obtain a voucher for Almack's."

Beck shuddered. "I never set foot in there. Not that

they'd have me."

"Too rakish?"

"Quite."

"Well, you needn't come. We're not trying to determine if you and I will suit."

No, they weren't.

"I'll work something out," he said. "In the meantime, we need a way to communicate. We can't keep meeting in the park. It won't matter if we aren't trying to see if we suit because everyone else will be. If they aren't already."

Lavinia nodded, her lips pressed together in a pensive line. "Yes, I know. My mother was thrilled when she saw you enter the park, and she expected that you would come over. I think it's important we avoid each other for the next several days. And yet, how will we communicate about our objectives?"

"I actually have a plan for that," he said. "There's a hollow in the trunk of the tree in the southwesternmost corner of Grosvenor Square. If you want to tell me something, leave a note in the hollow. I'll check it every day."

She looked at him in admiration. "Well done. And if you need to tell me something?"

"I can do the same, but I'll understand if you can't get there to check every day."

"I'm sure I can come up with something. It's not unusual for me to take walks with my maid or a groom. I'll just have to come up with a reason to visit that same tree." She cracked a smile.

He had a sudden thought. "What if I signal outside your house that there's a message?"

"What sort of signal? Perhaps a sign that reads, 'There's a letter for you in Grosvenor Square'?" She laughed. "Sorry, I couldn't resist. Of course not that."

He laughed with her. "No, not that. Something more...subtle." He considered a moment as they sobered. "I'll tie something to the iron fencing in front of the house across the street."

"Oh, that's a brilliant idea! Far better than my suggestion." She smirked, and he chuckled again. Droll was perhaps not an adequate description of Lady Lavinia's humor. "And I'll see it easily since my bedroom faces the street—second floor in the corner."

"Now that we have that settled, we should turn back and on the way, you can tell me if you've identified a young woman for me to help."

They pivoted on the path, and he sensed a slight change in her body—she tightened up again, though not as much as when they'd departed. "What's wrong?" he asked, worried that she'd changed her mind about helping him.

"I'm not entirely certain I have a candidate yet." She worried her bottom lip, which he'd never seen her do before.

"All right, well let me know when you do. The editor of the *Morning Chronicle* is pestering me for a poem. You mentioned Miss Pemberton may not appreciate the attention. Should I not write another poem for her?"

"No, you should not. Actually, I do have an idea." Her voice trailed off along with her gaze. Then she took a deep breath, and he had the sense she was summoning courage. "My friend Sarah Colton."

He blinked at her in surprise. While he'd thought of writing about Miss Colton next, he'd abandoned that idea after learning how much Lady Lavinia disliked it. "She doesn't share your views on my interference?"

"On the contrary, she's a bit jealous." Lady Lavinia

winced. "If only you'd written to her in the first place."

"I might have if I'd met her instead of you that night."

Their gazes connected, and he was suddenly more aware of her hand on his arm than he'd ever been. Heat radiated from her touch, and he recalled the scent of lilies and honeysuckle—how she'd smelled when he'd kissed her neck.

She looked away first. "Yes, well, if you could write a poem about her, she would appreciate it. As would her mother. Apparently, she prays for it daily."

Beck groaned. "Perhaps this is a mess. I hadn't intended for it to become such a...*thing.*"

"It's too late now. It's *quite* the thing."

He hated all the trouble he'd caused, and he wasn't sure he'd successfully find her a husband. He wished there was something else he could do. Something he could control. A thought occurred to him. It was a small gesture, but he suspected she'd appreciate it. "Lady Lavinia, does your interest in geology extend to fossils?"

Her dark eyes brightened. "Oh yes, I have a small collection."

He did too. He'd gathered them around his home as a boy, and now they sat in a box in his study. They'd be much more appreciated in her possession. He made a mental note to write to his stepmother and have her send them to him.

"Would it be untoward if I asked you to call me Lavinia?"

Her question caught him off guard.

She waved her hand. "Of course it would be. But I don't care. We're friends, and my friends call me Lavinia."

"It wouldn't be appropriate."

"No, but our entire association isn't appropriate. As long as we're breaking the rules, we may as well go all in."

He smiled at her argument. "All right."

She tipped her head as she looked up at him. "Your friends call you Beck?"

He nodded. "My given name is William Beckett. I was Viscount Beckett before I inherited the title. Everyone has always called me Beckett or Beck. Except my mother. She called me Will." A long-buried pang of sadness crested over him—like a giant wave from the sea, a disruption in the rhythm.

"When did she die?" Lavinia asked softly.

"When I was fifteen."

"You miss her."

He nodded. "I do, but I was lucky to gain a stepmother I love and who loves me."

"Bother, we're nearly back," Lavinia said. "But I think we've said all we need to."

Not really. He was enjoying their conversation far too much. On the other hand, he was eager to get home and empty the words milling about his head onto foolscap.

"Look for my sign," he said. "I'll let you know when Horace arrives and when you should come to the park to meet him."

"Very good. And you'll write a poem to Sarah. Make it good, please—your best. She likes dogs, if it helps to know that. And horrid novels, but maybe don't write about that."

He laughed again. "I'll write something deserving of your praise."

"Don't write it for me. Write it for her future

husband."

"Yes, of course."

They walked to her mother, and he left rather quickly, both because he was eager to write and play his guitar and because he didn't want to make small talk with the countess. Or encourage her to think he was going to court Lavinia.

That wasn't going to happen. They were friends, and he liked that, despite the oddness of it. A rake and a young unmarried lady were the unlikeliest of friends. And if Society knew of it, there would be hell to pay.

Luckily, Beck didn't believe in hell. He couldn't. Many would say his sister was there, and that was a notion he simply couldn't endure.

Chapter Seven

❦

Grant her high favor and be glad
For the smile she bestows, dear lad.
Give your care to this charming miss
Love's reward is elegant bliss.

-From A Ballad for Miss Anne Berwick
by The Duke of Seduction

THE REEVES ROUT was a terrible crush, and Lavinia had a hard time finding Sarah and Fanny, particularly without her spectacles. It was moments like these when she wished she just wore them anyway. Perhaps she would start carrying them so she could whip them from her reticule and use them for a brief time.

Squinting through the throng, she finally caught sight of Sarah, who was nowhere near the wall. But why should she be? The Duke of Seduction's *Ode to Miss Sarah Colton* had been published that very morning, and Sarah was currently experiencing the effect.

After seeing the poem that morning—Beck had truly outdone himself—Lavinia had rushed to visit Sarah, along with Fanny. Sarah had been so happy that Lavinia knew she'd done the right thing in asking Beck to write it for her. And Lady Colton was ecstatic. In fact, their visit had been cut short so they could go shopping for something special for tonight's rout.

Which was exactly what Lavinia's mother had done.

Leaving her mother's side, Lavinia made her way to Sarah, who stood beside her mother. As Lavinia cut her way across the large drawing room, she heard a snippet of conversation that made her stop and listen.

"I just can't see that it will help the poor gel. She has the personality of a mouse, regardless of what the Duke of Seduction says."

Lavinia gritted her teeth as she recognized the speaker—Lady Nixon, one of the ton's most malignant gossips. She was talking to her closest friend, who was equally toxic, Mrs. Law.

Mrs. Law sniffed. "I must agree. It doesn't seem the Duke has been able to help Miss Pemberton or Lady Lavinia land husbands. Perhaps his magic has worn off."

"Pity. I've so enjoyed his poetry. Today's ode was simply magnificent." Lady Nixon let out a sigh.

Lavinia thought of a few things she might like to say to the old biddies, but took herself off before she created a scene that would mortify her mother. Unfortunately, Sarah was no longer where she'd been. Lavinia squinted in search of her and saw her speaking with a gentleman. Ah, well, she'd find her later.

Instead of returning to her mother, Lavinia went in search of Fanny before recalling that she wasn't coming tonight. Lavinia did, however, see Miss Pemberton, who was just finishing a promenade with a gentleman. After he departed, Lavinia swooped in.

"Good evening, Miss Pemberton."

The other woman's sherry-colored eyes lit with recognition. "Lady Lavinia, how lovely to find you here. I see your friend Miss Colton is the latest recipient of the Duke of Seduction's…kindness."

"Yes, she's quite thrilled."

"Unlike us," Miss Pemberton said drily.

"I don't *hate* it," Lavinia said, immediately wondering why she had. Now that she knew Beck was behind it all, she felt a bit less annoyed. "But it will be nice to be forgotten."

"Hopefully soon. Things have begun to settle down, for which I'm grateful."

"I just overheard Lady Nixon and Mrs. Law discussing the Duke's failure since you and I are not betrothed."

Miss Pemberton let out a sharp laugh. "Clearly it hasn't deterred him from continuing his ridiculous campaign. Have you had any luck with determining his identity?"

Lavinia didn't hesitate to answer. "No. I don't think we'll ever know."

"Unless the editor of the *Morning Chronicle* is susceptible to bribery." Miss Pemberton appeared quite serious. "Do you suppose he is?"

"I'm sure I don't know." Lavinia laughed, hoping Miss Pemberton was jesting, and was rewarded with a grin. Relaxing, she asked, "What would you do if you learned his identity?"

"Besides demand he stop? Part of me would like for him to suffer some sort of public discomfort, but I am not a vindictive person. I should just feel better if I could unburden myself on him." Her lips widened in another smile.

"I can understand that." Lavinia had *done* that.

They stood somewhat near the door, and Lavinia saw the subject of their conversation enter the drawing room. Beck was accompanied by another gentleman. He was a bit shorter than the marquess, with ink-dark hair and a stocky build. His gaze darted about the room, making him appear a trifle nervous.

Lavinia had never seen the man before and wondered if that was Beck's friend from Oxford. She kept an eye on them while she spoke with Miss Pemberton a little while longer. Beck and the man exchanged pleasantries with their hosts, and then Lady Reeves came toward Lavinia.

Lady Reeves smiled warmly at them. "Lady Lavinia, I'd like to introduce you to a new arrival if you have a moment."

"Certainly." Lavinia looked to Miss Pemberton, who inclined her head and with her gaze encouraged her to go.

Lavinia followed Lady Reeves to where Beck stood with the other gentleman.

"Lady Lavinia, may I present Mr. Horace Jeffries?" Lady Reeves said. "I believe you know Lord Northam."

"Indeed I do." Lavinia curtsied to Beck and then to Mr. Jeffries. "Pleased to meet you, Mr. Jeffries."

"The delight is all mine, I'm sure." Mr. Jeffries slid a glance toward Beck, who tipped his head an infinitesimal degree. Turning his attention to Lady Reeves, Mr. Jeffries thanked her for the introduction, then asked Lavinia if she wanted to take a turn.

"I'd be honored," Lavinia said, feeling a bit strange to be leaving on the arm of someone who wasn't Beck. Her gaze lingered on his before she turned to walk away with Mr. Jeffries.

"I understand you live in Oxford," Lavinia said.

"Yes. Lord Northam invited me to town for a few days. I do like to get to London now and again, especially to visit the museum."

"I love the museum. How do you know Lord

Northam?"

"We attended Oxford together. I was already there when he arrived. I helped him with scientific subjects and arithmetic. He often sacrificed his studies in those areas to play music and read."

Beck had told her he played a bit. It sounded as though he'd misled her about how much he played. "You've heard him play?" she asked.

"Oh yes, he's wonderful." He sent her a pained glance. "But I don't know that he still does. He was always rather bashful about it. He only plays for his friends. And not even all of those."

Mr. Jeffries must be a special friend to Beck, then. Lavinia wondered if she was. Would he play for her if she asked?

Are you daft?

Apparently. Just when and how would the Marquess of Northam play guitar for Lady Lavinia without doing so in a public setting? And it didn't sound as though he did that. She'd have heard of it if he did. A charming, rakish marquess who played guitar beautifully would be the talk of the ton.

"How nice," she said, imagining a young Beck sitting idly beneath a tree with an open book as he strummed his guitar. "I'm not musical in the slightest."

"Neither am I. I much prefer research and academia." He glanced at her with curiosity. "Northam did tell me of your passion for in geology. What an extraordinary interest for a young woman."

She couldn't quite tell if he approved or not. Many gentlemen looked down their noses at her. "I found a fossil when I was nine, and I became a bit obsessed with the history of the earth."

He grinned. "Brilliant! I grew up with an extensive

garden, and from a very young age, I was always curious about the plants—how they grew, how they were the same and different, why they flourished in some environments and failed in others. How remarkable that your childhood curiosity has remained. No doubt because you've nurtured it as I have."

"As much as I can. It's not terribly popular for a young woman to have a passion for geology."

His brow creased. "Yes, yes, I can imagine. Pity you couldn't attend Oxford."

"Someday, women will be admitted there, I'm sure. Just as women will one day be fellows of the Royal Society."

"I believe they will, Lady Lavinia. Northam was always advocating for women at Oxford, but I daresay for a different reason." Mr. Jeffries laughed, seemingly unaware that he'd said something slightly untoward. "If memory serves, Northam fell rather deeply in love with a woman during his first year there. Her father was head of house at some college, can't remember which, but not ours. When she wed someone else, he was devastated. I recall he wrote a copious amount of exceedingly lovelorn songs and poems." He waved his hand. "That was a bit redundant. What is a song except a poem put to music?"

Lavinia wondered if Beck would mind that Mr. Jeffries was sharing this information. He seemed a rather private person. In fact, he seemed nothing like the carefree rake he presented to the world.

And yet, she was fascinated to learn these things about him. "It sounds as though you and Lord Northam were quite close."

"Oh, indeed. He and Ware endeavored to include me in their mischief, but I was never quite as boisterous as they were."

They'd completed their circuit of the drawing room, and Lavinia saw that Sarah was now free. Their gazes met, and Sarah inclined her head for Lavinia to join her.

"Here we are back where we started," Mr. Jeffries said.

Lavinia withdrew her arm from his. "Thank you for the promenade, Mr. Jeffries."

"As I said, I'm only in London for a few days, but perhaps we'll meet again."

"I'd like that," she said.

He smiled and offered her a bow before departing. She watched him walk right out the door and suspected he wasn't coming back.

Lavinia went to join Sarah whose eyes were sparkling. "You look as if you're having a splendid evening," Lavinia said.

"Oh yes. But you were right that it's strange. I find myself wanting to ask people if they never noticed me before. I don't, however, in fear of their answer." She grinned.

Lavinia laughed softly. "Best not to ask."

"Who were you with just then?" Sarah asked. "I didn't recognize him."

"Mr. Horace Jeffries from Oxford. He's a botanist."

"A scientist? However did you manage to meet him?"

Lavinia couldn't actually say without revealing her association with Beck. "Lady Reeves introduced him."

Sarah blinked with interest. "And did you like him?"

"I did, actually." She thought back over their conversation and realized most of it had been about Beck. Had she liked him because of that? She glanced around to see if Beck was still there but didn't see him. That didn't mean he'd gone, just that her eyesight at a distance was as terrible as ever. She focused on Sarah. "So you're enjoying yourself overall?"

"Yes, it's very busy. In fact, here comes another gentleman. But perhaps he's here for you."

"I doubt that," Lavinia said with a smile. She hoped not. She wasn't in the mood for another spin around the drawing room. Not unless it was with Beck.

Was that true?

She took her leave of Sarah and went in search of him. It did seem that he'd gone already. And since Mr. Jeffries hadn't come back to the drawing room, she wondered if they'd left together. Where had they gone? Probably to a club or wherever Beck went to do rakish things. Although she couldn't imagine Mr. Jeffries joining him in such activities. Or maybe she just didn't want to think of them doing that.

Disappointment curdled in her gut. It had been five days since she'd walked with Beck in the park, and they hadn't needed to correspond. She realized she missed him and that she had nothing to look forward to with him. It wasn't as if he could meet her in the library.

Lavinia left the drawing room and nosed around until she found the library. Beck wasn't there, of course. In fact, it was open to the rout and there were several people inside, mostly older men, conversing. Which meant she couldn't peruse Lord Reeves's bookshelves.

There was nothing for it. She'd have to return to the drawing room and suffer the rest of her evening. Alone. No, not alone. Thanks to Beck's pen, she was rarely ever that anymore. And damn if she didn't miss that.

❦

SHORTLY AFTER BECK entered his study the following day, Gage came in with his the day's post. "There's a package here, my lord," the butler informed him as he set it and a small stack of letters on Beck's desk.

Beck picked up the parcel and found it to be a bit heavy. "I asked my stepmother to send some things from Waverly Court." He was keen to open it, but he was also eager to play. His gaze drifted to his guitars in the corner.

"I'm sure the household would enjoy it if you played. Of late, your music has taken on a livelier tone. I caught one of the maids dancing as she worked yesterday." Gage said this with humor, his eyes twinkling.

Beck hadn't realized it, but what Gage said was true. His writing was also lighter and…easier. The poem for Miss Colton had flown from his fingertips.

"Whoever she is, I hope you're able to continue the association for quite some time." Gage was well aware of Beck's preference for short-term love affairs and disinclination to marry.

"There isn't anyone," Beck said even while his mind drifted to Lavinia. Her brazenly witty smile and her sharp, intelligent eyes formed an image in his mind.

"I'm surprised to hear it. Changes in your music are almost always accompanied by a new affair."

Beck glanced up at him. "There is certainly no affair."

"No affair isn't the same as no woman. Which is it?"

"Can't it be both?" Beck didn't want to discuss it for fear he'd mention Lavinia. He didn't want to talk about her to Gage. He didn't even want to talk about her to himself. "My friend Horace Jeffries will be by later. We're to take a ride in the park."

Horace was staying with his aunt while he was in town. Beck had offered his hospitality, but Horace said his aunt would be disappointed if he lodged elsewhere. Which was fine with Beck. Visitors in his home put him a bit on edge because he didn't play with others about. Though he might have made an exception for an old friend such as Horace.

Gage took the hint and didn't pursue the topic of women. "Very good, sir." He turned and left, closing the door behind him since he knew Beck would likely play.

First, however, Beck opened the package from Waverly Court. Inside, he found his fossil collection, or most of it, anyway. A few larger pieces sat in his study in a case, while he'd deposited these smaller ones in this box of childhood memories.

Some were quite small, barely spanning his fingertip. Many were beautiful spirals of a shelled creature from who knew how long ago. His favorite was the largest in the box, a rock with the partial skeletal outline of a fish. He smiled, eager to share them with Lavinia.

There were other items in the box he'd forgotten about—a handful of toy soldiers, a bent stick he'd used as a pistol, a few drawings he'd made, and a small stack of letters. He flipped through them, recognizing his mother's and father's handwriting. Then his heart froze for a moment as he saw one in a different hand— Helen's. He recalled that his mother had given him one of her letters as a keepsake after she'd died. He'd wanted something she'd written.

Opening the foolscap, he blew out a breath as he

began to read. The missive was addressed to his mother, and in it, his half sister detailed her activities during the Season. Beck remembered his mother would spend half the Season with her in London and half at home with him in Devon. This must have been written during the part of the Season when Mother had been with him.

The letter was heartbreaking as Helen wrote about her feelings of loneliness and inadequacy. Beck had thought her beautiful and gentle—she was petite and dark-haired with a rather shy and quiet demeanor. In hindsight, he could see how she would be overlooked. Because he saw it happen to young women like her today. Which was why he'd become the Duke of Seduction, and he'd be damned if he'd regret it.

He continued reading, and his breath caught when he reached a certain passage:

> *Just yesterday, a pair of particularly horrid young women (SW and DC) told me I'd likely be better off if I were dead, for then I wouldn't be a burden to my family. Am I a burden? Father says no, but if I don't marry this Season, I will be a spinster, and then I shall be a burden for all the days to come. I am trying my best. I do think it might be working. There is one gentleman who has asked me to dance twice now—at Almack's the other night and again last night at the Wendover ball. He's charming and handsome and so kind. I am trying not to have high hopes, but it is nice to have a small beacon of encouragement.*

The letter finished shortly thereafter, and Beck found himself rereading that section three more times. Anger roiled through him, and he was careful not to crumple the foolscap. He gently folded it and returned the letter to the box.

Beck sat back in his chair and stared, unseeing, across the room. Who were SW and DC? Two young women. Who were not so young anymore, since that was sixteen years ago. They'd be older than Beck. But they were likely still in Society. He'd find someone who was on the scene in 1802, and he'd hunt down SW and DC.

And then what?

He clenched his jaw. He wanted to rail at them, to make sure they knew that those thoughtless words had changed—nay, ended—a life. No one knew what had really happened to Helen, but oh, how he wanted them to. He wanted them to know and to fester in guilt and regret.

But he couldn't do that. Not without disclosing what Helen had done. And no one could know that.

Gradually, his eyes focused on his guitars. He stood and crossed the room, his insides churning with fury and despair. He picked up an instrument and began to play. It wasn't the cheery music Gage had requested. This was dark and wrapped in emotion—a tangle he wasn't sure he could work out.

Beck completely lost himself, surfacing only when Gage opened the door. The butler had that slightly uncomfortable look he reserved for when he had to interrupt. "I beg your pardon, my lord. Mr. Jeffries is here."

Damn, it was that late already? Beck really had submerged himself. "Thank you. Show him into the drawing room. I'll run upstairs to change."

After setting his guitar down, Beck raced up the back stairs to his chambers on the second floor and quickly changed with the assistance of his part-time valet, whom Gage had clearly sent up directly from the lower level where he served as a part-time footman.

A short time later, Beck strolled into the drawing room and smiled at his friend. "My apologies, Horace, I was caught up."

Horace chuckled, his dark brows waggling. "I'm familiar with how that happens. How many times did you keep us waiting at school because you weren't quite finished playing?"

"Too many to count." Beck had heard another student play guitar shortly after arriving at Oxford and fallen in love with the sound. He'd purchased his own instrument and begged that student to teach him to play. Soon, he was on his own, picking out the most atrocious of melodies. "Shall we head to the park?"

"You said you've an extra mount for me?" Horace asked.

"Yes, I'm sure they'll be out front directly, if they aren't already." Gage, in his exceeding efficiency, would have seen to it.

Horace slid him a cautious glance. "Do you think Lady Lavinia will be at the park?"

"Probably. I've seen her there a few times." Probably? He counted on her being there. He realized she was the best thing about the park. She was so much more interesting and *real* than just about anyone else in Society.

"Then perhaps we shouldn't go," Horace said.

Beck stopped as they moved into the hall. "You don't want to see her? I thought your introduction went well?" They'd left the rout last night and met up with Ware and a few other gentlemen at the club.

"It did. I'm just…" His neck colored a bit and he

glanced away. "I'm not very skilled at this courtship business. I'm not entirely sure I'm marriage material."

"I happen to know that Lady Lavinia isn't entirely sure if she's marriage material either, which is why I thought you might suit." And yet he found himself relieved that Horace might not be interested.

Horace peered at him with sharp interest. "How is it you know so much about her?"

"We have a rather, er, unorthodox friendship."

"I'm the last person to understand the rules of Society." Horace shook his head. "But I do know that young, unmarried women aren't supposed to have friends like you."

"Which is precisely why it's unorthodox and, er, secret. She's an intelligent woman who deserves better than Society's Marriage Mart has to offer." Beck realized it sounded as though he should court her. But he never planned to court anyone. Not after that first disaster.

To his credit, Horace said nothing—maybe because he knew all the regretful details. "Well, if it's the same to you, I'd prefer to stick to Rotten Row and leave the socializing to those with far better skill than I."

"It's entirely up to you. I wouldn't even be going to the park if you weren't here."

"Ah, I did interrupt you, then." Horace looked at him apologetically. "We don't have to go."

"Don't be silly," Beck said. "I don't see you very often. Besides, Felix will be there, and he'll be gravely disappointed if we don't show up."

"If you insist."

"I insist." Beck led him outside where their mounts waited. It didn't take them long to ride to the park. They entered through Grosvenor Gate, and paused for a moment to navigate traffic. Beck couldn't help but survey the crowd for Lavinia. He saw her almost immediately. She wore a spring-green frock with a matching bonnet that covered her dark red-brown locks. He didn't worry that she'd see him or Horace at this distance.

They turned their horses toward Rotten Row and were instantly greeted by two ladies who were also on horseback, Lady Fairwell and another woman whose name Beck couldn't remember. Lady Fairwell smiled brightly. "Good afternoon, Lord Northam. Do you recall Mrs. Goodacre?"

"Certainly." Vaguely. "Allow me to introduce my friend, Mr. Horace Jeffries from Oxford."

Horace inclined his head toward them. "I'm a botanist. Just in London to visit with my dear friend Northam."

"Pleased to meet you, Mr. Jeffries." Lady Fairwell directed her sultry gaze toward Beck. "I haven't seen much of you."

Beck didn't want to linger. "No, and I hope you won't think us rude, but we're on our way to Rotten Row."

"Don't let us keep you," Mrs. Goodacre said with a warm smile.

Beck and Horace steered themselves toward Rotten Row, and Beck breathed a sigh of relief. Felix was waiting for them.

"What took you so bloody long?" he demanded without rancor.

Horace rode up alongside Felix. "We were stopped by a couple of women, one of whom was either Beck's paramour or wants to be and he isn't interested."

"How do you know that?" Beck asked, blinking at

Horace in disbelief.

"I've had plenty of experience with women in your orbit," Horace said, chuckling. Felix joined him, and Horace turned to him and said, "And yours."

Felix shouted with laughter. "You know us too well, Horace."

"It's a bit like the good old days at Oxford, I must say."

Felix looked from Horace to Beck. "We should celebrate like that, then. I've the perfect place in mind—Madame Bisset's."

Horace smiled. "I think you took me there last time I was in town."

"And if memory serves, you enjoyed yourself immensely," Felix said.

Beck stifled a groan. Madame Bisset's was one of London's most elite brothels, catering to the highest echelons of Society. Beck didn't visit often, but sometimes he was in the mood for a transaction that didn't necessarily feel like a transaction, which was Madame Bisset's specialty. The women treated you as if they were your personal mistresses—and they were every bit as skilled.

Normally, Beck would agree to go without a second thought, but he wasn't in the mood. The idea of a transaction just didn't interest him right now. He didn't want to say that, however. His friends would ask why, and Beck didn't have an answer. The last thing he wanted to do was dwell on that.

"Sounds like a splendid evening to me," Horace said pleasantly. "What say you, Beck?" Since they were alone, he'd reverted to his familiar name.

He forced a smile. "Splendid." It would be fine— he'd play cards, or chess, with whomever Madame

Bisset sent him to. They were like mistresses in every way and would satisfy any whim, even if it didn't involve sex.

They decided to race along Rotten Row, an activity for which Beck was most grateful. Riding fast would banish all the things he didn't want to think about: Lady Fairwell, why he didn't want to visit a brothel, and his sister Helen. Only now he was thinking of her and, more importantly, the women with the initials SW and DC. He was going to discover who they were and then he'd find a way to avenge his sister, whatever the cost.

Chapter Eight

Sweet love, sweet air, sweet charity,
Her eyes, hair, gaze, bring clarity.
Love gained, love lost, but love restored.
Sweet love, sweet air, sweetly adored.

-From The Nature of Miss Rose Stewart
by The Duke of Seduction

THE MOMENT LAVINIA saw the red ribbon tied to the iron railing in front of the house across the street, her heart began to beat faster. She immediately told her maid to prepare for a walk, then went to the sitting room to inform her mother she was going out.

"Perhaps I'll go with you," the countess said, looking toward the window that faced the small rear garden. "It's rather fair today."

Lavinia blinked in surprise. Her mother didn't generally like physical exercise, unless it meant shopping or gossip. Lavinia didn't *want* her along—not today. Not for *this* walk. "I won't be gone long, and I'm just about to leave." She'd already donned a pelisse as well as her hat and gloves and was carrying her reticule so she could put Beck's message inside. She held her breath while waiting for her mother to respond.

Mother looked her up and down. "So you are. All right, then. Don't wear yourself out so that you won't want to go to the park."

She already didn't want to go to the park. "Yes, Mother."

Turning hastily, Lavinia met her maid, Carrin, in the hall. "Ready."

The footman opened the door, and Lavinia preceded Carrin out to the pavement. She waited for the maid, a soft-spoken woman five years Lavinia's senior, to join her before turning to the left and walking toward Grosvenor Square.

"Are we going anywhere in particular, my lady?" Carrin asked.

"Not really," Lavinia lied. "I think I'll just let my feet guide me." She sent Carrin a warm smile.

Once they were well enough away from the house, Lavinia pulled her spectacles from her reticule and set them on her face. She sighed happily as the sights around her came into sharp focus. Every time she put them on, she wondered why she took them off. Of course she *knew* why—her mother.

Carrin wouldn't tell the countess. She thought it a travesty that Lavinia wasn't allowed to wear them.

As they entered Grosvenor Square, Lavinia instantly found the tree. It was easy to spot, particularly since they were entering from the southwest corner. That was likely why Beck had chosen it.

The center of the square was a lovely green lawn with shrubbery and trees, and the whole was surrounded by a short, wrought iron fence. She turned to Carrin. "Let us go into the square."

They strolled to an opening in the fence, and Lavinia led her through to a path. After they'd walked for a moment, she said to Carrin, "I believe I saw a squirrel. Wait here."

Lavinia hurried to the tree and was glad for an adjacent shrub that partially shielded her as she walked around and found the hollow. Sticking her hand inside, she found a small bag.

Lifting it from the tree, she wondered at the contents, for it was rather heavy. She shoved her hand back into the hollow and felt around for paper, but there wasn't anything else.

The bag had a drawstring, and she tugged it open to see what was inside. Her breath caught as soon as she realized what it was. Rather, what *they* were.

She pulled the first rock out and held it up, staring at the spiral and the even grooves that marked the stone. It was beautiful. And so small. She'd seen drawings of such a thing, but she didn't have anything like it. Her fossils were all plants.

"Do you like it?"

The low, masculine voice stole across her neck, reminding her of the way his lips had caressed her there once. She turned to see Beck leaning against the tree, his gaze heavy, his lids low over his eyes.

"Where did you come from?"

"Nowhere." He pushed away from the tree, his eyes lighting with surprise and something else she wasn't quite sure of. Excitement maybe? No, not that strong. "You're wearing spectacles."

She'd forgotten. Instinctively, she lifted her hand to her face and began to take them off.

"Don't." He stepped toward her and took her hand in his, gently lowering it back to her side.

She stared at him, aware of his proximity in a way she never had been before. "You like them?" she asked softly.

"Very much."

"Supposedly, they detract from my face."

"They help you see the world in crystal clarity, and as a woman of science, you shouldn't view it any other way. That thirst for knowledge only enhances your face—and everything else about you."

A smile curled her lips. "Why, Lord Northam, I do believe you're a poet."

He put his finger to his lips, which she realized were rather supple. She really did like wearing her glasses. "Shhh. Don't tell anyone." He grinned, and her chest squeezed, making it a bit difficult to take a deep breath. Oh dear.

She ripped her gaze from his and looked into the bag. "What else is in here?"

"More like that one, in varying sizes. That's probably the easiest one to find in Devon. My favorite is the largest." He reached into the bag and pulled out a rock that was bigger than the palm of his hand. It was mostly flat with the partial skeleton of what looked to be a fish.

Lavinia gasped. "My goodness, is that real?"

"Touch it." He placed it in her hand.

But it wasn't enough. "Hold these," she said, thrusting the rock and bag into his hands. Her reticule hung from her left wrist, so it wasn't an impediment. She removed her glove, then took the stone back from him, running her bare fingers over the ridges of the fish's bones. "This is extraordinary."

"Watching your delight is extraordinary."

His words slid over her like a seductive song. She fought to look at the rock instead of him. She wasn't entirely sure what was happening here today—with him—and she wasn't sure she wanted to know.

She slipped the rock into the bag, which he still held,

then put her glove back on. "Thank you for sharing them with me."

He pressed the bag into her hand. "They're yours."

She couldn't help but look at him now. "You're giving them to me?"

"I can think of no one better to possess them."

"But they're so special. And valuable."

"I don't know about the latter, but they are certainly special—to you. They've been sitting in a box in my study in Devon for years. I don't remember the last time I looked at them, and that's a shame."

"Yes, it is." She would look at them and touch them every day. Even now, she was burning to study them. "Have you any idea how old these must be?"

He laughed softly. "Not the faintest."

She joined him, giggling. "It's debatable, but suffice it to say they are very, very old."

"Someday you will have to tell me all about this debate. But I'm afraid we are pressed for time today."

Someday? When would that be exactly? They weren't even supposed to be meeting. They were supposed to communicate by letter. Still, she wanted that someday. "Are you by chance going to the Kilves' dinner tomorrow night?" Lavinia had spoken to Violet and knew he'd been invited.

"Yes. The duchess is a friend of yours, isn't she?"

Lavinia nodded. "We met last fall."

"So you'll be there too?" He looked almost...relieved.

"Yes, but I had to prevail upon my father." The countess had almost persuaded Lavinia's father that they shouldn't go given the scandal surrounding the Kilves and the Romseys. Lavinia had put up a good argument as to why it wasn't really a scandal at all—

nobody had been harmed, everyone was quite happy, and why wouldn't they want to align themselves with two dukes? They'd had quite a row over it, but in the end, the earl had sided with Lavinia.

"Why?"

"My mother listens to too much gossip. There are those who think the Duke of Kilve and the Duchess of Romsey behaved badly, and of course the Duke of Romsey is typically known as the Duke of Ruin. Because his wife died, and for a long time, he was suspected of killing her. Not officially, of course."

"Wasn't he vindicated with regard to his wife's death?"

"He was, but you know how vicious and unforgiving Society can be."

"I do." The gravity of his tone and the curl of his lip gave her pause.

"Because of your sister," she said softly.

"Yes." He looked away, and she knew he didn't want to talk about it. She wouldn't press him. Someday, she'd like to know more about her, but not today.

There it was again: *someday.*

"You should go," he said. "We've lingered long enough, and I'm sure your maid is wondering where you are."

He'd seen her arrive with Carrin. Yet, he hadn't known when she would come. "How long were you waiting for me?"

He shrugged. "Not long."

Warmth spread through her. He'd brought her the most precious gift, and he'd waited to deliver them in person. He could very well have written a note to leave with it. Heaven knew he was quite good at that.

"I wanted to thank you for the poem you wrote for

Sarah," Lavinia said. "It's really wonderful. She's overjoyed with the attention."

"I'm pleased to hear it. I only want to help." He hastened to add, "Those who want to be helped, that is."

She grinned. "Just so." She hated to go, but he was right, she must. "I'll see you tomorrow, then."

Her gaze settled on his, and a wave of awareness crested over her—starting at that spot on her neck and flowing through the rest of her body.

He inclined his head toward her wrist. "You should put the fossils in your reticule—if they'll fit."

"Oh yes, I should."

She tried to juggle both items, but Beck took the fossils while she opened her reticule, then he deposited them inside. She put her glove back on and looked up at him. "Thank you."

"My pleasure."

That word—pleasure—sent another flash of anticipation over her. She made herself turn and go.

As soon as she stepped out from behind the shrub, a cool breeze rushed over her. It was as if they'd been in a private world just for them, and she'd had to leave it.

Carrin came rushing toward her. "I was beginning to grow concerned."

"Sorry, I found some interesting rocks." Which wasn't a lie. She held up her reticule and jiggled the contents.

Carrin was well aware of Lavinia's interest in rocks and dirt and science. "How lovely. Perhaps you can show me later."

"Certainly." Lavinia would simply show her some other things from her collection.

They walked back home in relative silence. Lavinia

couldn't shake a sense of giddiness. Beck had utterly surprised her with the fossils. They were without question the best gift she'd ever received.

But it was more than his generosity. It was the way he made her feel. When he looked at her. When he touched her. When he said things like, "That thirst for knowledge only enhances your face—and everything else about you."

She suppressed a shiver. Something was kindling between them, and she couldn't afford to play with fire. Not with a rake with no interest in marriage. And yet, moving a little closer to the heat was almost too exciting to resist.

✦ɛ·3✦

BECK SPENT THE dinner at the Kilves' stealing glances at Lavinia, who sat at the opposite end of the table near her friend Miss Colton. That might as well have been Scotland given the length of the table, which had to support all twenty-six guests.

The women left the dining room, and port was poured for the gentlemen, who congregated at one end of the table. Beck sat between Felix and the Duke of Kendal, a man in his late thirties with black hair and green eyes and the ominous nickname of the Forbidden Duke. It was generally known that he didn't mind being called that because it kept people from bothering him. He didn't participate in many Society events, and when he did, such as this one, it was with people he considered close friends—or so Beck had learned during dinner.

Beck hadn't sat with the duke before now, after everyone had moved, and he found himself wondering, given the man's age, if he might have met his sister Helen or, more importantly, if he might know who SW and DC were.

The duke turned to Beck and asked how he knew the Kilves.

"I don't really," Beck said honestly. "Her Grace is good friends with Miss Colton, and I believe they wanted to round out the female-to-male ratio, and so they invited some of Mr. Colton's friends."

"It's good of you to come. I never would have accepted such an invitation." The duke chuckled. "In my youth, I would have. I was more…gregarious then. Like you."

"Are you trying to politely say you were known for rakish behavior?"

The duke sipped his port. "Drinking, gambling, women, all of it. But then my father died, and I left it all behind. I don't miss it even a little."

Beck didn't really consider himself a drinker or a gambler, but women…he relied on them for inspiration and, of course, he enjoyed sharing pleasure. Since he'd started writing as the Duke of Seduction however, he seemed to need them less. At least as far as inspiration went.

This line of conversation gave Beck the opening he needed. "My half sister was out, likely when you were carousing—Lady Helen Beckett. Did you know her?"

The duke shook his head. "I hope not—for her sake. I was a horrid young man in retrospect. I caused problems for several people with my rather debauched behavior. How is your sister now?"

"She passed away, I'm afraid. That was sixteen years ago, and I was fairly young. I thought it might be nice to talk with someone who knew her."

The duke nodded sympathetically. "I understand. My wife was out then and might have known her." He winced. "She didn't have a very good experience, I'm afraid."

Beck wanted to ask for more information but didn't. "I'm sorry to hear that." He finished his glass of port.

"She fell for the charms of the wrong gentleman, and there was a scandal. She had to leave London. Fortunately for me, she came back nine years later as companion to my stepmother."

"I vaguely remember that, what, seven or eight years ago?"

"Seven, yes."

The Duke of Kilve announced they should join the women in the drawing room. The Duke of Kendal finished his port and stood. Beck also rose and told him he'd enjoyed their chat.

When they arrived in the drawing room, their hostess announced that they'd decided to play hide-and-seek. For those who wanted to play, they could hide anywhere on the first two floors. They'd already decided the Duke of Romsey would be seeker.

His Grace was an affable fellow who agreed to the role with glee. "Just be warned," he said. "If I find my wife first, you all may be waiting awhile." He winked at the duchess, whose blue eyes gleamed with emotion.

Beck could practically feel the love between them. It made his heart clench and reminded him of the way he'd felt at sixteen when he'd met Priscilla. Three years his senior, she was the most beautiful woman he'd ever seen. Her laugh moved him to write the most god-awful poetry, which he'd attempted to put to song shortly after taking up the guitar.

"All right then, you'll count to fifty?" The Duchess

of Kilve asked the Duke of Romsey.

"If I must."

Beck wasn't certain he wanted to play. His gaze immediately went to Lavinia, who'd already risen. Clearly, she was going to.

Well, if she was…

"One, two," the duke started counting, and everyone scattered from the room.

Beck didn't want to obviously follow Lavinia, not when he was fairly certain where she would go. He left the drawing room, noting that her parents and the Coltons had remained, and paid attention to where people went.

Now he just had to find the library. He walked upstairs and turned to the right as one of the ladies came out of the room on the left side, closing the door behind herself. "That's the library—someone's already gone in there."

Beck nodded and pretended to consider where to go. After the lady had disappeared to the other side of the house, he slipped into the library and closed the door behind him.

The room wasn't overly large, and it was—seemingly—empty. It also wasn't terribly well lit, with a low fire burning in the grate and a pair of sconces flickering on the wall on either side of the fireplace.

She was either beneath the desk or behind the curtain. He couldn't see the underside of the desk from the door. It wasn't a pedestal as Lord Evenrude's had been.

Circling around, he saw no one hiding there. That left the draperies on the window. He moved to the far wall and instantly noted the slight lump behind the blue damask. Moving forward, he reached for the fabric but hesitated before he pushed it aside. What if it wasn't her?

The fabric moved, and she bared her face. "You found me." Her dark gaze registered surprise. "Oh, it's you!"

"It's me."

"Are you still looking for a place to hide?"

"I am."

She reached for his lapel and held the drapery wide, pulling him into the darkness beside her. "He'll be done counting shortly. If he isn't already."

"I should probably hide somewhere else," he said, though he was loath to move. Ensconced in the dark with Lavinia, he was acutely aware of her heat and the intoxicating scent of lilies and honeysuckle.

"Yes, I suppose you should." She turned toward him, and they were so close, her breasts brushed against his chest. "Sorry," she murmured.

God, *he* wasn't. He was only sorry he had to leave.

"Before you go, I wanted to thank you again for the fossils." She whispered, her breath tickling his neck as she spoke. "I can't stop looking at them. They're absolutely extraordinary. I hope I have reason to visit Devon one day so I can hunt for my own."

"I hope you do too. Consider yourself welcome at Waverly Court any time."

"That's very kind of you."

He heard the smile in her voice and resisted the urge to run his fingers over her mouth so he could feel the curve of her lips. He really should go—

But first, he wanted to ask her something. "Do you know the Duchess of Kendal?"

"Yes, but not well. Fanny's sister is a good friend of hers. Why?"

Why indeed. Beck wanted to enlist Lavinia's help to see if the Duchess might be able to help him learn who SW and DC might be. However, if the Duchess had been part of a scandal, she might prefer to leave those memories in the past. Furthermore, he wasn't sure he should include Lavinia in any of this.

And yet, he found he simply couldn't resist. "Do you know what happened with the Duchess when she was out in Society—maybe sixteen years ago? The Duke mentioned something, and I was curious. Because my sister was out at the same time." He added the last because he felt he had to share a reason for his inquiry. Still, he hated bringing Helen up since he didn't want to answer too many questions about her, particularly regarding her fate.

"She was compromised. A gentleman—I can't remember who—wooed her. They were caught kissing, and he refused to marry her. She was ruined. It was horrible because it wasn't even her fault. It's so unfair. Men can kiss whomever they want, and women are blamed for any indiscretion."

"The key is to not get caught. It sounds as though this gentleman was rather inept."

"Are you saying it was his fault?" She sounded surprised. "Most would argue they were at least both to blame."

"Certainly she retains some culpability, but a decent gentleman would ensure they could kiss and not get caught."

"And how would they do that?" Something in her tone changed. Her voice lowered, and it felt as though she'd moved just a hair closer.

If he leaned just a tiny bit forward, he was sure he'd feel her breasts again. God, how he wanted to. "They might hide themselves behind a drapery in the library."

"During hide-and-seek?"

Beck's cock lengthened and grew stiff as the air around them heated. "Probably not. In that case, someone is actually *looking* to find them."

"And yet here we are." Her voice had changed again, going nearly breathless.

"Yes, here we are."

"Are you going to, then?" she asked, her breasts grazing his chest as she edged herself against him. "Kiss me."

"By God, I think I am."

"Oh, good."

He wrapped his arms around her waist and pulled her to his chest. Lowering his head, he swept his mouth over hers, finding her in the darkness as if his body instinctively knew hers.

She clutched his back and held him tightly as his lips moved against hers. He cautioned himself to go slow despite the passion raging through him. He'd been celibate forever, it seemed, and yet not all that long. No, just since he'd met her, he realized in just that moment. Had his inner self been waiting for this?

He ended the kiss, inviting frustration. But it had to be done.

"That's it?" Her question tossed him off guard. "I know there's more to it than that."

Hell, she'd never been properly kissed. "We don't have much time."

"Then you'd better be quick about it." There was an edge of challenge to her tone, but mostly it was sultry demand. And he was powerless to refuse her.

He moved one hand up to the back of her neck and curled his fingers around her nape. His lips found hers again, and this time, he angled his head and licked along the crease of her mouth.

She opened on a soft gasp, inviting him into her lush, velvety softness. His tongue slid along hers, coaxing her in long, delicious strokes to kiss him in return. She responded with seductive immediacy, her fingertips dancing along his neck.

The heat inside him blazed into a bonfire of need and desire. She pressed herself against him, bringing them more than chest to chest—her pelvis was tucked into his. It was sweet temptation, and he fought to hold himself in check.

They really didn't have time.

Her tongue thrust into his mouth, and he groaned softly, clasping her more tightly. He couldn't get enough of her. And damn, nothing was more true than that. He had to let her go.

Now.

He ended the kiss and took a step back while also pushing her back slightly. He needed to put distance between them. If he didn't, he wasn't sure he trusted himself to walk away.

"I'm going to hide beneath the desk now." He was a wreck of himself. His voice was dark and hoarse, and his cock raged with near painful need.

"All right." She sounded a bit dazed. "If you must."

"I must." He forced himself to reach for the drapery, pulling it open to step through it.

Light spilled in and revealed the flush of her cheek and the red rose of her kiss-swollen lips. He stifled another groan. She was beyond stunning, and he wasn't sure he'd ever wanted a woman more.

"If you ever have reason to do that again, I invite you to do so," she said, her gaze a mix of seductive innocence and wholesome desire that nearly sent him to his knees.

He didn't answer, because he heard a sound from outside. Letting go of the curtain, he dashed back to the desk and threw himself beneath it just a moment before the door swung open.

Well, that had been a near thing. What the hell was he doing, kissing an unmarried young lady whom he was trying to help find a husband?

More importantly, why was he trying to find a reason, as she'd said, to do so again?

Chapter Nine

❦

Angels take flight to see her face,
Delicate beauty, heaven's lace.
She is a song, she fascinates.
A stirring ballad she creates.

-*From* The Virtue of Miss Anne Berwick
by The Duke of Seduction

AFTER TWO MORE rounds of hide-and-seek, everyone returned to the drawing room. Conversation sprang up around the room, and Lavinia maneuvered herself to the corner where Beck was standing by himself.

"I was hoping someone might suggest music, and you could play guitar," she said.

He glanced over at her, but his expression was unreadable. "I didn't bring a guitar."

"That's a shame. I'd love to hear you play. Mr. Jeffries told me you are quite good."

Beck's dark blond brows arched briefly before he cast her another quick look. "What else did Horace say?"

She detected a sardonic edge to his tone. Overall, he seemed a bit tense. She moved closer to his side—but not too close. "He mentioned you fell in love."

Beck scowled but didn't look toward her. "Horace talks too much."

"Are you angry with me?"

He exhaled. "No. I'm angry with me." He still didn't look at her.

"Because of what happened in the library?" She nodded. "I'm a bit angry too, actually. Well, not angry. Frustrated."

Now he turned his head and looked at her. "You are?"

"Yes. I wish we'd had more time."

"*Lavinia.*" The single word came out low and thick, what she imagined lava might sound like.

She took a tiny step closer and blinked up at him. "Yes?"

He frowned. "You're flirting. And you're not good at it."

"I know." She curled her lips into an eager smile. "Maybe you can teach me that too."

He opened his mouth, then snapped it closed. His gray-green eyes were a storm of emotion she couldn't read. "No." His gaze moved past her. "Here comes Felix."

She pouted. "Bother."

He lowered his voice to a bare whisper, his gaze moving from her to the approaching Felix—or so she assumed since she didn't turn around. "Lavinia, you mustn't flirt, and we mustn't repeat what happened in the library. I am deeply sorry I took advantage."

"You didn't," she said softly. She narrowed her eyes. "And you're also not in charge of me."

Any further conversation was prohibited by the arrival of the Earl of Ware. He clapped Beck on the shoulder and said he was going to leave.

"I'll join you." Beck bowed to Lavinia. "Have a pleasant evening." He was particularly accomplished at behaving as if they were barely acquainted.

Fine. She could do that too. "I'm sure I will." She gave him a wide, brief smile and dipped into a not very deep curtsey. Then she turned and found Sarah, rescuing her from Lady Colton and Lavinia's mother.

They circuited the drawing room until they found Fanny, and the three of them moved to a corner where they deposited themselves onto a small settee with Lavinia in the center.

"While this has been a diverting evening, it hasn't furthered my marital prospects," Sarah said.

"Because there's no one with potential here," Fanny observed. "The only bachelors were your brother, Ware, and Northam. Taking your brother out of things, that leaves Ware and Northam, and neither are decent marital prospects."

Sarah nodded in agreement. "No, and that's such a shame. Hide-and-seek certainly lends itself to clandestine meetings. If only there'd been someone worth meeting. I should like a stolen kiss."

Lavinia stared straight ahead into the room even as her heart picked up speed. The imprint of Beck's lips on hers, the touch of his hand on her neck, the sound of his whispered words weighted with urgency and desire heated her until she wished she'd brought a fan.

"Have you never kissed anyone?" Fanny asked.

Sarah shook her head. "We played some kissing games last fall at a house party, and while Lavinia was fortunate enough to be kissed on the cheek, I received nothing." She peered around Lavinia at Fanny. "Have you kissed anyone?"

Fanny nodded, and Lavinia turned her head toward her. Both she and Sarah said in unison, "You have?"

"Yes."

"But you're younger than us." Sarah sounded woefully disappointed.

Fanny blushed. "It was just a kiss, though a very nice one."

"How did you manage that?" Lavinia asked. "I don't recall you going off with anyone." Which didn't mean she hadn't—neither she nor Sarah knew Lavinia had been alone with Beck.

"I met him at Stour's Edge—my brother-in-law's country house—at Christmas. I was out for a walk, and I got a bit lost. He was visiting the neighborhood."

"Who is he?" Sarah asked.

Fanny's cheeks colored pink again. "I only know his given name—David. We thought it best to leave our...encounter shrouded in a bit of mystery." She laughed. "I haven't seen him since and don't expect to."

Sarah's gaze softened. "Was it lovely?"

Fanny nodded, her eyes shining. "It was magnificent. Not a day goes by that I don't think of it. Of him. He may have ruined me for future suitors. That is probably why I haven't been overly interested in anyone so far this Season."

"Fanny has a secret admirer. Like the Duke of Seduction but not." Sarah laughed.

"I have a secret," Lavinia blurted, her voice nearly a whisper. She didn't want to keep this from her friends, and frankly, she had to tell *someone*. Beck's behavior was confusing and irritating and she didn't know what to do.

Sarah blinked at her in surprise. "You do?"

Lavinia nodded. She gave Sarah an apologetic look. "I should have told you sooner. At least the first part— when he kissed my neck."

Sarah's eyes widened. "Who kissed your neck?"

"Northam."

"Aha!" Sarah's expression gleamed with triumph. "I knew there was something between you."

"Keep your voice down," Lavinia urged. "There is nothing between us. I thought we were friends. But then we kissed in the library—"

"Tonight?" Sarah asked, cutting into her tale.

"Yes. During hide-and-seek."

Sarah leaned around Lavinia and gave Fanny a knowing look. "I told you it was perfectly suited for that."

Fanny laughed softly. "I don't think anyone would dispute it." She directed her attention to Lavinia. "What happened?"

"We both chose to hide in the library. We got, er, close. It seemed the natural thing to do."

"And when did he kiss your neck?" Sarah asked. "You said that was the first part."

Lavinia thought back. "Oh goodness… three weeks ago? Before—" She caught herself just before she said "he." "Before the Duke of Seduction wrote about me. It was the Evenrude ball—the night we met you, Fanny."

At Fanny's nod, Lavinia continued. "I went to the library to read a geological manuscript, and while I was seated on the settee—my back was to the door—he kissed my nape."

"You didn't hear him come in?" Fanny asked.

"No. I was too engrossed."

"Unsurprising," Sarah said with a soft smile. "Why did he do that?"

"He thought I was the woman he was meeting to…you know." Lavinia left her name out, as she'd promised him she wouldn't tell anyone about it. Just as she'd said she wouldn't tell anyone he was the Duke of Seduction. That information, however, was burning her tongue. Still, she was nothing if not loyal, so she'd simply go home and unburden her feelings about his interfering in her life to her diary. Yes, she hadn't done that in quite some time, and she found she had a bit to say on the matter.

Sarah giggled. "Oh my. What did he do when he discovered you weren't her?"

"He apologized. Profusely. I was rather angry."

"As you should have been," Fanny said. She leaned close, her eyes expectant. "But wasn't it exciting?"

Exciting? At the time, it had given rise to panic. But since then, she'd thought of it—and him—so often that she supposed she could attribute some adjective to it. "It was...memorable."

"Clearly, for you and he have developed an association—you talked at the Fortescues', you've promenaded at the park, and he even took you home in his curricle after you pretended to faint." Sarah's eyes narrowed. "I asked if he was courting you, and you said no. Yet you kissed him tonight."

There was so much Lavinia could reveal—about his secret, about their alliance, which came from that secret, about him giving her fossils... But she couldn't say any of that, not without crafting a giant lie. Better to simply omit.

Suddenly, she wanted to leave.

"Yes, I kissed him. Or he kissed me." Lavinia waved her hand and hoped she portrayed the appropriate level of insouciance. "It was a mutual curiosity, and one that won't be repeated. Northam is a rake, and I shouldn't want to be courted by one such as him."

"Don't write him off for that," Fanny said with determination. "My sister did that with West and ended up being wrong about him. She has said multiple times that she'd never been more glad to be wrong about someone."

Lavinia supposed she could be wrong about Beck, but he'd certainly demonstrated his penchant for "rakish things," to use his words. She'd seen him talking with Lady Fairwell at the park. What if he was still carrying on with her?

"I don't know that I'm wrong about Lord Northam," she said, rising from the settee.

The others stood with her, and Sarah said, "I suppose time will tell."

It would, and in the meantime, Lavinia wouldn't wait around to find out.

⊷ɛ·3⊷

STROLLING INTO BROOKS'S the following evening, Beck went directly to the small drawing room where he might run into Felix. If he was there. It was a bit early yet, and Beck would be content to simply sip a whiskey.

Or five.

He'd slept late and spent the day closeted in his study with his guitar and pen. It had taken Gage to pull him out of his thoughts and force him to bathe and go out this evening. Gage was nothing if not attuned to Beck's moods.

And his mood had been rather dark following last night's encounter with Lavinia. Rather, encounters. First there had been the kissing, then there had been her attempt at flirtation. He'd botched both.

Fine, maybe he hadn't botched the kissing. It had

been quite nice. Quite nice? It had been sublime. He'd messed up in that he shouldn't have kissed her in the first place. Just as he shouldn't have gone into the library looking for her, because that was precisely what he'd done. Actually, in hindsight, he shouldn't even have joined the game. Hell, he could do better than that. He shouldn't have gone to the damn party to begin with.

But he had. And he'd kissed her. Furthermore, it had been divine. He'd drunk himself silly last night in an effort to banish her from his mind. He'd slept fitfully, dreaming of her. Then he'd awakened early and frigged himself, and still she lingered as he fell into an exhausted slumber that lasted until afternoon.

Immersing himself in music and words had helped, though the outpouring of emotion had been dark and dissonant, leaving him feeling unsatisfied and a bit…empty.

He was used to that feeling. It came to him now and again, less often since he'd become the Duke of Seduction. However, since he'd found the letter from Helen a few days ago, he found himself falling back into the old pattern.

A footman brought a glass of whiskey as soon as he sat at a table. Beck thanked him and took a sip of the rich, pale amber liquid. It was heavy and spicy and exactly what he wanted. He needed fortification.

He couldn't continue to fixate on Lavinia. She was a charming and intelligent young woman who deserved a husband who would give her light and love. And science. Beck definitely couldn't do that.

What Beck needed to do was find out who had told his sister she was better off dead. That needed to be his priority. He considered speaking with the Duchess of

Kendal, but if she'd been embroiled in a scandal, she might not wish to discuss that time period. It was also possible that she didn't know Helen or who those other women might be. No, he'd be better off finding someone else who could help him.

Beck sipped his whiskey and looked about the room, cataloguing the handful of gentlemen in attendance, none of whom were better than acquaintances. From the corner of his eye, Beck saw someone enter. He turned his head, hoping it was Felix, who would undoubtedly be able to help him think of someone to talk to. Which would mean revealing his sister's secret. On second thought, maybe he couldn't do that.

Only it wasn't Felix.

It was Lavinia's father, Lord Balcombe. And he was walking straight toward Beck.

Hell.

Beck finished his drink and prayed the footman would come immediately with another.

He didn't, however. Instead, the earl arrived at Beck's table and bid him good evening. "Do you mind if I sit?"

Yes. "Please." Beck gestured to one of the empty chairs at his round table.

"When I saw you sitting here, I thought I should come over so we could have a talk. I regret I didn't get a chance to speak with you at the Kilves' last night. Perhaps I should have played hide-and-seek." The corner of his mouth ticked up, and Beck wasn't sure if he was trying to hint at something. Did he know what had happened in the library? No, how could he? Unless Lavinia had told him...

She wouldn't have done that. Beck would stake all the secrets he harbored on that.

"It was an enjoyable evening," Beck said.

Thankfully, the footman arrived with two more glasses of whiskey, which he deposited in front of them on the table.

The earl scooped his up in his fingertips and held the glass aloft. "To new relationships and looking to the future."

Beck held up his whiskey, then took a robust drink. He wasn't sure what Balcombe was about, but he had a sinking feeling the earl had a specific purpose for this meeting.

Balcombe set his glass down. "Fine whiskey here at Brooks's." He looked over at Beck, his dark eyes assessing. He squinted slightly, and Beck wondered if the man also suffered from myopia. "My wife and I require your assistance with our daughter. Well, more help than you've already provided."

The sinking feeling intensified, and Beck had the sensation that the floor beneath him was turning to dust. "I beg your pardon?"

"You needn't prevaricate," Balcombe said pleasantly, but with a touch of steel. "We know you're the Duke of Seduction." He pursed his lips and let out a soft, nasal sound. "Such a ludicrous nickname."

How the hell did they know that? Gage never would have revealed his secret—not that they would've learned such a thing from his butler. That left Lavinia. Why had she told them? Had she been angry with him after he'd told her they couldn't kiss again?

Beck set his ire and his burning curiosity aside. "How do you want me to help her beyond what I've already done?"

"It seems your...efforts aren't bearing the same fruit as some of your other subjects. Lavinia is unique and perhaps requires an additional nudge." Balcombe sipped his whiskey, behaving as if this were a friendly conversation he had with regularity. "We'd like you to court her."

Beck bit back his instant refusal. "I do not wish to marry."

"We're not asking you to marry her. We want you to court her so that other gentlemen—those who've expressed an interest—will accelerate their courtship."

As angry as Beck might be with Lavinia for exposing him, he hated that her parents sought to manage her life in this way. "Why not wait for things to take their natural course? Is there some reason you need to rush into a wedding contract?"

The earl's eyes darkened, and he leaned slightly forward. "I don't care for your insinuation, Northam. I came here prepared to make a deal, but you may force my hand. I won't hesitate to reveal your hidden identity to the world."

It was to be extortion, then. "I wasn't insinuating anything," Beck said with heat. "I find your management of your daughter's marital affairs overbearing."

"You may keep your opinions to yourself. I'll ask if I'd like to hear them."

Beck gripped his whiskey, his hand choking the glass as he brought it to his mouth and took another healthy drink, not quite finishing it. He set it back down on the table, perhaps a trifle too hard as the liquid sloshed up the sides of the tumbler. "Has it not occurred to you that I am providing a service to young women, including Lady Lavinia? Just because she is not yet betrothed doesn't mean she won't be. You can see my poems have elevated her visibility."

"Yes, but we want her wed this Season. You'll court her, and things will move with alacrity."

"And if they don't?" Courtship often led to a betrothal, and Beck wasn't prepared to agree to that. Hell, he wasn't prepared to agree to any of it.

"We'll deal with that problem should it arise. The countess and I are confident your interest will spur a few men in particular to make their move. Let us worry about that maneuvering."

Maneuvering? Christ, would they manipulate the other suitors as well? Any anger he had toward Lavinia dissipated. For all he knew, they'd done something to manipulate her too.

The earl cleared his throat and straightened, adopting the stature and tone of someone conducting a business transaction. "You'll call on Lavinia tomorrow and walk with her in the park some time this week. And dance with her at your earliest convenience. We will be attending the Halliwell ball and expect to see you there. If you fail to meet our terms, we will publish your identity as the Duke of Seduction in the *Times*."

Beck glared at the man across the table. "Your manipulation is rather despicable."

"No more so than your meddling and unsolicited 'help.'" Balcombe finished his whiskey and stood. "See you tomorrow."

Fury raged through Beck as he watched the man leave the room. He was so focused on the earl's retreating back—and staring daggers into it—that he failed to notice Felix approach.

He sat down in the chair Balcombe had abandoned. "What the devil was that about? You look as though you'd like to run him through."

"I would, actually," Beck said tightly.

Felix cast a look toward the door through which the earl had departed. "Why?"

Beck couldn't explain without telling Felix everything. And he might—just not right now. He was too angry. "Never mind. I don't want to discuss it."

The footman came over and swept up Balcombe's empty glass, then deposited a fresh one for Felix.

"I hope you don't mind my saying so, but you seem a bit off lately," Felix said, picking up his glass and taking a small sip. He swallowed, flexed his lips, then took another. "Have you been writing? Playing?"

"Both."

"You aren't seeing anyone right now, are you? Perhaps we should visit Madame Bisset's again. I had a grand time the other night."

"No, thank you. I'm not up for that this evening."

Felix surveyed him a long moment. "You're in another of your moods. I hope this doesn't last long."

His moods could last a few hours or a few weeks. Or, as in the case of Priscilla's rejection, months. Beck hoped this wasn't one of those times.

He finished his whiskey and decided he should engage in "rakish things," reminding him of what he'd said to Lavinia at the Fortescues' musical performance. "Let's go play cards."

"Brilliant." Felix plucked up his whiskey and stood.

Beck rose and followed him into the card room. Tomorrow he would call on Lavinia and pretend to court her. She would be extraordinarily baffled given how he'd acted last night. He'd either have to convince her he was earnest in his desire to court her or tell her the truth about her parents' extortion. Unless she already knew.

God, had she come up with this scheme after he'd

refused her advances last night? She'd tried to flirt, and he'd rejected her. He'd told her they couldn't repeat what they'd done in the library. He knew he'd disappointed her. However, he apparently hadn't realized how much.

Disappointment washed over him too. He'd liked her so much. And now he didn't know what to think. Tomorrow, hopefully, he'd find out.

Chapter Ten

If wit were gold, her purse boundless.
If humor air, her world groundless.
If grace were rain, she'd fill the seas.
Her love's warmth the cold heart unfreeze.

-*From* A Song for Lady Lavinia Gillingham
by The Duke of Seduction

LAVINIA HAD ALLOWED herself to stew about Beck's rakishness for most of yesterday, but she didn't plan to give him such time today. Though it was difficult not to think of him, because every time she looked at her expanded fossil collection, he was *right there*.

And she refused to return them.

So instead, she focused her energy on planning a geology-themed excursion. She often tried to find places around London where she could take a short jaunt. It took some planning—convincing her mother to go with her, which hadn't happened in a few years, or taking some other chaperone, such as her sister-in-law if she was in town.

Lavinia had a destination in mind and a chaperone. Hopefully, her mother would agree to both. In the meantime, she'd write to Diana and ask if she'd chaperone. It was rather helpful to have a married friend who was a duchess to boot.

As she sat down at the desk in the upstairs sitting room, the butler came in to announce the arrival of Sarah. Lavinia hadn't been expecting her. "Send her up, please."

The butler nodded and left. A few moments later, Sarah, who'd come up to this sitting room dozens of times, came in wearing a tense expression. She removed her gloves and took her bonnet from her head.

"Is something amiss?" Lavinia asked.

"Not amiss, but I do have something to share." She perched on the small settee and waited for Lavinia to sit in the chair angled toward her.

"You're causing me concern," Lavinia said.

"I don't mean to. I just—" Sarah dropped her gloves in her lap and set the bonnet on the settee. "After what you told us about Northam the other night, I felt I had to tell you what I've learned."

Instantly, Lavinia thought of his secret identity, but doubted that could be it. "What's happened?"

"Anthony saw him—Northam—at a brothel last week. He was there with his friend, Mr. Jeffries, and Felix, of course."

Lavinia felt a bit sick. Which was ridiculous. Beck was a rake. He likely went to brothels quite often. In fact, he'd probably been many times during their acquaintance. Perhaps he'd even gone to one after leaving Violet's party the other night. After they'd kissed. "Well, I guess we have our answer regarding his reputation." And it stung.

"Still a rake," Sarah said flatly. "I'm sorry. I knew you'd want to know."

"You were right. Don't be sorry. I expected nothing from him. That kiss was a curiosity, nothing more."

Lavinia ignored the constriction in her chest and swallowed past the bitterness in her throat. "Enough of that. I'd like to take an excursion to the Charlton Sand Pit about ten or eleven miles east of town. I'm going to ask Diana to chaperone. Would you like to come?"

Sarah brightened, which did wonders for Lavinia's mood. "Of course! But do you think your mother will allow Diana to chaperone?"

"I hope so. I believe she and Violet won her over with their wonderful party the other night. The scandal surrounding them is starting to recede."

Sarah nodded in agreement. "Yes, it seems to be." Her eyes lit with an idea. "Should we plan a picnic and include Fanny?"

"Oh yes, let's!" Lavinia felt better already.

"If your mother refuses to allow Diana, perhaps Fanny's sister would chaperone."

"A splendid alternative. I'll speak to Cook about preparing the picnic. We'll leave midmorning."

Sarah's brow creased. "Why do you want to visit the sand pit?"

"Through excavation, they've uncovered an amazing strata of dirt. I'd like to see it." Lavinia had read about it in *Philosophical Transactions*, the Royal Society journal.

"How wonderful." Sarah was always so supportive of Lavinia's interests. "I look forward to seeing it too. When shall we go?"

"Later this week, if we can manage it. Perhaps Thursday or Friday."

Lavinia's mother swept into the room, her gaze settling on Sarah. "Good afternoon, Miss Colton. I'm afraid Lavinia has a gentleman caller."

Sarah's widening eyes connected with Lavinia's. Who could it be? She'd met so many gentlemen the past couple of weeks, but none of them had called. She also hadn't encouraged any of them to, a fact she needed to change.

Lavinia rose from the chair and smoothed her hand down the side of her day gown. "Who is it, Mother?"

"The Marquess of Northam."

Swallowing an inelegant sound of disgust, Lavinia looked to Sarah, who was busily tying her bonnet beneath her chin. She gave Lavinia an apologetic wince, then tugged her gloves on.

"Come down to the library, Lavinia," the countess said, turning and departing the sitting room.

Lavinia groaned softly as she made her way toward the door behind Sarah, who turned to say, "I'm sorry. But do let me know how it goes. Later at the park?"

"Yes." Lavinia nodded, then trailed Sarah downstairs.

Sarah looked back over her shoulder and gave her an encouraging glance and a small wave before moving into the entrance hall.

Squaring her shoulders, Lavinia went to the library, which was really just a larger sitting room where they kept a few bookshelves. Inside, Beck stood in profile near the front windows, his hat in his hand. He turned to face her as she entered and offered a courtly bow. "Good afternoon, Lady Lavinia."

Lavinia darted a glance toward her mother, who'd come in behind her. Beck bowed to her and offered a greeting. It was all very stilted and formal while Lavinia fought to hide her frustration and hurt.

Hurt? Why should he have hurt her?

Because he'd kissed her while still carrying on with Lady Fairwell and going to a brothel. She'd thought him better than that, but why? He was an unapologetic rake, and she'd known it. She'd kissed him in spite of that, and even now couldn't bring herself to regret it. Those moments in his arms sparked a heat she worked to quash.

How she wished she could say precisely what she thought of him. The presence of her mother prevented such satisfaction.

"Would you care for refreshment?" the countess asked, spurring Lavinia to stifle another groan. She wanted this over as quickly as possible. What was he even *doing* here? He had no interest in courtship.

"No, thank you. I'd like to take Lady Lavinia for a turn around the back garden, assuming you have one?"

This seemed to please her mother, for she smiled quite brilliantly. "Yes, of course."

Beck turned his head toward Lavinia in invitation. She wanted to tell him she'd rather take a turn with the devil, but then decided this could very well be the same thing.

Notching her chin up, she turned and strode from the room, turning right to lead him to the morning room, where they could exit to the garden.

She didn't wait for him or her mother, who followed them to supervise from the morning room. Lavinia opened the door and stepped outside. Beck came out behind her and closed the door, then offered his arm.

"I suppose I have to take that?" she said with considerable rancor.

"I'm sure it would please your mother, and I'm afraid that is my primary goal today."

She stared at him, utterly confused. In the end, she curled her hand around his arm, and they began a circuit of the garden. Suspicious curiosity overtook her other emotions. "Why are you trying to please my mother?"

His brow furrowed. "Because—"

Lavinia's other emotions weren't content with being pushed aside. "You know, I don't actually care. I don't know why you're here, nor do I care about that either. I'm not interested in taking a turn about the garden with an unapologetic rake who visits a brothel, is likely still carrying on with a married woman, and kisses me at the same time." She tried to remove her hand from his arm and go back inside.

He put his free hand over hers and squeezed her close. His gray-green eyes bored into hers with intensity. "Well, I am not interested in being manipulated. Just walk with me, dammit."

"Manipulated? Who is manipulating you?"

"I thought you might be, but I gather it's just your parents." He started walking, albeit slowly, dragging her along.

"Explain."

"Your father approached me at Brooks's last night. He informed me that I am to court you, or he'll expose me as the Duke of Seduction." He looked down at her, and she detected anger in his gaze. "What I can't understand is how he found that out." His tone held an accusatory edge.

She stopped again, and this time, he let her remove her hand from his arm. Turning to face him, she touched her chest, irritated he would doubt her loyalty. "*I* didn't tell them."

"It had to be you. The only other person who knows is my butler."

His butler? Just her and his butler? That knowledge prompted a slight flutter in her belly. Followed by a sharp queasiness. "Your butler wouldn't have told them."

His gaze didn't move from hers. "No."

"I swear I didn't tell anyone—not even Sarah." Though she'd wanted to, and if they hadn't been interrupted today, she might have. She'd been that annoyed with him. "I only—" She clapped her hand over her mouth as her eyes widened. "My diary. I wrote about it in my diary." She sent a livid glance toward the house. "She reads my bloody diary?"

"Apparently."

She looked at him in abject apology. "I am *so* sorry."

"Not as sorry as me. Now they are using this information for extortion—I am to court you, or they'll expose me."

"They asked you to marry me?" Oh God, this was too awful. She knew they wanted her wed, but to resort to such despicable tactics was unconscionable.

"No. They believe my courtship will prompt others to come forward. They are rather impatient to see you betrothed."

The sick feeling in her gut increased. She glanced toward the house again and squinted. Her mother was standing inside the door, watching them. Lavinia spun about and took his arm once more, pulling him farther from the house to the opposite corner of the garden.

"They're horrid." It was all she could manage to say right now. Her parents would see her wed at any cost. Given their haste—and apparent desperation—Lavinia was afraid they'd betroth her to nearly anyone. She needed to accept the inevitable: she was going to wed this Season, and if she wanted a husband of her own choice, she'd best find one.

"I wish there was something I could say to ease your distress," he said softly.

She appreciated that, but the period for emotional

reactions was over. It was time to act. "You were going to help me find a husband. That is more important than ever since I seem to be running out of time."

"What about Horace?"

She paused again and narrowed her eyes at him. "The same Mr. Jeffries who went to a brothel with you? Be honest with me—is he a rake like you?" She wouldn't have guessed it based on their introduction, but what did she know about him really?

Beck gestured toward the bench that sat in the corner of the garden just a few feet away. "May we sit?"

Wordlessly, Lavinia withdrew her arm from his and went to perch on the bench. He sat down beside her—not too close—and stretched one leg out as he angled himself toward her.

"Horace does like women, though I'm not sure I'd classify him a rake. Honestly, I'm not sure I'd classify myself a rake anymore either. Yes, I went to Madame Bisset's with Horace and Felix. I played chess."

Lavinia blinked at him in confusion. "You can play chess there?"

His mouth cracked in a brief smile. "Or cards or backgammon or any number of things. The women there provide whatever entertainment a man desires—and it needn't be, er, sexual." He averted his gaze from hers as he spoke the last.

The implications of what he was saying only made her more curious. "Were you even a rake at all?"

He looked at her then and promptly burst out laughing. Whether it was due to the absurdity of the question or the tumult of emotions she'd gone through in the past quarter hour, she joined him. It was a long moment before they quieted, and she could only imagine how this looked to her mother. If she could even see them. There was a well-placed shrubbery that afforded a measure of privacy for their location.

"Without going into specifics, I've behaved in plenty of rakish ways. However, I am not seeing Lady Fairwell any longer—much to her dismay—and sometimes I prefer a game of chess to something…else."

The memory of his lips on hers stole over her, and she couldn't imagine preferring chess to that sensation. She was, however, pleased to hear that he wasn't entertaining Lady Fairwell any longer and that he hadn't gone to Madame Bisset's for the typical reason. Which was silly because he wasn't a potential husband. He wasn't *really* courting her. Or so he'd said.

Did she want him to?

She turned toward him slightly. "Just so I understand, you are not courting me with the intent to marry. You are courting me to provoke others to launch a courtship."

"That is what your parents want, yes."

Her bloody parents. "I won't let them reveal your secret—I promise."

His gaze softened. "I appreciate that, but are you sure you'd be able to stop them?"

"I will if I become betrothed. So that must be my primary goal." The knowledge that her freedom, such as it was, would soon be curtailed filled her with dread. Unless she could find a husband that supported her interests. Would he let her do things such as take excursions to the sand pit?

"And Horace is out, it seems," Beck said.

Lavinia clasped her hands in her lap. "Is he? If you have reason to doubt his fidelity, then yes, I'd prefer to look elsewhere."

"I'm not certain," Beck said. "However, I'm also not

certain he's ready to wed. He's a bit awkward, if you didn't notice."

"I did, but I actually found it endearing. Plus, he revealed all sorts of tantalizing information about you." She flashed him a smile, and his eyes darkened and narrowed slightly. His expression made her heart skip, and she realized she wanted to kiss him again.

Blast it all, he was *not* courting her.

She forced herself back to the matter at hand—her future husband. Recalling the various men she'd met over the past few weeks, the only one who stood out was Sir Martin, and that was largely because of his scientific leanings. Since she was short of time and, apparently, of acceptable potential suitors, she would have to determine if he would suit.

"At this point, I think Sir Martin Riddock is my best option. However, I have an idea that might help me see if anyone else would suit. I am taking a picnic to the Charlton Sand Pit later this week to look at the stratification that's been exposed there. If Sir Martin could come, and perhaps a few other eligible bachelors, I could ascertain their attitudes toward my scientific interests. It's the perfect setting since I will be researching and discussing geology."

"You're taking a picnic at a sand pit?" He smiled as he gave his head a shake. "Of course you are. And this is a brilliant idea. In fact, if you'll permit me, I'll speak to Felix, and he can turn the excursion into quite the thing. Then you'll have a plethora of gentlemen to choose from, and you'll be the star of the day as you explain the importance of the stratification to everyone."

Lavinia's pulse quickened. To think that she could speak about geology in front of people gave her a heady sensation. The goal of finding a husband faded to the back of her mind. "Do you think people would come?"

"Most definitely. Felix can persuade just about anyone to do just about anything."

"Thank you." This was better than she could have imagined. "That would be wonderful. The Duke of Seduction is a very helpful gentleman."

His answering smile made her heart turn over again. "He tries to be."

Anticipation coursing through her, she stood before she did something foolish. "I'll endeavor to ensure this faux courtship is brief."

"Take all the time you need," he said.

No, she wouldn't do that. She feared even a pretend courtship with him could lead to something that just might leave her wounded. She took his arm, and he escorted her back toward the house.

"Shall we plan for Thursday?" she asked.

He nodded. "I'll talk with Felix immediately and leave a note in the tree confirming things."

"I won't be able to get there today," she said. "I'll be in the park later, however. Perhaps you should come and promenade with me—my parents will be expecting that."

"Yes, that will kill two birds with one stone." He opened the door for her to the morning room, and she preceded him inside.

Beck took her hand and brushed a kiss over the back of her knuckles, sending a shiver up her arm and over her shoulder straight to that spot on her neck. She drew her hand away perhaps a bit too quickly. "I'll see you later at the park," he said softly before turning to bow to her mother.

After he was gone, the countess tugged Lavinia to the settee. "Tell me everything he said."

Lavinia bit her tongue before she could respond, *Including how you and Father are extorting him to court me?* Instead, she smiled pleasantly and told her they'd discussed the weather, music, and rock stratification.

At that, her mother flinched. "He couldn't have wanted to hear about that."

"Actually, he was quite intrigued," Lavinia said haughtily.

The countess gave her a condescending look and patted her knee. "I'm sure he was just being kind, dear. You mustn't test a gentleman's patience." *Because he was only feigning interest?* That was certainly what her mother obviously thought. Her parents' manipulations made her ill.

Lavinia jumped to her feet. "I'm feeling a bit peaked. I should go rest if I'm to go to the park later."

Her mother stared up at her imploringly. "You *must* go to the park."

If Lavinia didn't know better, she'd think her parents would gain some sort of prize for marrying her off with the utmost haste. Their urgency coupled with their deviousness was wholly disturbing. She exhaled with sudden weariness and decided she *did* need a rest— from her parents. "Yes, Mother, I must do many things. And I'm confident you'll ensure I do them."

She swept from the room, her back rigid, and vowed to look to the future where, no matter what, she wouldn't have to deal with them anymore.

THE PAST FEW days had been a whirlwind of activity.

Beck had promenaded with Lavinia in the park twice and danced with her at a ball once. He'd also watched as Sir Martin had paid her specific attention, along with two other gentlemen. He tried not to watch too closely because it made him distinctly uncomfortable.

He didn't see the point in exploring why that was, so he didn't.

Meanwhile, Felix had organized the picnic of the Season. A multitude of vehicles and riders on horseback descended upon a green space near the Charlton Sand Pit early Thursday afternoon.

Lavinia was already there—Beck knew from the planning that she was to be one of the first to arrive. She'd taken up a position near an exposed wall of rock and dirt in the sand pit. It was a beautiful stratification of bands of varying texture and color. Throughout the afternoon, she talked with people about the history of those bands, sometimes going deep into discussion about the potential age of the Earth. Some people shook their head with doubt, but most were fascinated by her knowledge.

Beck was a bit infatuated. Was there anything more attractive than an intelligent woman? He didn't think so. One of the reasons he'd fallen so hard and so fast for Priscilla had been her intellect. Her father was a scholar at Oxford, and she'd learned from him and his colleagues. She wasn't a scientist like Lavinia, but a literary historian. Her love of words was part of what had inspired Beck to write.

The young spring day was cloudy but not cold, and, thankfully, dry, which made it a perfect occasion to spend time outdoors. The picnic area was a bit rambunctious. Felix had set up a shuttlecock net and bowls, and a group was currently playing a rousing game of blind man's bluff.

Beck watched the festivities with amusement but didn't particularly want to join in. What he wished he could do was sit beneath a tree and play his guitar. But of course he hadn't brought it and never would. Not to an event such as this. Not to any event.

"Excuse me, my lord?" A feminine voice drew him to turn. The woman addressing him was tall with light brown eyes and a charming smile. He recognized her as the Duchess of Kendal.

Beck offered her a gallant bow. "Good afternoon, Your Grace."

"Good afternoon. We met at the Kilves' dinner party."

"I remember."

"You spoke with my husband that night—he told me of your conversation. I hope you don't think me presumptuous, but I wanted to tell you I did meet your sister. Lady Helen was a kind and gentle soul. I'm sorry to hear she passed. I did wonder what had happened to her, but I lost touch with nearly everyone after I left town."

Beck tensed upon hearing the duchess had known Helen, but relaxed slightly at her compassionate recollection. "Thank you for your kind words."

"That was a nasty Season." A slight tremor flitted across her shoulders. "Not just what happened to me—though, in hindsight, several of the gentlemen seemed rather predatory."

Beck thought of the man Helen had mentioned in her letter. Had he behaved like that? "It seems as though it was very competitive."

"Quite. Some of the young ladies could be ruthless in their pursuit of matrimony."

He nodded in agreement. "That was my impression. My sister mentioned a couple of those women, but only by their initials—SW and DC. I don't suppose you recall who they were?"

She pressed her lips together, her eyes narrowing slightly. "I don't even have to think about it. They possessed the most acidic tongues that year. In truth, they haven't improved much over time, particularly Lady Abercrombie."

He had a name at last. "She's one of them?"

"Yes, she was Susannah Weycombe then, and DC refers to her closest friend, Dorothy Cranley—she is Lady Kipp-Landon now."

Satisfaction curled through him, but knowing their identities wouldn't truly grant him victory. He vaguely knew who they were, but wasn't entirely sure he could pick them from a crowd. He glanced around, wondering if they were here.

The duchess gleaned his thoughts. "They wouldn't be here. They aren't in this circle. I doubt the Earl of Ware would invite anyone like that."

No, she had that right. "True, but sometimes things get out of hand with one of Felix's events."

"Is that so? Well, that sounds like it could be good or bad." She grinned briefly, then fixed him with a sympathetic stare. "Does it help you to know who those women are? I sense it's somehow important to you."

"My sister had a difficult time of things, and they were part of that. I don't know that it helps, but I certainly appreciate knowing who they are so I may give them the cut direct. Should the occasion ever arise."

"I wouldn't blame you. They tried to befriend me

when I married Titus, but I may have ensured they were excised from my mother-in-law's considerable sphere of influence." She shrugged without a bit of concern, provoking Beck to laugh. "And my husband *may* have punched Lord Haywood, but I daresay he deserved at least that."

Beck had met Haywood, who was more than a decade his senior. He was known as a bit of a gambler and a drinker. "Haywood is the man who—?" Beck didn't want to say and knew she would understand the question.

"The man I was foolish enough to meet alone? Yes. He possessed an exceedingly charming demeanor. I had no idea he wasn't sincere in his pursuit of me." Her lips quirked up into a self-deprecating smile. "It turned out he was pursuing many young women. With no apparent intent to wed any of them."

"He strung them along with empty promises."

"He certainly did me," she said. "And I was the perfect target—young, foolish, and desperate to marry."

Exactly like Helen. Had she fallen prey to Haywood or someone like him?

"I'm happy things worked out for you." Beck smiled at the duchess despite his sorrow at how things *hadn't* worked out for Helen.

She let out a light laugh. "Exceedingly well, thankfully! And now I must be off. I have children to attend at home." She glanced about briefly before returning her attention to Beck. "First, I must find Ware and thank him for this charming affair. Did you happen to listen to Lady Lavinia talk about the stratification in the sand pit? It was absolutely fascinating."

"I did, and I agree."

She bid him farewell, and Beck found himself drawn back down to the sand pit. There was no one there at present, and he wondered where Lavinia had gone. He meandered to the exposed layers she'd talked about earlier. Removing his glove, he ran his bare fingers over the lowest band of dirt, wondering at what things might have lived on it.

His mind turned to a more recent history—that of his sister's last Season. Now that he knew who those women were, he wanted to ask them why they'd tormented Helen.

Beck's family knew little of the circumstances of Helen's death. Could these women shed any light? Would Beck trust anything they said?

The satisfaction he'd felt at learning their identity faded away. The helplessness and despair and anger he'd nurtured for years flooded back over him, driving him from the sand pit toward a copse of trees away from the revelers. People were beginning to depart. Good. He'd hide until then. He didn't want to see anyone in his current mood. He'd leave, but he'd come out with Felix and would have to find someone else to take him back. The only person he thought he could suffer right now was Felix, and so he'd wait.

The only other person?

Lavinia filled his mind—her wit, her beauty, her keen intellect and confidence. Yes, he could suffer her quite well. Too bad their courtship wasn't real.

Chapter Eleven

Beasts in the field fall at her feet.
The stones of mountains, from their peak.
Stars from heaven, like rain to sea.
All wish to be near; close to she.

-From An Ode to Miss Anne Berwick
by The Duke of Seduction

THE DAY WENT by so quickly that Lavinia hardly knew where it went. She was particularly grateful to Sarah for bringing her food at the sand pit, for she'd been so wrapped up in talking to people about the geology of the place, she hadn't taken time to eat.

When things had finally begun to calm down, she'd been attended upon by three different gentlemen, most notably Sir Martin, who'd found her geology discussions enlightening. It was a shame her mother wasn't here. The countess would be delighted with the attention Lavinia was receiving.

Lavinia, on the other hand, found herself looking for just one man—the one who was falsely courting her and probably wouldn't need to do so any longer. She saw him dodge into a stand of trees away from the picnic area.

Glancing toward where the picnic was being cleaned up, she stole toward the trees. A light breeze stirred her skirts as she stepped behind the shoulder-high hedgerow that stood between the grassy expanse and the copse.

"Beck?"

He stepped from behind a tree. "Are you following me?" The question was light, but there was a crease in his brow—she could see because she'd donned her spectacles, something she'd done throughout the day as needed. Indeed, she'd worn them in front of Sir Martin, and he'd said they made her look brilliant.

"I saw you come into the trees, and here I am, so I suppose I *am* following you. I wanted to thank you for arranging today."

He leaned against the tree he'd stepped around. "You're wearing your glasses."

She adjusted them on her face unnecessarily. "Yes."

"I like it when you wear them." He glanced toward the picnic area, which was shielded by the hedgerow. "I didn't do anything to arrange today—that was entirely Felix's management."

"But Felix wouldn't have done it if you hadn't asked."

The corner of his mouth lifted. "True. It seemed a grand success for you. I'm so pleased."

The warmth in his tone showed her how much he meant it. "Yes, everyone was quite interested in geology. I can hardly wait to tell my mother."

Beck laughed. "Will she believe you?"

Lavinia shrugged. "Probably not."

"Aside from that, I meant success in your marital quest. You seem to have several suitors who may be serious—or have I read that wrong?"

She reached for the tree next to her and ran her gloved hand over the bark. "No, you are correct. Sir

Martin in particular seems as though he'll come up to snuff. He plans to call on me."

Beck pushed away from the tree and took a step toward her, decreasing the distance between them. "Will that make you happy?"

Happy. She wasn't sure if that was the right word. "It won't make me *un*happy. I like Sir Martin. He's certainly not dull to talk to, provided I can keep him focused on science instead of horses."

"Do you think you'll be able to keep him from speaking of horses for an entire marriage?" Beck asked.

"Of course not, but I can put up with that."

"That's not a particularly favorable perspective of your marital future with him."

No, it wasn't, but neither was it terrible. So she didn't love Sir Martin, but she was learning that love was perhaps a luxury she couldn't afford. Better to wed someone she liked well enough than allow her parents to manipulate her into a union with someone she detested. "I'm running out of time, as you know, and Sir Martin is my best option at present."

Beck moved closer. "I was hoping you'd find love," he said softly. "Have you ever been in love?"

She shook her head, captivated by his sultry gaze and the seductive timbre of his voice.

"I was—as you know. Her name was Priscilla. She was three years older than me, and so intelligent and so beautiful, it stole my breath. I thought of her night and day. I could scarcely eat or sleep for want of her company. I began to write love poetry—horrendous verses of maudlin tripe."

Lavinia's chest squeezed, and she knew exactly what he meant when he talked about losing his breath. Jealousy, bitter and thick, clogged her throat. She somehow found her voice. "I've never felt that way."

"Good. When it's not reciprocated, it's the worst feeling in the world."

"She didn't love you?"

He shook his head. "I was too young, too desperate, too bad at poetry, probably."

She laughed and immediately clapped her hand over her mouth until she reined in her amusement. "Sorry."

He smiled. "Don't be. I love the sound of your laugh."

Every drop of laughter evaporated. When he spoke to her like that and looked at her as he was now—as if she were Priscilla—she only wanted him to touch her, to kiss her again. "Did you ever kiss Priscilla?"

"Why would you ask me that?" the question was a near whisper.

"If you had, I'm sure she wouldn't have spurned you."

He took another step toward her, bringing them so close, they almost touched. "How do you know?"

She couldn't keep from staring at his mouth. "From experience, of course."

"Lavinia, you are tempting me to do it again." He sounded hopeful.

"'Temptation is the marriage 'tween stark curiosity and need.'" It was a line from the first poem he'd written about her.

His gaze lit with admiration. "You're quoting myself to me."

"It's a beautiful line."

He reached for the ribbon of her bonnet and teased it between his thumb and forefinger. "I wrote it about you."

"You barely knew me then," she breathed.

"And how well do I know you now?"

"Not well enough." She grabbed his coat by the lapels and pulled him against her. Standing on her toes, she pressed her mouth to his.

His arms came around her and held her tight to his chest as his mouth plundered hers. She'd thought of his kiss for days, and now that his lips were on hers once more, she realized she hadn't remembered it quite right. This was so much better.

His body was warm and hard, and he smelled of pine and grass. Or maybe that was just that they were outside. No, it was him. He smelled of outside, and damn if that didn't make him the most attractive man in the history of men.

Well, in her history of men.

Good Lord, could her mind possibly travel down a rabbit hole while Beck was kissing her? Apparently it could, but it didn't matter. She was drowning in wonder and delight, and she didn't ever want to come up for air.

She clutched at his shoulders and neck and pressed herself into him. She'd relived that kiss in the library, plotting what she would do if she were afforded a second opportunity with him. And here it was.

Tilting her head, she was vaguely aware that she knocked his hat from his head with the brim of her own. She slid her tongue along his, reveling in the sensation of their coming together. Her breasts tightened and her core heated, and she became aware of other ways in which they could join.

Did she want that?

Oh, for the love of God, Lavinia, stop thinking!

She pushed her thoughts away and concentrated on just feeling. His hands clasping her back, his lips and tongue mating with hers, his body urgently pressing into hers. She wanted more.

Tentatively, she pushed her hips to his. His hand came down and gripped her waist, pulling her into him. He moved against her, and she gasped into his mouth as friction sparked between her legs.

He pivoted her body and guided her back two small steps until she felt a tree against her back. His mouth left hers, but only to nip and lick at her jaw and ear. She tipped her head back until it met the bark, closing her eyes as he worked magic over her flesh.

"Your collar is too damned high," he muttered, pushing it down and away so he could access her neck.

She had to agree. And yet he was managing quite well, it seemed. His hand moved up her side, gliding over her until he cupped her breast. The touch was woefully inadequate given his gloves and her clothing, but her body reacted as if it were more than enough.

Her nipple tightened as he caressed her through the gown, all while he kissed her neck. She pulled him harder against her, wanting to feel as much of him as she could. His hand left her breast, and she might have whimpered softly. Yes, she definitely whimpered. And she didn't care.

He reached down and lifted her skirt. Cool air rushed over her stocking-clad leg as his hand brushed along her thigh. His fingertips grazed the apex, lightly touching her flesh. Then he stilled.

"Forgive me."

She tugged on the hair at his nape. "Look at me."

He lifted his head and stared into her eyes.

"There is nothing to forgive. At least not if you don't stop. If you do, I'll *never* forgive you."

"You want me to continue?"

"Whatever you were going to do…" She could barely find the words. She felt utterly brazen. But him touching her there was a sensation she didn't want to let go. "Do it," she begged.

"Have you ever done that before?" he asked quietly. "Orgasm, I mean."

"I don't know that word." She'd talked about sex— briefly—with other young ladies, but until Diana, none of them had possessed any practical experience. And the conversations she'd had with Diana since her marriage had been woefully devoid of exciting details. She'd only said it was marvelous, and she dearly hoped Lavinia was as lucky in finding her husband as Diana had been.

"It describes what your body does when it releases with sexual satisfaction. Think of pent-up anticipation for an event and the rush of sensation when that event occurs." While he spoke, he touched her gently, his fingertips sliding over her flesh.

She opened her thighs, giving him better access because it seemed she should. She wasn't sure what he meant to do, but knew it had to be more. That anticipation he mentioned was building inside her. She clutched at his neck and held on tight as he slipped his finger along her crease.

She sucked in a breath just before he kissed her. It was short but wondrous, and his mouth continued across her cheek, his lips dragging across her flesh. He whispered in her ear, "I could try to make you come— to your orgasm, that is—by just touching you here." He pressed his fingers against the top of her sex and moved them back and forth, creating a delicious friction. "Or I could put my finger—or fingers—inside you and make you come that way. Which would you prefer?"

Oh God, how could she possibly know? "Can't I choose both?"

He laughed softly. "Lavinia, you never fail to surprise and intrigue me. And in this case, excite me. How I wish we had a proper location and far fewer clothes. I would show you all the ways I could make you come. With my fingers. With my mouth. With my cock."

Good Lord, he *was* a rake. His words enflamed her already heated body. She was desperate to come, to feel this thing he was talking about. "I don't care what you do, but please do it." She clasped his nape and made him look at her. "*Please.*"

His gaze was dark and seductive as his fingers began to move over her sex. He concentrated on that first part, rubbing her flesh. With each stroke, the anticipation grew. Then he kissed her again, his mouth sweeping over hers and his tongue driving deep into her mouth.

A moment later, his finger mimicked his tongue, sliding into her sex. She groaned as lights danced behind her eyes, and her legs began to quiver. He worked his finger in and out of her, slowly at first and then picking up speed. Then his thumb found that other spot, and he pressed while he penetrated her.

His movements grew faster, then his hand focused on the outside for a moment before his finger—or was it fingers now?—plunged into her again. Back and forth, he alternated his focus, and her passion increased apace. She was so close to what he'd described. She could feel it in her bones, in the blood coursing through her fevered body.

He broke the kiss and pressed his lips to her ear. "Come for me, Lavinia."

He speared into her and pressed the heel of his hand against her. She knew precisely what he meant by the word release. Her body felt as if it were coming apart. Her muscles tightened first, clenching everywhere as sensation rioted through her. Then came the release, a loosening of all the ecstasy that had built within her. But his hand didn't still, and she tightened again. And whimpered again. She was glad for the tree at her back, for she would surely have slumped to the ground. On and on it went, his hand coaxing her to heights she never dreamed existed.

Then finally, her body wilted. Spent, she worked to catch her breath. His hand was gone from her flesh, and her skirts dropped down around her legs. He took a step back and bent to pick something up from the ground. His glove, she realized. She hadn't even noticed him taking it off. And then his hat. That she remembered.

"That was rather ill-advised," he said, his voice sounding rather tight.

"Perhaps." Lavinia straightened her bonnet, her glasses, and her dress. Her face was probably flushed, but there was no help for that. Hopefully, a breeze would cool her off. "I won't regret it however, and I hope you don't either." She winced. "Unless… I shouldn't have urged you to do that." She hadn't urged. She'd *begged*. She was completely shameless.

He came back toward her and took her hand, pulling her away from the tree. "My dear Lavinia, if I hadn't wanted to do it, I wouldn't have. But now you must go. We've been gone too long, and I can only hope our absence—at the same time—hasn't been noted. You go back, and I'll follow later. I'll be the last to leave with Felix anyway."

What he said made sense. And also filled her with a bit of dread. What if their absence had been noticed? They hadn't been here *that* long, but apparently long enough…

"I really did want to thank you for today, and now I've even more reason to." She gave him a saucy smile, then kissed his cheek. "You are a kindhearted gentleman, just as Fanny and Sarah thought about the Duke of Seduction. I'm sorry I presumed you were anything else."

A storm gathered in his eyes. "I'm still a rake, Lavinia. Lest you forget, just consider what happened here. Kindhearted gentlemen don't seduce unmarried women in the forest."

"Is that what you did? I'm the one who asked you to go on. Perhaps I'm the one who seduced you." She lifted her shoulder, then turned and walked away, feeling supremely satisfied.

Yes, from her perspective, the seducer had just become the seduced.

⁂

A LIGHT DRIZZLE began to fall as Beck and Felix rode back to London in Felix's coach. "Glad I didn't drive the phaeton," Felix said, glancing out the window.

Beck barely nodded in response. His brain was stuck on Lavinia and his transgression and the unfulfilled desire still teeming in his body.

"I still can't believe they were fucking in front of everyone."

Blinking across the coach at Felix, Beck tensed. "What?"

Felix had crossed his arms over his chest as he

stretched his legs out as far as he could. "That finally snagged your attention."

"Who was fucking?" Beck was afraid to ask—what if someone had seen them? But no, Felix would have said something immediately, and they'd already been in the coach nearly a quarter hour.

"No one. I was trying to see if you were listening." Felix narrowed his eyes at Beck. "What the devil is wrong with you today? You've been brooding all afternoon."

"Not *all* afternoon." Really, not until he'd spoken with the Duchess of Kendal.

"Don't be a dolt. What's going on?"

"Nothing." Beck inwardly winced, thinking that it might be nice to unburden himself and Felix was someone—one of the only people, really—he could trust.

Felix's lips flattened into a straight line. "You've become rather secretive of late. And I noticed you disappeared for a while. As did Lady Lavinia."

Shit. If Felix had noticed, who else had done so?

"Don't worry," Felix said. "I doubt anyone else was paying attention. The only reason I put it together is because I've seen you with her the past few weeks. There's something going on there." He unfolded his arms and waved his hand. "Oh, you can deny it or ignore it or pretend there's nothing, but I'm not stupid. And if I see it, you must ask yourself who else does."

"Her parents."

Felix stared at him. "What?"

"Her parents will notice. That's the point. I'm supposed to be courting her."

Felix's eyes widened, and his jaw loosened. "You plan to wed? That seems an important thing you might share with your closest friend."

"I do not plan to wed. I am being extorted." Beck exhaled and scrubbed a hand over his face. He sank back against the squab and let his legs sprawl in front of him. "I have a secret, and her parents are using it against me. I'm to pretend to court her to encourage others to step up their suit."

"What's this secret?"

"I should have told you before now. I'm the Duke of Seduction."

Felix blew out a whistle. "I'll be damned. I knew you could write, but I never would've imagined you'd do that." He leaned forward slightly. "Why did you?"

Beck turned his head and stared at the window, where slender rivulets of water sluiced down the glass. "I wanted to help those young ladies who are overlooked, who deserve a chance at happiness."

"On the Marriage Mart. Which you despise." His tone was heavy with disbelief. "I still don't understand."

"I don't think I ever told you why I hate the Marriage Mart."

"I assumed it was because of Priscilla. Because she broke your heart. You swore off marrying anyone."

"That was sort of true. However, there was more to my bitterness. My sister Helen failed on the Mart." He moved his gaze back to Felix's as darkness moved through him. "It was more than that, however. People were cruel, and I'm starting to wonder if she was pursued by a knave who drove her to the unthinkable."

Felix paled. "Your sister died. You're saying she—?"

Beck hesitated, even though it seemed Felix had deduced the truth, which he should have after what Beck had said. Still, it wasn't something his family discussed, and to say it out loud brought his family's shame into the light. Beck hadn't even known what had really happened until after his mother had died a few years later. Then, in a fit of despair, his father had revealed everything.

"Yes, she was poisoned and likely by her own hand. Or so it seemed to my parents. She'd spoken of not wanting to endure another Season and of an end to her loneliness and suffering. She'd always possessed a dark nature, and it seemed to engulf her." Beck's throat tightened. He recognized that feeling of loneliness, of helplessness, of utter darkness. But it didn't swallow him. Not yet, anyway. Not as long as he had music and words to keep himself from the abyss.

"She killed herself." Felix wiped his hand over his brow. "I'd no idea. And why should I—you wouldn't want that getting out." He leaned back against the seat. "You think a man pushed her to do it?"

Beck rested his elbows on his knees and dropped his head into his hands. "I don't know what to believe. I only know two women told her she'd be better off dead, some man was pursuing her, and then she died of poison. It never sat right with my father."

"You'd like to know what happened," Felix said softly.

Beck lifted his head slightly and peered over at his friend. "Wouldn't you?"

"Yes. How can I help?"

Exhaling, Beck dropped his head back to his hands. "I don't know. Today, I found out who those women were. I'd like to ask them what they know. I want to know who this man was."

"I would too," Felix said. "Who are these women, and how can we get information from them?"

Pushing himself up into a sitting position, Beck tipped his head back against the squab. "I've been thinking about that—hence my broodiness." He said the last with a wry tone, provoking a brief smile from Felix. "I think I'm going to write a poem addressed to them."

"Hell, that's brilliant." Felix sat straighter. "Not your typical poem, of course."

"No. This one will carry a far different purpose."

"How will that get them to talk to you?" Felix asked. "You've kept your identity secret, and I can't imagine you'd want to reveal yourself over this."

"No. That's the part I'm trying to work out."

Felix cocked his head to the side. "What if you use the poem as leverage? Threaten to continue to write them unless they tell you what they know about Helen."

It wasn't a terrible idea. "And how will I communicate that? I can't put that in the newspaper."

"No, but you can send them a letter via the newspaper—so they won't know who wrote it."

It also wasn't a great idea. "If I ask about Helen, don't you think they'll puzzle it out?"

"Damn. Of course they will." Felix banged his head back against the cushion. "You need an intermediary— someone who can ask them what they know without leading back to you."

"Well, if you think of something, let me know. In the meantime, I wrote to my sister Margaret and asked if she recalled a gentleman who may have been paying attention to Helen. They corresponded regularly, and I'm hoping Helen might have told her."

"I shall hope so too." Quiet reigned for a moment before Felix asked, "Then what will you do?"

Once he found out who had wooed his sister and perhaps driven her to kill herself? He didn't know. "I want the truth. Until I have that, I can't say what I'll do."

Felix nodded slowly. "I'll stand at your side no matter what." He said this with such ferocity that it warmed Beck's chest.

"Thank you."

"Now, about Lady Lavinia," Felix said, abruptly turning the conversation in a far lighter direction. Or was it? Beck had overstepped propriety in spectacular fashion and feared he would eagerly do so again. Which meant he should stay away from her. Hell, he should stay away from her anyway. Sir Martin was going to call on her, and a week from now, she could bloody well be betrothed. Their faux courtship was no longer necessary.

"There's nothing about Lady Lavinia. I told you—it was a fake courtship."

"There's nothing fake about disappearing with someone for a quarter hour," Felix said with a sardonic arch of his brow.

Beck scowled. "I think I'm done revealing things today."

"Fair enough." Felix fell mercifully silent for quite a while. However, as they neared the city, he spoke up again. "Perhaps it's time you gave love another chance. Priscilla was an awfully long time ago."

It wasn't that Beck hadn't given it a chance. He'd simply never encountered it. And the desire he felt for Lavinia wasn't love. He wanted her—desperately—but love?

Beck eyed his friend. "You might take your own advice. But then I don't think you've ever given it a first chance."

Felix's gaze iced over, and Beck felt the chill. "No, I haven't, nor do I plan to."

Beck knew that, of course, but Felix had pushed, and dammit, Beck would push back. He wasn't foolish enough to continue, however. For all his good nature and ability to create amusement wherever he went, there was a wall around Felix's heart that no one penetrated. Not even his closest friend.

Settling back for the remainder of the ride, Beck focused his mind on what he would write. He'd draft the poem as soon as he got home—what better way to channel his anger and frustration?

And his unsatisfied lust.

Chapter Twelve

❧

Wicked are those that wound with words,
Lashing at grace like flies on curds.
Lies in their mouths, sitting in wait,
Ugly, soiled, rancid with hate.

-The Evisceration of a Pair of Vicious Parrots
by Anonymous

"I THOUGHT THAT went exceedingly well!" Lavinia's mother exclaimed with a bright smile as soon as Sir Martin had left. She'd sat in the corner, her hawk-eyed gaze trained on Lavinia and Sir Martin as they'd talked. After a quarter hour, Lavinia had asked him to take a turn in the garden in order to alleviate the constancy of her mother's attention.

"Yes," was all Lavinia would say.

"What did you discuss in the garden?" the countess asked as Lavinia stood from the settee.

"Science." That would ensure Mother wouldn't ask for details. And really, they had discussed science—astronomy mostly, although Sir Martin did ask some questions about the Charlton Sand Pit. He asked her where else she'd like to visit and seemed interested in accompanying her. That should have filled her with happiness, if not excitement, for it seemed a union with him would allow her to pursue her passion for geology.

And yet, she felt a bit…empty. She'd thought of almost nothing but Beck since yesterday. The way he flirted with her. The way his stare seemed to bore straight into her soul. The way he touched her—with an intoxicating combination of reverence and need. The way her body came alive in his embrace.

"You'd accept him, then?" Mother asked.

"Oh yes," Lavinia said, her mind wholly focused on the blond-haired, gray-green-eyed rake who'd stolen her heart.

Her heart? Had he done that?

"Lavinia!"

She blinked, drawing her head from the clouds. "Yes?"

"You need to get ready to go to the park." Her mother rolled her eyes. "Goodness, girl, sometimes I think you live in another world."

Because sometimes it is preferable to living in yours.

Lavinia offered her a sweet smile and dashed upstairs to change into a walking gown for the park. Would Beck be there? She hoped so.

After choosing her gown with far more care than usual, she met her mother downstairs and they walked to Hyde Park. Sir Martin would not be there and had apologized for his absence. Lavinia expected another gentleman or two to approach her, but only watched for Beck.

She didn't immediately see him, but then she was without her glasses, so most people were a blur. Still, she'd come to recognize his stature and stance, even with her myopia, and it seemed he wasn't there.

Ah well, it was early yet. She did, however, see Jane Pemberton, who approached her with a smile. "Good afternoon, Lady Lavinia. Can we take a short walk?"

She shot a glance toward Lavinia's mother.

Lavinia didn't care what her mother thought. In any case, the countess was still riding a wave of giddiness from Sir Martin's call, so Lavinia would take advantage of it. "Yes." She looped her arm through Jane's, and they started along the path.

"You've become quite popular," Jane said. "I've heard so many wonderful things about yesterday's picnic excursion. I'm sorry I missed it."

"I am too. It was great fun." Her mind drifted toward the best part, and she quickly reined it back lest she fall completely and irretrievably down the rabbit hole.

"Still, most people are talking about that poem in the *Chronicle* this morning."

"What poem?" Lavinia hadn't read it, and her mother hadn't mentioned anything. So she doubted it was one of Beck's. And yet, who else published poetry in the *Morning Chronicle*?

Jane's eyes widened. "You didn't read it?"

"I rarely read the *Morning Chronicle*."

"Not even since you were the subject of the duke's poems? I check every day to make sure he hasn't written about me again. It's so peculiar that he wrote about me only that one time. I think I'm the only one who only had one poem, not that I mind, of course. In fact, it's almost as if he realized I didn't like the attention and stopped."

Lavinia kept her expression from revealing that Jane had the right of it. "Wouldn't that be enterprising of him?" She diverted the topic away from the Duke of Seduction. "Was today's poem about someone new?"

"Most assuredly. It was a new sort of poem altogether. In fact, it may not have been written by the

Duke of Seduction, for the author didn't sign it." She sent Lavinia a knowing glance. "However, I have to think it was. The cadence and word usage are too similar."

What had Beck written? She wanted to rush home and read the newspaper for herself. "Who was it about?"

"The author didn't make that entirely clear, but the use of initials and the description of the subjects' behavior has led most to believe it was written about Lady Abercrombie and Lady Kipp-Landon."

They were close friends and two of the worst gossips with the nastiest tongues in London. Lady Kipp-Landon *could* be pleasant, especially in the absence of Lady Abercrombie, but Lavinia sought to steer clear of them.

She was still confused. He—if it was Beck—obviously hadn't written about them to help them find husbands. Both women were married with children and in their middle thirties. "You said it was a different sort of poem."

"It's called *The Evisceration of a Pair of Vicious Parrots.*"

Lavinia's breath stalled in her chest.

Evisceration. Her word. That was most certainly Beck. Why had he written it? She glanced about, wondering if she'd see him today—*hoping* she'd see him.

"Well, that sounds rather unpleasant."

Jane's lip curled. "They deserve it, in my opinion. They are two of the most judgmental harpies in all of Society. Lady Abercrombie doesn't even pretend to be nice in most cases. She'd sooner give someone the cut direct. Two years ago, I saw her trip a young lady who was deemed one of the Season's brightest jewels. I tried to go and call her out for it, but my mother wouldn't allow me." Jane waved her hand. "Anyway, we shouldn't waste time talking about them, even if it is to revel in their well-deserved public humiliation." She turned her head toward Lavinia. "What we should discuss is Phoebe Lennox."

Lavinia was glad for the change of subject even though her brain was likely to hold on to that poem— at least until she had a chance to talk to Beck about it. "Oh? Isn't her wedding tomorrow?"

"It is. I saw her last night, and she was rather distressed. She said she'd seen Sainsbury speaking rather intimately with another woman."

There was no harm in speaking. "What do you mean by intimately?"

"They were very close, touching hands and so forth. Phoebe said she saw him lean in to whisper in her ear, and he kissed the woman's neck." Jane's mouth turned into a deep frown. "If it's true—and why would Phoebe lie—he's disgusting.

"What is Phoebe going to do?" Lavinia asked. "It's not as if she can cry off. The wedding is tomorrow."

How horrid to have to marry a man you suspected of being unfaithful. It happened, of course, and plenty of women were unfaithful too—Lady Fairwell came to mind—but Lavinia hoped it wouldn't happen in her marriage. A feeling of unease crept over her. Beck, for all his pleasing attributes, had helped many a woman be unfaithful.

"I don't know," Jane said with concern. "She was rather in a dither about it last night. I was hoping she'd be here today, but I don't see her."

"Perhaps she'll be at the Sutton ball tonight."

"I doubt it since the wedding is in the morning." Jane's eyes narrowed. "But I shall be on the lookout for

Sainsbury, and he'd better behave himself."

Lavinia arched a brow at Jane. "This time, you won't be held back?"

Jane blew out a breath. "If my mother is in the vicinity, she will try. But so will I." She winked at Lavinia, who smiled in response.

They returned to Lavinia's mother, who waited with Mr. Chapman, one of the gentlemen who'd displayed interest in Lavinia the day before. He was a widower with two small children and a small estate in Kent. He'd liked hearing that Lavinia enjoyed the outdoors, since his children did too.

Lavinia wasn't certain how she felt about taking on an entire family, particularly without meeting his offspring. Still, he was nice enough and possessed a charming smile even if he did lack hair, which she knew because his hat had been knocked askew at one point yesterday.

During their promenade, she continued to look for Beck and continued to be disappointed. She also didn't see Sarah or Fanny, and by the time she returned to her mother, she was more than ready to go home. She knew she'd see her friends at the ball tonight. She only hoped she'd see Beck too.

They had much to discuss, not the least of which was whether he'd *eviscerated* two of Society's worst gossips. Lavinia was eager to learn why.

THE POEM ABOUT Lady Abercrombie and Lady Kipp-Landon was *the* buzz of the Sutton ball. It seemed no one held any doubt as to whom the author had been writing about.

Good.

Beck hadn't wanted to name them, but neither had he wanted to shield their identities. He'd no idea what would come of it, but he was glad everyone was discussing the misdeeds of two of Society's worst gossips.

He'd heard the following exchange between two middle-aged women shortly after arriving:

"It's about time someone took them down several notches. I daresay their social calendars will be rather sparse, and really, that's as it should have been for some time."

"But everyone's been so afraid of them and their ilk. I suspect others like them may find themselves similarly cut."

"Then perhaps they'll adjust their behavior."

"One can only hope."

Indeed.

Still, he didn't feel truly satisfied. None of this helped him learn the identity of the man who'd pursued Helen.

But perhaps his dissatisfaction was also due to a second source. He'd heard another snippet of conversation this evening:

"Sir Martin called on her this afternoon. It seems a betrothal is in the offing."

"The Duke of Seduction manages success again!"

He didn't feel very successful. He felt hollow as he watched Lavinia dance with Sir Martin.

She was beautiful, even when she spent half her time squinting across the ballroom. He hoped to God, Sir Martin would allow her to wear her spectacles after they wed.

After they wed?

Hell, he couldn't think of her the way he did if she

was married to another man. And he sure as hell couldn't look at her on another man's arm for another moment.

Spinning on his heel, he left the ballroom and went in search of Sutton's library. It was at the back of the house on the ground floor through a sitting room, which made it quite far removed from the festivities upstairs. That suited him spectacularly.

Even better, Sutton had a fully stocked sideboard. Beck helped himself to a tumbler of whiskey, which he downed in short order.

What the hell was he doing? Why hadn't he just left instead of coming in here? He'd no reason to stay. He didn't have to pretend to court Lavinia any longer, and frankly, being in her orbit and knowing she was on the verge of marrying someone else was enough to take him back to the age of sixteen when Priscilla had been beyond his reach.

Setting the glass back on the sideboard, he turned to go. The door to the library, which really looked as though Sutton used it as an office, opened.

Suddenly, he had his answer as to why he'd not only remained, but why he'd come here.

Lavinia stepped inside and closed the door behind her. "I knew I'd find you in the library." She looked toward the bookshelves. "Any good books on geology?"

"I didn't look." He couldn't keep himself from looking at her, however. He devoured her from the top of her cinnamon-colored hair to the toe of her persimmon-colored slipper. Christ, was he hungry again? Yes. For her.

She came toward him, her eyes relaxing the closer she got. "I read what you wrote in the paper."

He should have realized she would know he'd written it. "How do you know I'm the author?"

She cocked her head to the side and gave him a dubious stare. "I doubt I have to answer that. I've read your poems dozens of times. I know your writing. And so do others."

He inwardly winced. He'd been afraid of that, but what did it matter? It wasn't as if anyone knew he was the Duke of Seduction. He shrugged. "I don't particularly care. It needed to be done."

She stepped in front of him and took his hand. He felt the heat of her through their gloves and wished he could toss the garments away. Her gaze found his. "Why?"

"They hurt my sister. Years ago. They told her she'd be better off dead." He didn't know why he told her. The words simply tumbled from his mouth.

Her forehead creased, and she touched his face, her white cotton-clad fingertips grazing his cheekbone and jaw. He closed his eyes briefly, relishing her caress.

"I'm so sorry," she whispered. Standing on her toes, she brushed her lips against his.

He edged backward. "Lavinia. You said it yourself— we can't keep meeting in libraries."

"That was before yesterday." Her eyes were dark with desire, and his body reacted, hardening and tightening with lust. "I can't stop thinking about what happened. What you did."

"Yesterday was a grievous mistake. I vastly overstepped."

Her eyes narrowed. "I *asked* you to."

"Yes, well, I shouldn't have listened to you. And I especially shouldn't now. Not when it seems your betrothal to Sir Martin is imminent."

"It isn't."

His stomach dove into the floor. "You're already engaged?"

She put her hands on her hips and glared at him. "No, but would that help? You don't seem to have a problem conducting affairs with women who are married."

It was a punch to his midsection, and it took his breath away. "Lavinia, I am not going to have an affair with you." Even as he said the words, he wondered if he'd really be able to say no. She was right; he'd had no trouble carrying on with married women. He was suddenly and thoroughly disgusted with himself.

She exhaled and relaxed her arms at her sides. "How am I supposed to marry someone else after everything that's gone on between us?"

The pain in his midsection spread through him. He wouldn't let it take over. Straightening, he inhaled a deep breath. "I wish I could change what happened. You deserve far better. I've enjoyed our friendship, but that's all it can be. I am not the marrying kind, Lavinia." He corrected himself. "*Lady* Lavinia."

She stared at him a long moment. "I don't think we can maintain a friendship. You see, I don't want to change anything that happened, and knowing you do will only make me sad. Furthermore, it seems clear to me that we share an attraction, and you just said you enjoyed our friendship. I think you *could* be the marrying kind if you wanted to." Her gaze was dark with disappointment and something else he didn't want to consider. "I'm afraid this must be good-bye." She turned and went to the door, turning her head to look at him before she left. "Good-bye, Lord Northam."

The moment she was gone, he went to the door and

rested his forehead against the wood. He wanted her. But he couldn't see past the darkness just now. It engulfed him until he felt as if he couldn't breathe.

He wasn't sure how long he stood there, but eventually, he opened the door and escaped the house. He went home and buried himself in a tangle of words and whiskey.

Gage roused him early, speaking softly and encouraging him to go upstairs to bathe and dress. Why was Gage bothering him? Beck didn't want to go anywhere. He'd passed out on the chaise in his office plenty of times.

Blinking his heavy eyelids open, Beck looked about at the empty decanter and the tumbler lying on its side near the chaise on the carpet. Sheets of foolscap littered the floor and the end of the chaise.

"The wedding is this morning, my lord," Gage said softly.

Wedding. Oh God, she was getting married already? Anguish and regret pulsed through him with astounding force, pushing him to a sitting position. His head pounded in concert with the thumping of his heart.

"Where?" Beck rasped.

"St. George's, of course." Gage looked at him with concern as he always did after a night like the last.

Wait. Last night. He'd just seen her last night, and she said she hadn't been betrothed. Not yet anyway. And he certainly hadn't given her a reason not to be.

He put his hand to his head and began to massage his temple. "It's not Lavinia's wedding."

The creases in Gage's brow deepened. "No. It's Miss Lennox's wedding."

Beck sagged with relief, and the ache in his head

lessened a degree. Of course it was Miss Lennox. He meant to watch her leave the church and see that she was off to a happy life.

"You don't have much time," Gage said. "Cook is preparing a headache tonic. I'll bring it upstairs while you dress."

Beck rose from the chaise with considerable effort. "Thank you." As he wove his way upstairs, he thought of Lavinia. He was afraid he'd been an ass. No, he *had* been an ass. What he'd said was true—he wasn't the marrying kind. And yet when he thought of her marrying someone else, he simply couldn't bear it. The fear he'd just felt when he'd thought it was her wedding this morning… He didn't want to feel that again.

Once he'd downed the tonic and was bathed and dressed, he went back to his office and scrawled out a note. His horse was waiting outside, but instead of taking him east toward St. George's, Beck turned west toward Grosvenor Square.

After stashing the note in the tree, he cut over to Park Street to tie the ribbon tucked into his coat around the railing across from Lavinia's house. He stood there for a moment, staring up at her chamber, willing her to come to the window. But it was still early, and she didn't.

Now, he rode east, and when he arrived across from the church, he waited. His heart had begun to lift once he'd written the note, and he'd felt better when he'd put the ribbon across from Lavinia's house. Seeing Miss Lennox happily wed would readjust his mind and bring him back from the dark.

He continued to wait.

After some time, he began to grow concerned. Then people—a small group—filtered from the church and climbed into their coaches and drove away. Alarm gripped his chest.

Beck climbed from his horse and tied him to a post before crossing the street. A gentleman leaving the church looked toward him. "Northam?"

Pulling his attention from the doorway, Beck turned to the man. It was Lord Haywood. Knowing what Beck knew now, he had to fight the urge to hit the man in the face and knock him to the ground. And then kick him for good measure.

"If you came for the wedding, don't bother." Haywood's tone was heavy with scorn.

"No, just passing by," Beck said, masking his dislike for the man in the interest of obtaining information. "Whose wedding?"

"My cousin, Sainsbury. His bride called it off, the ridiculous chit." Haywood's lip curled. "A gel shouldn't be allowed to do that."

What had happened to change Miss Lennox's mind? The anticipation Beck had felt a few moments earlier dissolved in a cloud of unease. "Why not?"

"Because it's a commitment," Haywood said. "And commitments should be honored." He had the gall to prattle on about making a commitment and seeing it through after leading the Duchess of Kendal on the way he did?

Beck had to hold his hands at his sides lest he hit the man. "I have to imagine she had good reason." Beck's feeling of discomfort increased, and it had nothing to do with Haywood's lack of self-awareness.

Haywood snorted. "She's convinced herself she has. Silly chit will regret this, however." He looked back toward the church. "Ah, here's my cousin, then." He turned, and Beck took the opportunity to leave.

Climbing back on his horse, he rode home, his mind churning with what could possibly have happened to cause Miss Lennox to cry off. He handed off his mount to a groom and walked up the steps as a footman opened the door.

Gage stood inside the reception hall. "The Earl of Ware is in the sitting room." He held his hand out for Beck to deliver him his hat and gloves.

"What the devil is Felix doing here this early?" And he'd waited for Beck to come home?

"He's rather insistent upon seeing you."

The disquiet simmering within Beck increased yet again. He turned and went into the sitting room to find Felix standing in front of the window. "I was about to come out into the hall."

"What's so bloody important that you're here at this hour?"

"What's so bloody important that you weren't?"

"I went out." Why not just tell him? He already knew Beck's secret. "I went to see Miss Lennox leave the church after getting married. Only she didn't get married. She cried off, apparently."

Felix's eyes widened. "Why?"

"I don't know. I ran into the groom's cousin— Haywood—and he didn't offer a reason." Beck had to wonder if she'd never really wanted to marry in the first place. He couldn't help but think of Lavinia's initial outrage at his interference in her and the other ladies' lives. He should have left them alone. The darkness he'd managed to banish earlier slithered back over him.

Felix frowned, his expression grim. "You don't look happy."

"She became engaged to Sainsbury because of me."

Felix's eyes narrowed. "That's absurd. Did you throw

them into a compromising position that required them to wed?"

"When you put it like that, it does sound absurd." He was letting the darkness take over, and he—usually—knew better. However, he was in a rather deep dither after the way he'd mucked things up with Lavinia last night. "Still, I played a part. If not for my poetry, she might not have attracted Sainsbury, and whatever happened to cause her to cry off may not have happened."

"Instead of concerning yourself with something you may or may not have affected, let us turn our attention to something that is entirely due to your idiocy."

Beck inwardly flinched beneath the weight of his friend's ire. "What did I do?"

"What didn't you do is probably the better question. Sir Martin is going to propose to Lady Lavinia today—her father has already agreed to the betrothal."

Oh hell. Beck's knees wavered. "How do you know that?"

"Late last night at the club, Sir Martin announced his good fortune."

Now Beck sat, his frame sinking into a chair.

"Why are you sitting?" Felix took a step toward him, his gaze blazing. "You've no time to lose."

He'd already lost Lavinia. What did time matter? "For what?" He looked away from Felix.

"Good Lord, man. Your evasiveness the other day spoke volumes. It's evident to me you care for her and that there's something between you. If you're certain she feels nothing for you, then I suppose there's nothing to be done. However, if you have even a chance at happiness, don't you think you should try before it's too late?"

Beck cocked his head to the side and gave Felix a suffering sidelong glance. "You offering me advice in matters of the heart is rather baffling, don't you think?"

Felix threw his hands up. "I am no expert, that's true. But I put up with your anguish after Priscilla, and I know how wrapped up you can get in your own head. I'd rather not lose you for another series of weeks or months. Furthermore, you are not *me*. You are William Beckett, and you need love in your life—you *want* it. Do you want her?"

He couldn't lie. "Yes." The word was a croak, a broken plea.

"Then go get her."

Beck didn't hesitate. He jumped up from the chair and found Gage still in the hall, still holding his hat and gloves. Grabbing them, Beck made haste out the door—and to the future.

Chapter Thirteen

◆❦◆

Sweet song! Her words make flowers bloom.
Sweet visage! Her love slays the gloom.
Great heavens! She drives black cruel night
From those who see her grace alight.

-From An Ode to Miss Rose Stewart
by The Duke of Seduction

LAVINIA'S MOTHER BUSTLED into her bedchamber. "Time to wake up, dear. That must have been a rather horrid headache. You never sleep this late." She pushed open the heavy drapes and moved to stand at the edge of Lavinia's bed.

Rolling over to avoid her mother's gaze, Lavinia exhaled. "Yes. And I may spend the day abed." What reason did she have to get up? She closed her eyes against the offending daylight.

"Oh no, not today. Today is the day you will be engaged to marry!"

Lavinia's eyes flew open, and she sat up, turning toward her mother. "What?"

"Sir Martin approached your father last night at the club and asked if he could propose today. Isn't that wonderful?"

No, it was *terrible*.

Why? She'd already decided he was her best option.

But she didn't want him. She wanted Beck. Who didn't want her.

She resisted the urge to bury her head under her pillow. "What time is he coming?"

"My goodness, you don't sound very excited, but then you did say you wanted to spend the day abed." Mother's brow pleated, and she frowned. "Are you still ill?"

"Yes." She actually *was* ill. Or felt like she could be.

"Well, rest for a bit, and I'll have some chocolate and rolls sent up." Occasionally, her mother could be quite caring and thoughtful. "I'm sure Sir Martin won't call for a while yet." She gave Lavinia an encouraging smile before departing.

With a groan, Lavinia threw herself back onto the bed and stared up at the ceiling. Anger and sadness warred inside her as she directed all manner of ill thoughts toward Beck. A few minutes later, a maid arrived with a small tray and set it on the table situated in front of the window that faced the street below.

After she left, Lavinia pulled herself from the bed and trudged to the table. She picked up a roll and nibbled the corner as she pulled the drape aside, hoping it was gray and rainy outside to match her dismal mood.

A blue ribbon tied to the railing in front of the house across the street made her heart stop.

Beck.

What the devil was he doing? He'd been clear last night—she had nothing to hope from him. Unless he'd changed his mind.

She had to know.

If she rang for her maid and asked to dress for an excursion, she couldn't slip out unnoticed. And if she told anyone where she was going, she wouldn't be allowed. Mother would insist she stay home to await Sir Martin's arrival.

Which meant she had to dress herself. No matter. She possessed clothing that could be donned without help. It would be a simpler costume, but once she put the pelisse over it, she would look quite put together.

She worked quickly and was able to ready herself in astonishingly rapid time. But then she was exceptionally motivated. Now the trick would be to steal from the house without attracting notice. That left the main staircase out of the equation. Her mother was probably in the front sitting room watching for Sir Martin's arrival, even though it likely wouldn't happen for a couple of hours yet.

Oh, Sir Martin. She did feel bad for not wanting to marry him. He was a nice gentleman—if a trifle overbearing—but compared to Beck, it would be like settling for a potato pie when there was maybe a roast rack of lamb available.

She had to see if the lamb was on the table.

Lavinia went to the door and had to step back as it opened inward. Carrin's eyes widened as she took in Lavinia's costume. "Oh! You're already dressed."

Pulling Carrin into the room, Lavinia peered into the corridor to make sure no one was there before closing the door. "I need to go out," Lavinia said, realizing she could both use Carrin's help and trust her to keep a secret.

"I can see that," Carrin said with a hint of sarcasm that made Lavinia smile.

"I didn't realize you could be so droll, Carrin. I need to *sneak* out. My mother can't know I'm leaving."

Carrin's eyes widened again, but only briefly. "You

want my assistance?"

"Yes, please."

Carrin gazed at her shrewdly. "Give me your hat, gloves, and pelisse. I'll secret them downstairs. And take them out to the mews."

Lavinia began to understand Carrin's plan. "I'll step out to the garden, then steal back to the stables."

"Where I will give you the rest of your garments and you will be on your way."

Lavinia stared at her maid in awe. "How have I never realized or appreciated your brilliantly devious mind?"

Carrin shrugged. "It's apparently never been necessary before."

Lavinia removed her gloves. "Well, I am deeply grateful for it now."

A short time later, Lavinia made her way to the garden without incident. She was fortunate to evade her mother's notice entirely. Carrin was waiting for her in the mews and helped Lavinia don her garments. "You don't wish me to come with you, my lady?"

Lavinia shook her head. "I may only be gone a few minutes." She just had to dash up to Grosvenor Square and back. Unless…what if he was waiting there for her as he had been before?

She wouldn't know until she got there. Impatience stabbed through her as Carrin sought to place a pin in her hat. Lavinia raised her hand. "Never mind the pins. I'm sure it will be fine."

Carrin glanced up at the sky. "It's a bit breezy."

"Then I'll hold on to it," Lavinia said.

After thanking the maid one more time, Lavinia left the mews and cut out to Park Street. Her pace was swift as she strode to Grosvenor Street and then over to the square, aware she was without escort. If anyone saw her, it could be a bit of a scandal. Perhaps she *should* have brought Carrin…

She clutched at her hat, holding it atop her head as she reached the square and quickly marched to the tree, her gaze raking the area. In her haste, she hadn't brought her spectacles, which she now regretted. She'd have no idea if someone of her acquaintance could see her—but thankfully, there were few people about.

There was also no sign of Beck, which she found disheartening. But she still had the tree… She thrust her hand into the hollow and pulled out the folded foolscap.

My dearest Lavinia,

Her heart cinched, and she struggled to swallow. That didn't sound like a man who didn't want her.

I'm afraid I was hasty in our discussion last night. I hope I might speak with you in the park today. I look forward to seeing you.

Yours,
Beck

Yes, *hers.*

Only she couldn't wait to see him at the park. By then, she'd be engaged to Sir Martin. Without hesitating, she spun on her heel—again holding on to the damned hat—and started walking, then stopped abruptly. Where was she going? She knew Beck lived on Brook Street, and she *thought* he lived on the corner. But which one?

Bother!

She started across the square toward Brook Street and hoped it would just become apparent. Didn't she deserve some good luck?

Suddenly, she had it.

Coming toward her, his hat pitched low over his brow, was Beck. He paused when he saw her. She squinted as she tried to see his expression, but it was hopeless.

They both rushed forward at the same time, and they both looked around to gauge who might be seeing them.

"Where's your maid?" he asked gruffly. He looked about, then focused on her face. "And your glasses?"

"I left both at home. And don't say we can talk in the park later, because we can't. I'll be engaged to Sir Martin by then."

His eyes widened, and she sensed a bit of something in his gaze—relief, perhaps? "You're not already?"

She shook her head. "But he's coming to call soon."

He swore under his breath and turned her about, tucking her arm under his. He walked quickly toward Brook Street.

"Are we going to your house?" she asked.

He stopped just before they crossed over to the corner of Brook Street and turned to look at her. "We shouldn't."

"But we must." She dragged him forward after checking for traffic, and they continued to the corner. "Is this your house?"

"Yes." He escorted her quickly up the stairs. The door was opened immediately by a tall, rather handsome retainer—the butler, she'd guess. Beck glanced at him but said nothing as he guided her into a large drawing room. They didn't stop until he'd taken her into another room, in the front corner of the house, and closed the door behind them.

She looked about and instantly knew it was his office or music room or both. There was a desk that was obviously well used, with a variety of quills of varying sizes strewn about along with a stack of foolscap in one corner. There were also shelves of books she longed to peruse—even knowing he wouldn't have any about geology. And finally, in the corner were three guitars situated around a cushioned stool.

Her feet carried her to that corner, and she pushed aside the draperies to see he had a view of Grosvenor Square. She turned to him. "You can just make out our tree."

"Yes."

His gaze was intense as he leaned against the door, where she'd left him. He removed his hat and sailed it toward his desk, but it fell quite short.

"Lavinia." Her name had never sounded so seductive or so gorgeous coming from his lips. "I am not a gentleman. I've carried on with married women with no thought to their husbands. Despite that—and perhaps in part because of it—I've sought to help young ladies like you find happiness in matrimony. And yet, it seems I've held marriage in rather poor regard. I can only think it's because of the manner in which my sister was treated. A woman's life, her very existence, is reliant on whether she marries, and it's grossly unfair."

She couldn't have agreed with him more, and yet she wasn't entirely certain as to his point. She said nothing, waiting to see if he would get to it.

"Miss Lennox cried off. There was no wedding this morning."

She heard the pain in his voice and knew he felt

responsible. She strode back over to him and felt her hat slip once more. With a muttered oath, she tossed it in the same direction he'd sent his.

She continued forward until she stood before him. "It's not your fault."

His eyes were bleak. "She may not have become engaged to Sainsbury if not for me."

"She may not. Or she may have." Lavinia lifted a shoulder. "You mustn't torture yourself." And yet she could see he was. She began to glimpse another side to this man, a side he kept very well hidden.

She rested her hand on his chest, splaying her fingers over the front of his coat. "Jane Pemberton told me that Miss Lennox saw Sainsbury with another woman—this isn't your fault," she repeated, earnestly looking up at him. "Why did you turn me away last night?"

"Because it was the right thing to do."

"Are you going to turn me away today?" She flexed her hand against him briefly. "If you do, there is no going back. Sir Martin is coming, and I'll have to say yes. If not, my parents will find someone I may not like." She watched the torment in his gaze and whispered, "What are you afraid of?"

"You." The word was barely audible. "And me."

"Singly or together? I prefer the latter, and I don't think you have anything to fear."

"You don't know that. I'm…difficult."

She was beginning to see that. "I'm patient." She smiled, thinking of her own faults. "Mostly. And definitely when it matters." She stared into his eyes, longing to kiss him. "I'm running out of time, Beck. What did you want to say to me at the park? You'll have to say it now or not at all."

"Marry me."

She'd wanted to hear those words, and yet she couldn't quite believe he'd said them. Perhaps because he sounded as if he were being stretched upon a rack. "Forgive me, but your offer doesn't sound particularly compelling."

He slipped down the door until he was on his knees before her. His gaze was naked with need and a host of emotions about which she could only speculate. The humor she'd tried to hold close to her breast as protection fled in the face of his...desperation.

"Lavinia, marry me. I'm prone to dark moods, and as I said, I haven't behaved as a gentleman ought. But I can't imagine the future—my future—without you."

His words heated and delighted her, but she wouldn't make it easy for him, not even with the torment he was clearly enduring. "Will you be faithful to our marriage?"

"I haven't thought of or looked at another woman since I kissed your neck." He sounded rather surprised. But also proud and pleased. "I want only you. I can't imagine wanting *anyone* but you."

She shivered with need.

"Yes." She cupped his face. "Yes, I'll marry you. Now stand up and kiss me."

"I'll do more than that." He tore off his gloves and rose, then swept her into his arms, his mouth crashing down on hers with feverish intensity. His hands dug into her back as he clutched her close. It was the most delicious feeling in the world to be held by this man.

Who would be her husband.

She wound her hands around his neck and tangled her fingers in the hair at his nape. His tongue dipped into her mouth, and she met the invasion, exploring and tasting him as desire built in her core.

He arched her back, clasping her against him as she bent her knees just slightly. His hand moved lower, over her backside, holding her as he pressed into her.

She moaned into his mouth, wanting to feel what she'd felt at the sand pit the other day. He'd utterly ruined her for anyone else. If she'd wed poor Sir Martin, she'd only be comparing him to Beck.

He stood her up and pulled back, looking down at her clothing. Wordlessly, he tugged her gloves off and tossed them away, then began unfastening her pelisse.

She shivered, thinking it was fortuitous that she'd dressed so simply. Captivated by the spell he'd woven around them, she took her arms from his neck and let him divest her of her outer garment. He laid it gently over the back of a chair, which, while thoughtful, created a tension in her belly. She wanted him to move faster. She wanted him to touch her. She wanted to be sure this was real.

He came back to her and turned her around to unlace her day gown. It was quick work, and she felt the fabric loosen and air touch her flesh just above her corset and chemise. She pulled the garment forward and let it pool at her feet. He bent to pick it up as she stepped free of the muslin. He took it to the chair, where he carefully set it atop the pelisse.

She shrugged out of her petticoat and kicked it aside. When he made to pick it up, she said, "Don't bother with the rest. You are far too meticulous. Are you sure you're a rake?"

He arched a dark blond brow at her, and the edge of his mouth quirked up in a seductive smile that turned her insides to jelly. "Most definitely. Shall I show you?"

She swallowed but couldn't speak, only managing a nod.

He moved around her and unlaced her short corset. His lips moved against her neck, hitting that very spot he'd first kissed all those nights ago in the Evenrudes' library. The corset, which she hadn't managed to cinch very tightly, came loose and fell to her waist.

His mouth continued along her neck, moving up to her ear and then down again to nibble on the lobe. He licked along her jaw and back to her neck, dragging his lips to her nape. He clasped her above the corset and gripped her tightly as he kissed her back and shoulders.

Then his hands skimmed up her rib cage to the underside of her breasts. He cupped her through the chemise and she gasped, tipping her head to the side so he had full access to her neck and collarbone and shoulder. She'd never been more exposed to anyone, and it felt divine.

His fingertips tugged gently at her nipples as he swept her back against him, where she felt the firm press of his rigid cock against her backside. She wanted to turn, to kiss him, but she didn't want his touch to stop. Her breasts felt so heavy and full, and his caresses only increased the sensation.

He pulled at the edge of her neckline, loosening it and tugging the cotton down until her breasts were free. Then his hands were on her bare flesh. He was warm and hard, and she couldn't contain her moan. What he was doing somehow triggered a wave of desire in her core, making her want him *there*. She'd no idea her body worked that way and now wondered what else she didn't know. So many things. And he'd teach her all of them.

She tried to turn in his arms, but he moved one hand down to her abdomen and held her flat against him.

"Don't turn. Not yet." The hand on her breast

tugged at her nipple, pulling her flesh until she cried out. Sensation shot through her, weakening her legs. "I've got you," he whispered against her ear. His tongue traced along her flesh as he worked her breast and slid his hand lower.

She felt air on her legs and realized he was pulling up her chemise. She held her breath until the fabric was up around her waist with the corset. Anticipating what would come next, she parted her legs.

His fingers stroked gently along her folds. "Turn your head and kiss me, Lavinia."

She did as he bade, and his mouth captured hers. His tongue speared into her mouth as his finger slipped into her flesh. She whimpered, barely able to stand, but he held her fast against him, his hands arousing her body.

He rocked against her, and she felt the hardness of his shaft against her backside once more. She was at once lost in the throes of ecstasy and desperate for more.

Suddenly, he swept her up and carried her to the chaise, where he laid her down. He shrugged out of his coat and tore his cravat from his neck before he leaned down and, without preamble, took her breast into his mouth. He shoved her garments down, and she wriggled her hips as he pulled them free.

His lips and tongue teased her nipple, lightly licking and sucking then drawing hard on her flesh. She clasped his head and schooled herself not to rip his hair out. She could hardly stand it as need built inside her.

She didn't know how long he attended to her breasts, but with each lick and suck, her hips rotated and she began to rise up off the chaise. She wanted his hand back between her legs. Or better yet, his cock.

But he did neither. Instead, his mouth trailed down her abdomen, and she tensed, wondering what he intended. Unfortunately, she had to wait as he removed her half boots. She grew impatient, contemplating how long it might take him to peel away her stockings, but he surprised her by not doing so.

He clasped her knees and dragged her down the chaise, kneeling at the end. His fingers stroked briefly along her flesh before his lips were on her. His kiss was light, grazing over her curls. Embarrassment flamed through her, and she partially sat up.

"Beck, this can't be—"

"My favorite thing. I promise you. I've wanted to taste you here for so long. Let me, Lavinia, please." He looked up the length of her body into her eyes, and she was completely lost.

Her shame faded in the face of his stark desire—a desire she felt too. Willing herself to relax, she lay back. His kiss was gentle again, just his lips against her as his fingers teased her folds. Then he slid inside her as he lightly suckled that place at the top where he'd touched her the other day. A shocking burst of lust shot through her, and she bucked up off the chaise.

He pressed his hand on her pelvis and held her down as he licked along her crease. The sensation of his tongue against her gave her another jolt, but he didn't let her move. He pinned her down, captive to his mouth. And oh, the things he did with it.

Lavinia never could have imagined such pleasure. What he'd done the other day had possessed her mind and body so completely that she never thought she'd find its equal. But this was somehow better. His favorite, he'd said. God, it was becoming her favorite too.

Tension built in her muscles as his fingers slid into her channel, and he sucked on her flesh. Lights danced behind her eyes as she cast her head back against the chaise.

He took his hand from her pelvis and clasped her thighs, draping her legs over his shoulders as he buried his tongue deep inside her. Her orgasm exploded through her body, tightening everything as wave after wave of ecstasy enveloped her. She cried out mindlessly, her legs quivering as he held her through the storm.

Slowly, she came back to herself and started to cringe. She was spread so wantonly before him... And why shouldn't she be? She was to be his wife. And yet, she felt so exposed. Perhaps because he was still almost entirely clothed.

He sat back on his heels and looked up at her, his eyes gleaming with male satisfaction and lust. She propped herself up on her elbows. "Why are you wearing so many clothes?"

"I can't go talk to your father naked."

She flicked a glance down toward her spent body. "You think I can?"

His lips spread in a wicked grin. "No, but I do enjoy you like this. You have the most magnificent breasts." He prowled up her body and cupped one, taking the nipple into his mouth. Desire poured through her again, as if she hadn't just been swept away.

She pulled him down between her legs, and he groaned against her flesh.

"Lavinia, we should go."

"This is twice now that you've given me pleasure, and I haven't had a chance to reciprocate."

He lifted his head and peered down at her. "Do you

have the slightest idea what to do?"

She pursed her lips. "Given what I just did and your response, I'd say I have at least a *slight* idea. And that was nothing. Perhaps if I remove your clothing…" She plucked at the buttons of his waistcoat, and in her haste, one went flying. She followed its trajectory, then looked up at him with an apologetic smile as she pushed the garment from his shoulders. "Sorry."

His gaze darkened, and he put a knee down between her legs to brace himself while he pulled his shirt over his head. "You want me, Lavinia?"

She stared up at his chest and ran her palms over his heated flesh. "Oh yes."

"Then take me."

Chapter Fourteen

◆€·3◆

Man has no wit greater than her,
No judgment made, no slight or slur.
She is holy! Her words are might,
Yet silken, like sound taking flight.

-*From* An Ode to Lady Lavinia Gillingham
by The Duke of Seduction

"I HAVE NO idea what to do," she said, "but I daresay I'll work it out." She pressed her lips to his chest and trailed her mouth to his nipple, where she licked a circle around it.

"Uh, yes. I daresay you will." He barely ground the words out. How he'd managed to hold himself in check was a mystery to him. He'd nearly spilled his seed when her muscles had squeezed around his fingers, and she'd come apart in his mouth.

He might be a rake, but he was a rake on his knees, completely at the command of one woman. This woman.

His knee pressed against her heat, and she rotated against him, moaning softly against his chest. "How is it that I'm not satisfied after what you just did?" she asked with a soft innocence that would have made him laugh if he weren't strung so damn tight. "Is it that you maybe aren't very good at this?" He did laugh then, a strangled sound that didn't particularly resemble amusement. "That can't be right, for I did enjoy that *immensely.*" She'd been kissing and licking him between her words, driving him insane with her explorations. But now she stopped and peered up at him. "Am I, perhaps, insatiable?"

"God, I hope so." With a grunt, he gripped the back of her neck and angled her head so he could kiss her, his tongue driving into her mouth hard and deep as lust spiraled through him.

She clutched his shoulders as her pelvis moved against him once more. He adjusted his knee, rubbing along her folds, and she gasped into his mouth.

He set her back, pulling away from her almost ruthlessly as he stood to tear his remaining clothes off. His boots landed in some nether region of the room, and he may have actually torn the fall of his breeches, but he didn't care.

When he was nude in front of her, he watched as her gaze dropped to his cock. Her eyes glimmered with desire, and her tongue darted out to lick her lower lip.

It was enough—more than—to send him to the very edge.

He put his knee back between her legs, but lower between her thighs, and he clasped her sides, scooting her back up the chaise so her torso was elevated. "I would say we should wait until we are properly wed, but I'm afraid I can't do that."

She gripped his waist and pulled him down on top of her. "Lovely."

He paused, looking into her dark eyes. "But I will always stop if you ask me to."

"That's nice to know, but the only thing I'm asking you now is to go faster, please."

"Insatiable is probably accurate," he murmured just before he kissed her.

She sucked his tongue into her mouth and proceeded to demonstrate her natural skill at kissing. He lost himself completely to the devilish things she was doing to his tongue.

And she managed to pull him into her so that his cock pressed at her opening. She moaned, her fingers digging into his hips as she rose up against him. White-hot need burst inside him, and he had to hold himself back.

He moved his hand between them and found her slick passage. He teased her flesh, arousing her so that her kiss deepened and her legs opened wider.

Gripping the base of his cock, he guided himself to her sex and slid gently into her sheath. She was wet satin and heat, and he glided inside with relative ease. He'd no idea what to expect with a virgin, having no experience with them. Oh, but the farther he moved into her, the tighter she became. He pulled his mouth from hers and groaned in ecstasy.

"Is this all right?" he managed to grit out.

"I think so. It feels…odd."

"That is not encouraging." Hell, he wasn't going to last long. He needed to get himself under control. He pushed into her until he was fully inside, then took a deep breath, dropping his forehead against hers. "Just stay still a moment."

"I thought we were supposed to move." She brought her legs up and curled them around his waist. "Ooh, that feels better, you're against that spot, and oh *my*. I don't think I want to be still, Beck." She began to move her hips, and his cock jerked inside her.

"*Lavinia*." He pulled out of her, not quite all the way,

and drove back in. He tried to go slow, but feared he was failing miserably. "I want this to be… pleasant for you." He could barely speak.

"It's quite pleasant," she said, not sounding nearly as affected as he felt. "Do that again."

He stroked out and in again. "That?"

"Oh yes, *that*. But faster. I keep asking you to go faster. Is that normal?"

"Yes, especially at first. Someday, we'll go much slower, particularly when we aren't in a rush to go see your father."

She gasped. "Don't mention him right now!"

God, what was he thinking? He wasn't. She'd completely robbed him of coherent thought. He wanted to sink deep inside her body and lose himself completely.

So he did.

He cupped the back of her neck and kissed her with fierce hunger as he thrust into her relentlessly. He let himself go, and with every stroke, she met him with eager need. He wanted her to come with him so badly, but he was very close.

He kissed along her jaw and snagged her earlobe with his teeth. "Come with me, Lavinia. I can't hold back much longer."

"Don't hold back," she rasped, clutching his backside and pressing her fingers into his flesh. "Take me where I need to go. Please."

He moved faster, deeper. His balls tightened and blood rushed through him as his orgasm built to the peak. He lifted his head from her ear and shouted as he came, pouring his seed into her.

He wasn't so mindless that he didn't feel her muscles squeezing around him, bearing down as she came too.

She whimpered softly, her lips pressed to his chest as he continued to move.

He slowed but didn't stop, taking them both to the very end. When she quieted except for her breathing, he stilled. Then he started to pull back.

But she held him against her. "No, don't go. Not yet. I just want...a moment."

He kissed her damp forehead, her temple, her soft cheek. "Anything."

They lay together, entwined, until their bodies had completely quieted. He felt her shiver and rose up. "Are you cold?"

"No, just changed, I suppose." She gave him a saucy smile. "For the better."

Relief relaxed his frame. He felt that way too. "I need to speak with your father, and then we have to find out what happened with Miss Lennox." Her aborted wedding weighed in the back of his mind, even if it was entirely due to Sainsbury's behavior, which, knowing his cousin's reputation, wouldn't surprise Beck.

He started to rise but paused. "Am I allowed to get up now?"

She laughed. "Yes."

He stood, then helped her up. He pulled her close against him and kissed her, contemplating that he'd be able to do that anytime he liked after they were married.

Married.

He was going to marry this woman.

Fear and anticipation curled through him. He wouldn't be alone. When he thought of his days filled with Lavinia, joy burst in his chest. He broke the kiss and pulled his head up from hers. "I want to play for you."

Her cheeks were flushed, her breath short. "*Yes*. When?"

"Now. Just for a moment." He moved away from her and swept up his favorite guitar. He strummed his fingers over the strings, then plucked out a few notes as she found her chemise and drew it over her head.

He started playing one of the songs he'd written in recent days—since he'd met her. One of the melodies Gage liked.

She stopped dressing and just stared at him, rapt.

When he was finished, she clapped, her eyes glowing. "Aren't there words?"

"Yes, but I'm not a great singer."

"Says who? Do you sing for as many people as you play for?"

He laughed at the sarcasm in her tone. "Your taunt is well placed, my lady. I shall sing for you another time."

She grinned as she picked up her corset. "I shall look forward to it." Her face fell into a frown. "How long do I have to wait to be alone with you again?"

His mind went blank. "Not long? The banns could be read tomorrow." They could marry after the third Sunday.

"A fortnight seems an eternity," she said, making the same calculation he had. "What if you tried to get a special license?" Her shoulder lifted. "I told you I was impatient."

"Actually, I think you tried to tell me you were patient, but I'm beginning to see the truth of things." He winked at her. "I can certainly try." He moved to tighten her corset in place.

He focused on getting dressed lest he become distracted by her. His body was already stirring, and it wouldn't take much for him to take her in his arms again.

She began to tighten her dress by herself, but he rushed to help her. "I can do that," he offered.

"I did it myself earlier. I dressed entirely without my maid, actually. I was trying to sneak out."

"How enterprising of you."

When he was done, she turned to face him. "Is my hair a mess?"

Several locks had come loose. "It isn't a mess…" He went to the door and called for Gage.

"What are you doing?" she asked.

Beck stood in the door blocking Gage from seeing into the room. "Please bring a small looking glass?"

Gage's expression was impassive, but Beck was certain he knew what had transpired. "Right away, my lord."

After closing the door, Beck turned to see her clutching her gloves with a half frown.

He went to her and took her hand and brought it to his mouth so he could press a kiss against her wrist. "You need a mirror."

She exhaled. "I suppose."

Beck finished dressing—the tear in his breeches and his missing button weren't at all detectable, but knowing he was flawed and that their desire had made him that way filled him with a perverted satisfaction— as Gage rapped softly on the door.

Answering the knock, Beck took the mirror from his butler and left the door ajar. "Come in and meet my bride, Gage. This is Lady Lavinia.

"Lavinia, allow me to present Gage, the finest butler in England."

She smiled at him, perhaps a bit nervously, which he wasn't used to seeing in her. Had he erred in introducing them at that moment? He'd definitely presented them in the wrong bloody order. He was absolutely mangling this.

"I'm pleased to meet you, Gage. Thank you for the mirror." Her gaze fell to the glass in Beck's hand, which he'd neglected to give to her.

He held it up for her so she could tidy her hair.

"The pleasure is mine, my lady," Gage said. "Would you like me to send a maid to help you?"

"No, thank you." She sent him a smile as she adjusted the pins in her hair and remade her coiffure. She glanced at Beck to indicate she was finished, and he handed the glass back to Gage.

Beck crossed the room to retrieve his hat. "I'll be back later, Gage. I need to go and speak with Lord Balcombe."

"Very good, sir," Gage said with a nod. "I've today's post when you return. There's a letter from your sister, which I know you've been waiting for."

Beck stopped cold before he reached Lavinia to escort her from the room. He'd written to Margaret after reading Helen's letter from the box his stepmother had sent from Waverly Court. The need to read it nearly obscured everything else, but he had to see Lavinia home.

"I'll read it later," Beck said, anticipation curling through him as he guided Lavinia into the drawing room and back to the hall.

Gage rushed to open the door for them. "May I be the first to congratulate you both," he said with a smile as they left.

Lavinia turned her head and thanked him. When they were on the pavement heading toward Grosvenor Square, she said, "I like your butler."

"That's good." He began to think of what it might be like to share a house—his space—with someone and began to feel a bit strange. He blamed it on the letter awaiting him. He was desperate to read it.

They turned into Grosvenor Square and made their way toward Grosvenor Street. "Why are you expecting a letter from your sister?" Lavinia asked.

"I wrote to her about Helen. When I sent for the fossils I gave you, my stepmother sent everything that had been in the box, including a letter written by Helen. In it, she mentioned what Lady Abercrombie and Lady Kipp-Landon had said—that she would be better off dead. She also talked of a gentleman who'd danced with her. He gave her hope, and I wondered if Margaret might know who he was and what happened to take it away."

"Take what away?" she asked softly. "Her hope?"

He nodded, remembering his petite sister with her gray eyes and dark hair. She'd possessed a sweet and gentle soul, with a very dry sense of humor few understood. "She died alone and sad."

"How did she die?" Lavinia's query held a weight of empathy.

His heart constricted. He struggled to find the words, despite having already told Felix the truth. "She was poisoned."

Lavinia stopped near the corner of Park Street and turned toward him, her face suddenly pale. "Someone killed her?"

"No, they presumed she did it."

Lavinia lifted her hand to her mouth as her jaw dropped briefly. "Oh, Beck, I'm so sorry. Why would she…do that?"

He started walking, gently urging her along. He

didn't want to stand there and talk about this in the street, particularly when they were perhaps already drawing attention as they were unchaperoned. "She was very unhappy. Desolate, really. She had no luck on the Marriage Mart—she was too shy and too quiet. She didn't have any friends like you do." His voice hardened.

"No, but she had enemies. Or at least others were cruel to her. I understand why you wrote that poem." She stroked his arm as they turned onto Park Street.

She suddenly stopped walking, and her hand dug into his arm through his coat. She squinted down the street. "I think Sir Martin may be there already."

He looked ahead to her house and saw a coach out front. "Damn and the devil. This is going to be awkward."

"We can sneak in the back through the mews, and I'll have you wait in the morning room."

He looked down at her. "I can't let you confront them alone."

"Do you really want to come face-to-face with Sir Martin?"

His features creased in a slight wince. "Do you?"

"No, but I must," she said with a hint of resignation. "I owe him an explanation."

Beck couldn't help but feel sorry for the man. "And what will you tell him?"

She averted her gaze. "That we are better suited."

He sensed she wanted to maybe say something else but didn't press her. They were well and truly out of time. "No, we'll go in the front door," he said, looking at her in question. She nodded in response.

As they walked up to her door, he felt the tremor in her body. "I won't let anything happen to you," he whispered just before the door opened.

It wasn't a retainer, however, who stood on the threshold, but her father. And he looked ready to commit murder until his gaze settled on Beck. Then his brow wrinkled with confusion. He opened his mouth, then snapped it closed before stepping aside so they could walk into the hall.

Beck spoke up immediately. "I realize you're entertaining another caller, Balcombe, but I should tell you straightaway that I've come to ask your blessing that I marry your daughter."

"Well, that's a relief." The earl wiped a hand over his brow. "When I saw her walking back to the house on the arm of a gentleman, I was ready to call you out. My wife thought it was you, but I couldn't tell."

"You should wear glasses, as Lavinia does," Beck said. "As she *will.*"

Lavinia beamed up at him.

The countess stepped into the hall, her lips pursed. She came toward Lavinia, her gaze noting that she still clutched Beck's arm. "What is the meaning of this?" she hissed.

"Calm down, dear, they're to be wed. Poor Sir Martin is out of luck, unfortunately."

Now Lavinia withdrew her arm. "Will you please excuse me while I speak to him for a moment?" She gave Beck a half smile, and he watched her go into the room her mother had just left.

"This is going to be a scandal," the countess said, and Beck couldn't tell if that made her angry or pleased.

"It needn't be," Beck said evenly. "I'll be seeking a special license, so we'll be married with the utmost haste."

Lavinia's mother's face fell. "No, you can't. That *will* cause a scandal."

And it was clear to him that one would be *bad*. He gave her a bland smile. "We'd prefer not to wait."

"It's only a fortnight." The countess's tone had turned pleading. "That's hardly any time to wait."

"It's entirely up to Lavinia," Beck said. "She's had little say in things, and I insist she have the final word in this."

Sir Martin emerged from the room with Lavinia walking a bit meekly behind him. He looked exceedingly perturbed.

The baronet sized Beck up with a grim expression. "I understand congratulations are in order." He sent Balcombe a distasteful stare. "You might have mentioned she had additional suitors."

Lavinia's father smiled briefly and apologetically. "I'm afraid you both came up to scratch at almost precisely the same moment. Unfortunately, you endeavored to speak to me first, and Lord Northam went directly to Lavinia to ask for her hand. And in the end, it is her choice."

Beck glanced toward Lavinia and saw her gaze soften toward her father. He was glad for her.

"Good day, then." Sir Martin didn't bow to anyone nor did he even look toward Lavinia before he left.

The countess frowned again. "Well, that was *very* awkward." She turned to Lavinia. "You are in a heap of trouble, my dear. Sneaking out to meet a gentleman!" She speared an angry glance at Beck.

"My *fiancé*, Mother." She kept her serenity rather well, but then Beck supposed she'd had years of experience with her mother.

"And what's this nonsense about a special license?"

her mother continued. "You're my only daughter, and you'll be married at St. George's. The banns will be read tomorrow. If you're in such haste, you can wed two weeks from Monday." Her lips jutted into a pout. "But you will not deny me the pleasure of a church wedding and celebration breakfast."

Beck said nothing as he waited for Lavinia to decide. She looked at him in question, and he barely lifted a shoulder, silently communicating that he would do whatever she wanted.

Lavinia exhaled and lifted her gaze briefly toward the ceiling before turning to her mother. "Fine. Two weeks from Monday, and not a day more."

The countess visibly relaxed. "That barely gives us time, but I'll try to manage. We're going to be very busy, Lavinia." Her tone held grave importance. One would think she'd been asked to solve a national crisis.

Beck stifled a laugh.

"Excuse us for a moment, please," Lavinia said with considerable authority. "I need to speak with my fiancé." She took his arm and dragged him into the room where she'd gone to see Sir Martin, closing the door behind them.

"That is one nice thing about being engaged," he said wryly. "No one cares if we're alone together anymore."

She winced. "That makes me think of Miss Lennox. I do hope she's not ruined after calling off her wedding to Sainsbury." She looked up at Beck in horror. "I'm sorry. I shouldn't have brought it up."

He inwardly flinched. "No, it's fine." Was it? He still felt responsible and likely always would. He clung to the happiness of the past hour to keep any disquiet away. "I do want to make sure she's all right."

"I'll pay a call on her this afternoon," Lavinia said,

touching his arm reassuringly.

"Will your mother allow it? It sounds as though your time may be occupied with planning our wedding."

Lavinia rolled her eyes. "Not all of it. She'll prefer it if I let her handle most of it, believe me. I've never been as interested in that sort of thing."

"Perhaps it should be geology themed."

She laughed and brushed a kiss across his lips. "I adore you."

He froze for a moment. It wasn't the word love, but it was close. Did she love him? Did he love her? He hadn't loved anyone since Priscilla. He hadn't thought the emotion would find him again.

"Trust me," she said, drawing him back to the present. "I will make sure we have plenty of time for things we want to do before the wedding. We'll just need to be…creative." Her lips curled into a seductive smile, and he began to grow hard.

He took a step back from her. "I'd better go before I try to be…creative here and now." He leaned forward and kissed her cheek. "I'll see you soon."

"Tonight—at the Morecott Ball?"

He hadn't thought about his evening plans, but he supposed he must. And he'd take any chance he could get to see his soon-to-be wife. "Yes. I think it's past time I danced with you."

Her eyes glowed with anticipation. "Most definitely."

"And wear your spectacles." He went back to the hall, where he bid farewell to her parents who were still loitering, as he expected them to be. He and Lavinia might be afforded a modicum of privacy, but it wasn't as if he could seduce their daughter in their sitting room.

Not today anyway.

⟡⟡

AFTER BECK LEFT, Lavinia had to spend an excruciating hour with her mother planning the wedding breakfast. When she was finally free, she dashed off notes to Sarah and Fanny telling them her news and a third note to Jane Pemberton informing her of Miss Lennox's aborted wedding. Then Lavinia dressed in a more appropriate costume for paying calls and went downstairs to tell her mother she planned to visit Miss Lennox.

"Oh, I'll go with you," Mother declared. "I must learn what happened."

Lavinia gritted her teeth. "Mother, I'm not going to cull gossip. I want Miss Lennox to know she has support and friends during this difficult time." While Lavinia didn't know her very well, she thought it was important for Miss Lennox to understand she wasn't alone. And not everyone would be as thoughtless as Lavinia's mother.

A groom drove them to Albemarle Street where it looked as though there were several callers at the Lennox residence. As Lavinia and her mother made their way to the front door, two women nodded in their direction as they departed.

As much as Lavinia wanted to offer support, she also didn't want to overwhelm Miss Lennox.

The butler admitted them into the house and showed them to the drawing room on the first floor. Mrs. Lennox greeted them with a weak smile. "Good afternoon, Lady Balcombe, Lady Lavinia. How kind of you to call."

The countess pressed her lips into a sympathetic

line—not a frown, not a smile, but something meant to convey wordless support. Or pity. "We just wanted to make sure you know you have friends and support during this difficult time."

Resisting the urge to roll her eyes at her mother, Lavinia instead looked about for Miss Lennox, but she wasn't present. Lavinia turned to Mrs. Lennox. "Would Miss Lennox care for a visitor?"

"I think not," Mrs. Lennox said sadly. "She's been through quite an ordeal. She's not seeing anyone."

A young maid came into the room and went to whisper in Mrs. Lennox's ear. The older woman blinked in surprise, then turned her attention back to Lavinia. "It seems my daughter would like to see you. Her maid will show you upstairs."

Lavinia turned and followed the maid out and up the stairs. The maid led her to a sitting room at the front of the house, where Miss Lennox stood near the window looking down at the street. She glanced over at the maid and Lavinia as they entered. "Thank you, Hobbs."

The maid nodded and left them alone, closing the door behind her.

Lavinia wasn't sure what to say. Why had Miss Lennox chosen to see her and no one else?

Miss Lennox exhaled as she turned from the window and walked to a chair near the hearth. "Good afternoon, Lady Lavinia. Would you care to sit?" She gestured to the settee in front of the fire as she sank into the chair.

"Please call me Lavinia." She went to the settee and perched on the edge, waiting for Miss Lennox to guide the conversation.

"Then you must call me Phoebe." She stared into the fire for a moment. "I'm quite glad not to be Mrs.

Sainsbury."

"I'm glad you're glad," Lavinia said, not wanting to be intrusive as to what had happened to make her that way. "It's better than being sorry or having regret."

Phoebe turned her head toward Lavinia and smiled. "Yes. You understand. You don't feel sorry for me, do you?"

"I feel…bad that you apparently suffered an unpleasant situation. I can't imagine it's easy to call off a wedding." Lavinia couldn't even conceive of it, and she was planning one. "Particularly under the intense scrutiny of a London Season."

"Precisely. You *do* understand." She looked back to the fire and narrowed her eyes. "I expect most people will fault me for crying off, but I had exceptional reason."

"I don't wish to pry or make you speak of something you'd rather not." Lavinia wanted to be clear about her purpose in coming.

"You're very kind," Phoebe said. "But I knew that. That's why I invited you up. I saw you arrive, and you're the first person I've wanted to talk to. You're also intelligent, and you've suffered the notoriety of being one of the Duke of Seduction's subjects." She looked at Lavinia with a touch of admiration. "And you seem to have handled it with aplomb. I haven't seen you rush into an engagement—not as I was foolish enough to do." Her gaze darkened. "Marriage is not the shining beacon of feminine completion we're led to believe."

"Er, yes." Lavinia felt a bit disingenuous since she was now engaged. And she'd tell Phoebe—in a moment. First, she wanted to ask about Beck. Rather, the Duke of Seduction. "Do you blame him? The Duke of Seduction, I mean. Without his interference, you would likely not have had to deal with this…problem." That word was wholly inadequate.

"Possibly, but I don't blame him. No, the blame rests firmly with Sainsbury and his inability for fidelity or, at the very least, discretion." She shook her head and looked down at her lap. "Actually, I blame myself most of all. I was so anxious to marry." She lifted her gaze to Lavinia's. "That's what we're supposed to be, isn't it?"

"Yes." Lavinia's heart twisted for the other woman. Now she did indeed feel sorry for her—not because of Sainsbury, but because it seemed she'd learned a painful lesson.

"But you aren't," Phoebe said, her lip hitching up in a brief smile. "You and your friends defy convention. You cling to the perimeter, and you set your own terms. *You* blame the Duke of Seduction, I think. For your popularity."

"Er, yes." Lavinia said again, concerned that her discomfort might be plain. "I may not have been anxious to marry, but I did plan to. *Do* plan to, rather." She summoned a tepid smile. "I've just become engaged to the Marquess of Northam, actually."

Phoebe's jaw dipped with surprise. "Have you?"

Lavinia nodded. "Today."

"And are you happy about it?" Phoebe tipped her head to the side. "I can't really tell."

"Quite. We suit rather well. So in that respect, I must thank the Duke of Seduction." She nearly told Phoebe the truth—that Beck was him—but decided it was a secret that should stay a secret. In fact, the duke should retire his match-luring poems entirely. Instead, Lavinia would persuade him to write poems that would inspire young women like Phoebe to seek clarity and purpose for themselves and not rely on the expectations of others.

"Well, I'm glad it worked out for you," Phoebe said.

"And I'm sorry it didn't for you. Truly. But this will pass, and there will be other opportunities."

"Perhaps, but they needn't be marriage. If I've learned anything, it's that I'll marry for love or not at all. And he has to possess a good measure of honor and dignity—and display a high regard for women." She winced slightly and hesitated a moment before asking, "Aren't you a bit worried about Northam's reputation?"

Lavinia glanced away, hating that she'd asked the question and yet knowing it would be on everyone's lips the moment they learned he was betrothed. And to her of all people—someone who barely appeared on most people's societal landscape.

"I'm not." Lavinia had been, of course, but knowing he hadn't looked at or thought of another woman since they'd met was enough for her. She supposed he could be lying, but she didn't think he would do that. "Perhaps I'm naïve, but I believe he'll be a devoted husband."

Phoebe smiled warmly and clasped her hands together in her lap. "How wonderful. I do hope that will be the case." Her smile faded. "It's horrid, though, isn't it, that if he was unfaithful, people would look at you as if it were your fault. Men are excused from nearly anything. I'm sure Sainsbury will find another gullible young woman who will fall for his charms, just as his cousin did."

"His cousin?"

"Lord Haywood. He had a horrible reputation when he was a young buck, and he ruined at least one young woman and is rumored to have carried on with many more. Yet, he was able to marry an heiress just a few years later."

"Yes, I'm quite familiar with Haywood's transgressions," Lavinia said grimly. "Thankfully, the woman he wronged was able to find happiness."

"She's a peculiarity and very, very lucky. Most of us aren't." Phoebe waved a hand. "But I am not looking for sympathy. I will survive this, and I will be the better for it, whether I wed someday or not. In the meantime, I've persuaded my mother to allow me to return to the country."

"Oh, then you'll miss my wedding breakfast." Lavinia had planned to invite her.

"I'm afraid I must. I don't plan to discuss the details of why I called off the wedding, but people will talk anyway."

"I won't say anything," Lavinia rushed to assure her.

"I know you won't—at least not to anyone who will gossip. I imagine you'll talk to Jane about it and maybe your other friends."

"Only if you don't mind."

"I don't. It's going to be a spectacle in any case, which is why I'm leaving town." She rose. "I should start packing."

Lavinia took her cue and stood. "I'm so glad to see you're doing well. This *will* pass."

"It will, but whether I'm able to weather it with a decent reputation is yet to be determined." She shrugged. "I have no regrets—and that's what's most important." She looked intently at Lavinia. "Remember that. If for any reason you decide you don't want to marry Northam, you don't have to. Take the time of your betrothal—and I recommend stretching it out if you can—to make sure this is what you want. Once you're wed, there's absolutely no turning back."

A shiver tripped up her spine. She'd said something similar to Beck earlier that day, and he'd decided to plunge forward, without regret. She smiled at Phoebe. "I can't imagine anything happening to change my mind."

They said good-bye, and Lavinia went downstairs to the drawing room where her mother waited. Mrs. Lennox thanked Lavinia for visiting with Phoebe.

As she made her way outside, she couldn't stop thinking of Phoebe's advice and the fact that she didn't need it. Nothing would stop her from marrying Beck. They had friendship, attraction, mutual respect…and she loved him.

Yes, she was completely in love with him. And that was   all   that   mattered.

Chapter Fifteen

❧⋄❧

Like the skylark brings its sweet song to air,
Her wisdom and poise have none to compare.
Forgiveness! Compassion! Her heart unbound.
For mortals, her beauty shall be renowned.

-*From* In Praise of Miss Phoebe Lennox
by The Duke of Seduction

GAGE OPENED THE door for Beck and immediately took his hat and gloves. "Married, my lord?" He didn't bother disguising his shock.

"Yes." Beck started through the drawing room toward his office, expecting Gage would follow.

"I had no idea you were even considering it," Gage said. "Not that I expect you disclose everything to me."

"I wasn't considering it," Beck revealed honestly as he walked into his office and continued to his desk.

"Well, I trust you will be very happy and that this isn't a hasty…situation."

Beck could hear how carefully Gage chose his words. He always strove to be respectful, but also knew that Beck appreciated his counsel. Beck sat down behind his desk. "You're worried I compromised her and we have to marry."

"Didn't you?" The question was devoid of judgment or accusation.

"I proposed to her *first*." And he'd do it again. "She was on the verge of becoming betrothed to someone else, and I found I couldn't live with that."

"That sounds rather definitive," Gage said.

Because it was. Lavinia had become an important part of his life. He looked forward to every moment he might share with her and had begun to look for them as much as possible. Now, he could be assured of many, many moments for the rest of their lives. He'd never considered that, at least not since he'd had his heart broken. He didn't like to dwell on things that might never come true, and he'd never imagined he'd fall in love again.

Did that mean he'd fallen in love with Lavinia? He thought so. If he even knew what love was. He thought he had with Priscilla, but this was different. When he contemplated a future without Lavinia, it appeared far bleaker than any of the pain he'd suffered after Priscilla's rejection.

"Have you set a wedding date yet?" Gage asked. "I should like to prepare the staff for the change in the household."

Of course he would. As he *should*. Beck really hadn't given this much forethought. He ought to write to Rachel immediately. She would likely want to come to London for the wedding. "It will happen rather quickly," Beck said. "My bride has an impatient streak." He swallowed a smile, grateful for her inability to wait. "The banns will be read tomorrow, and the ceremony will take place two weeks from Monday."

Gage blinked in surprise. "That is fast. As fast as you can manage."

"Without a special license, yes." Which he would happily have procured, particularly if it would have pleased Lavinia. That she'd capitulated to her mother's wishes to give her the wedding she wanted for her daughter revealed her kind and generous nature. Which only made him love her more.

"Is there anything we should do before the new marchioness arrives? We don't have much time, but I'm sure we could effect some sort of change if any is required."

Beck stared at him blankly. For the first time, he realized he was going to have to share his home, which he'd always treasured as his private space. It was one thing to share Waverly Court with Rachel and his half brother, especially since he'd begun to expect that George would one day inherit the title. However, now that would not be the case. Everything in his life had changed in the span of this afternoon, and he was just now beginning to understand the impact.

Unease rippled through him, like a stone thrown into a lake, with echoes of movement disrupting the smooth surface. Beck might have a smooth surface, but underneath lurked a dark tangle, which Lavinia had glimpsed today. What would she say the first time he closeted himself in his office and didn't come out for a day? Would he still do that after they wed?

He leaned back in his chair with a huff and realized Gage was still waiting for him to respond. "I can't think of any changes right now, but I'll invite Lavinia to tour the house and solicit her opinion. She'll require an office of her own. With bookshelves."

"The upstairs sitting room?" Gage suggested.

That would work, but Beck wondered if he might like having her nearby. If she took the sitting room next door, they could install a door between the chambers and spend many afternoons as they had today…

And yet that would also mean she would be right next door—with specific access—during his darker periods. His gaze drifted to the letter to his desk, and he found he wanted to read that rather than think about this anymore.

It will be fine. You love her. She loves you. Probably.

Did she?

"I'll discuss it with her," Beck said. "Thank you, Gage."

Gage inclined his head and departed, closing the door behind him.

Beck picked up the letter from Margaret and began to read. He found himself speeding through her descriptions of her daily life and those of her family. Her eldest daughter had become engaged, which made him read more slowly. He couldn't quite believe she was that old, but then Margaret was twelve years his senior.

He continued reading, and when he saw Helen's name, his heart began to pound.

> *It's been so long since I thought of that time in Helen's life. She was so despondent at not finding a husband. I know it caused her considerable pain to hear of my marital happiness and our growing family. I was surprised at what she did, but I now realize I somewhat expected it. There was always a shadow across her, and I fear it was destined to swallow her. I did hope that she had found happiness with Lord Haywood, but it seemed even that was not to be. I do wonder what happened there. She told me he wanted to marry her, but when that didn't happen, I assumed, in her*

eagerness to wed, that she'd misunderstood.

Haywood? He was the man who'd danced with Helen and gotten her hopes up? It seemed Margaret doubted whether he'd promised to marry Helen, but Beck didn't for a moment. He was confident Haywood had led his sister on a merry chase.

Or did he just want to believe something—or someone—had pushed Helen to kill herself? What if it had been entirely herself? As Margaret wrote, Helen had always possessed a shadow. As he did. Only hers had seemed deeper and more pervasive. She was often melancholy and complained of feeling lonely. She'd sometimes mentioned not wanting to feel that way any longer, but as a boy, he'd never thought she meant it in a permanent way. He'd never imagined she would want to end her life entirely.

And yet, if she'd considered it, and then two horrid women had encouraged her along that path, would she have done it? Especially if another person, a man, disappointed her? Beck could see how she might have found solace in the unthinkable.

Shit. Did that mean he could see that for himself? Could his dark episodes ever push him to an inconceivable edge? He didn't think so—they hadn't yet. Apprehension tripped across his shoulders just the same.

He dropped the letter to his desk and blinked. His gaze settled on the chaise, and he couldn't help but think of Lavinia. The sultry tilt of her smile, the lush curve of her breast, the sheer joy of her curiosity and desire. Her optimism, her selflessness, her absolute zest for life. She was the perfect antidote to the poison in his soul.

He looked back at the letter and wanted to leap to his feet and drive directly to Haywood's house to interrogate him about Helen. What had he done to her? Had he led her on and abandoned her as he'd done to the Duchess of Kendal? The man had no shame. Just listening to him earlier outside St. George's had galled Beck. And now, knowing he was the man Helen had hoped would court her...

Fury raged within him. He stood and went to his guitars. For the first time, he wanted to pick one up and smash it against the floor. He forced himself to take deep breaths and calm his thundering heart.

He could not interrogate Haywood. That was not the way to glean information from a man like him. No, Beck had to come up with another plan, and one was already forming in his mind.

Tonight, after the ball, he'd execute it. And Haywood had better hope he had nothing to do with Helen's death.

The Morecott Ball was the best Society event Lavinia had ever attended. It happened that when you became engaged to marry a marquess, everyone—*everyone*—was kind and charming and effusive with their good wishes. That some of them were insincere didn't matter to her. Not tonight. Tonight, she was filled with joy and anticipation for the future.

When Beck arrived, Lavinia's breath snagged in her chest. He was almost sinfully handsome in his black evening clothes. The white of his cravat gleamed against his skin, and she dreamed of ripping it from him along with the rest of his garments.

Well, it hadn't taken long for her to become a complete wanton.

"Why are you smiling?" Sarah asked from beside her. "Oh, I see the marquess has arrived." She'd been utterly thrilled to hear of Lavinia's betrothal.

"We're going to dance," Lavinia said, perhaps unnecessarily.

"Seems like that's a bit overdue," Sarah said with pointed sarcasm and a smile.

Instead of going to the park that afternoon, Sarah and Fanny had called on Lavinia to hear all about how the engagement had come about. Lavinia had told them what had happened after he'd proposed, though not in great detail. They'd both gaped at her and then said, "Good for you."

They were the best of friends.

Beck came straight to them and bowed first to Sarah and then to Lavinia, whose hand he took and kissed. The next several minutes were filled with people rushing over to offer their congratulations and the arrival of Lavinia's mother, who preened over the entire scene.

Lavinia was glad when the waltz started so that she and Beck could be alone. Or at least away from the crowd around them.

She put her hand on his shoulder as he splayed his hand across her back. "I was going to suggest we rendezvous in the library later, but I daresay we won't be able to sneak away."

"Perhaps not," he said with an edge of disappointment. "There's always tomorrow."

She laughed. "At church?"

He narrowed his eyes in a thoroughly seductive manner. "I'll take you wherever I can have you."

A thrill of anticipation and something far more primitive shot through her. "I may drag you to the library," she muttered.

"Careful, Lavinia," he said. "Unless you want me to kiss you in the middle of a ballroom."

Desire swirled through her as she looked up at him, but his gaze was trained over her head. "I wish you would."

They were quiet a moment before she said, "I called on Miss Lennox today."

"Oh?" He glanced down at her, but only briefly. Did he have to concentrate on the dance steps? "I scarcely know Sainsbury, but I daresay she's better off."

She started with surprise. "You do?" He'd felt guilty earlier. What had changed? "Do you know why she cried off?" That was the only thing that made sense, and yet Phoebe had made it clear that Lavinia was the only person she'd told. She'd shared the information with Sarah and Fanny that afternoon, but both had sworn themselves to secrecy.

"Not particularly," he said, "but Sainsbury comes from bad stock."

Bad stock? She finally understood. "Haywood is his cousin." Yet, hadn't Beck known that earlier when he'd felt so bad about his role in instigating Miss Lennox's courtship with Sainsbury?

"Yes." He looked around the ballroom, and she decided he was acting a bit odd. Distracted almost. "I don't suppose Haywood is here tonight?"

"I haven't seen him." Why did Beck care?

"I don't plan to stay very long after we dance. Is that all right?"

She tried to will him to look at her. "Are *you* all right?"

His gaze dipped to her once more. "Certainly. I just don't enjoy this sort of scrutiny."

"If you want to go, I'll understand." She couldn't help but feel a bit disappointed. This was the one night she thought she might enjoy the attention, but without him, it would be far less sweet. She was, however, enjoying her view of the ballroom through her spectacles. She could see everyone and everything. It was marvelous.

Until she saw Sir Martin.

He stood near the doors to the patio, his forehead bunched into little lines. His expression could only be described as a glower. And it was clear he was looking directly at her and knew she was looking at him.

She looked away from him. "Oh dear, Sir Martin doesn't look very pleased."

"Where is he?" Beck demanded, sounding agitated.

"Over by the doors to the patio."

Beck turned his head as they moved. "I see him."

She looked up and caught Beck's eyes narrowing. "He's just disappointed."

"He'll have to learn to get used to it." He sounded annoyed.

Lavinia squeezed his shoulder. "He will. I can't say I blame him. I do feel as though I gave him false hope."

Now Beck's eyes latched on to hers with sharp intensity. "Did you promise him anything? Did you make any sort of commitment?"

She found the depth of his response slightly unsettling. "No."

"Of course you didn't. You have no reason to feel guilty."

"I didn't say I felt *guilty*." Her voice trailed off, and she wondered at his mood.

The dance came to an end, and Lavinia wished they had more time. Something had to be bothering him.

As they walked from the dance floor, Sir Martin approached them. Lavinia felt Beck tense beside her.

"I don't think I offered my congratulations to you earlier today," Sir Martin said. "After you brought Lavinia home from…wherever." He said this just loud enough that a few people nearby turned their heads.

Beck stiffened even more. "Sir Martin, I don't think your congratulations are necessary, but we do thank you." He took a step forward, and Lavinia moved with him. He bent his head toward Sir Martin's ear and spoke softly, but she could still hear him. "Say something like that again, and I'll make it hard for you to speak for a month." He smiled widely, then started toward the door to the patio, taking Lavinia with him.

As soon as they were outside, he removed her arm from his and stalked to the railing. The mostly dark garden lay below them. A handful of people were on the patio, and Lavinia hurried to Beck's side, keeping her voice low. "What did you just do?"

He stared out at the garden. "I threatened Sir Martin. I won't allow him to cast aspersions on you."

"He can't hurt me."

"You are far too kind, Lavinia. He may not be able to hurt you, but he will attempt to extract what revenge he can. By besmirching your reputation." Beck wiped his gloved fingers against his brow. "Hell, I've already done that."

"We're getting married. How does that besmirch my reputation?"

He turned his head to look at her briefly, his eyes sharp and narrow. "Because of *my* reputation."

She thought of her conversation with Phoebe that afternoon. "I suppose. But I don't care. What people say or think can't hurt me. You're not a rake any longer, and I've no doubt you'll be the best of husbands." She edged closer to him as he turned his gaze back to the garden. "Unless you decide to behave like this all the time."

His shoulders dipped briefly, then he took her hand and pulled her down the stairs to the garden. She expected him to lead her onto the path, but instead, he took her back into the house through what appeared to be the breakfast room. Then he opened a door and tucked them both into a small closet that went completely dark as soon as he closed the door.

With her free hand, she felt for the shelving at her right to find her bearings. "What are you doing?"

"I just…" He took a deep breath and let go of her hand. "I told you earlier that I was difficult."

"Yes. I can manage difficult." She put her hands on his chest and felt the strong beat of his heart through his clothing. "What's wrong with you tonight?"

"Nothing."

Frustration simmered within her. "I don't believe you."

"Nothing I want to talk about right now. I want you to enjoy tonight."

"I was. I will." Except he was leaving. "I wish you would stay a little longer."

"I can't." Suddenly his bare hand caressed her neck, and he drew her head forward as his lips closed over hers.

Her irritation melted into desire as he devoured her mouth. She curled her arms around his neck and stood on her toes to kiss him with abandon. He ripped his mouth away from hers and dropped savage kisses along her jaw and neck, leaving her breathless. His hand curled around her side and slid up to cup her breast.

She gasped softly, recalling the feel of his mouth and fingers on her earlier that day. Heat radiated in her core, and she was desperate for him to touch her again.

"Touch me," she whispered.

"Where?"

"Everywhere."

He kissed the flesh above her bodice, his tongue dragging over her and sending delicious sensation to every part of her. He reached down and pulled up her dress, reminding her of the day at the sand pit.

She didn't want to be the only one being touched. She wanted—needed—to do some touching of her own. She pulled off her gloves and let them fall heedlessly. Then she gripped his nape and took his mouth in a searing kiss.

He moaned softly, stoking her desire. She slid her hands down his front and searched for the buttons of his fall. She moved clumsily at first, but soon his pantaloons fell open.

Meanwhile, he'd lifted her skirt and held it at her waist while his other hand stroked up her thigh and found her sex. He deepened the kiss, and she thrust her hand into his smallclothes, finding his shaft.

He pushed forward, his cock sliding into her hand as surely as it had moved into her earlier. Had it been just today? And here she was, desperate for him again. Maybe she *was* insatiable. She had to be since they were in a closet engaging in sexual activity during a ball. Though she realized this was usual behavior for him.

She suddenly froze. A moment later, he did the same, lifting his head from hers. "Lavinia?"

"Is this what you did with all the other women?" She detested the jealousy in her voice, but couldn't help it just the same.

He took his hand from between her legs and cupped her face. "No."

"Please don't lie to me. I know you had assignations with women like this. At balls and such. That's how we met, in case you forgot."

"How could I?" he asked with a wry tone that didn't immediately soothe her. "First, I did meet with women...like this." He exhaled softly. "Second, and most importantly, I'm not lying. This is far different from anything I've ever done or experienced." He stroked her cheek, her jaw, and she could feel that his mouth was just a breath from hers. "Don't you know how different you are, Lavinia? How precious and wonderful? I never loved any of them."

Joy loosed inside her and spread. "You love me?"

"More than anything. More than music. More than words. More than my life."

Nothing he said could have meant more to her. She felt very foolish for her jealousy. "I'm a petty woman, aren't I?"

"You're entitled to any emotion you feel—and I shall do my best to answer your concerns. But know this, Lavinia: I love you. I *love* you."

"Oh, Beck, I love you too." Her heart felt as if it would burst from her chest.

He kissed her again, more gently at first, then with increasing urgency as she moved her hand against him. His hand descended to her sex once more, and she tightened her grip around his cock.

He gasped, breaking the kiss, and she worried she'd hurt him. She loosened her hold. "I'm sorry. I have no idea what I'm doing."

"You're doing magnificently. Please don't stop."

She gripped him again. "That's not too tight?"

"No," he answered, the tightness of his voice giving her a moment's pause until she realized that was how he tended to sound when he was aroused. And judging from the length and girth of his shaft at present, he was most definitely aroused. "Please move your hand."

She slid her palm along him to the tip and then back down. "Like that?"

"Yes, please. Faster."

Oh, he liked faster too. How lovely. She smiled to herself as she quickened her pace. He answered by teasing her folds and slipping a finger inside her. Desire blossomed into blatant lust, and she couldn't help but move her hips forward, seeking more of him.

"Lavinia, put your foot on that shelf."

"Which shelf?"

"*Any* shelf."

She lifted her foot and found one. The position opened her up to his touch, and he thrust two fingers into her, drawing a cry from her lips.

"Now take my cock from my clothing so I can get to you, please."

"You're being so polite," she murmured, grasping his flesh and using her other hand to peel his clothes away.

"It's taking a great deal of effort." It sounded as though he was gritting his teeth. He tucked her skirt behind her leg so it was pinned between her thigh and the wall. Then he clasped her waist and lifted her slightly as he nestled himself between her legs. "Guide me into you, my love."

She struggled to get him at just the right angle, but after several tries and a tweak of his hips, he penetrated her. Pleasure instantly washed over her, giving her the promise of ecstasy to come.

"Now hold on to me, no matter what."

He trapped her against the wall with his body, lifting her as he drove deep inside her. She closed her eyes and tipped her head back as her foot found another shelf. Her other foot sought a place to ground them, so he could work less at holding her up and focus more on thrusting into her. God, she needed him to move.

She braced her foot against the door, opening herself wider to him, then clutched his neck as he slammed into her. It wasn't a slow build. She was thrown up to the pinnacle, where she floated for just a few moments, then ecstasy rushed through her, taking her higher still.

He kissed her, their lips and tongues fighting to cling together between their frantic breaths. Then he thrust particularly deep, and his entire body tightened. He groaned into her mouth, trying, she could tell, to stay as quiet as possible. She could only imagine what this must sound like outside their haven. So she didn't.

After a few more strokes, she felt him relax—just slightly—as his body came back under control. She caressed his face and felt sweat along his brow.

He withdrew from her and eased her legs down until she was standing on the floor. "All right?"

She nodded, then realized he couldn't see her. "Yes. A little wobbly."

"Sorry. And a bit messy." His tone held a shade of regret.

"That's what petticoats are for, silly." She reached down and lifted her dress to expose her undermost petticoat that no one would ever see, then awkwardly used it to dry him off, pushing his hands aside.

"You didn't have to do that," he said.

"I wanted to." She set to tidying herself.

He kissed her lips, her cheek, her forehead. "You are the most thoughtful woman."

"I'm sensible."

He laughed. "Yes. Very."

She sensed that he'd relaxed and felt relieved. "I suppose I should return to the ball."

"I'll escort you back."

"No, you go," she said. "I'll say I was in the retiring room. That way, we won't look so obvious."

He groaned softly. "I didn't mean to cause a stir. But what am I to do? You're irresistible."

"And insatiable."

"Yes, and never change." He kissed her again. "Ready?"

She let out a breath, not quite ready to leave him, but knowing she must. "Yes."

He opened the door a bare sliver, just enough to allow a faint bit of light. He plucked up her gloves and handed them to her.

She worked them on as he found his own and did the same. "I'll see you at church tomorrow, then?"

"Yes."

She patted her hair and pressed her hands to her cheeks, thinking she would definitely stop by the retiring room first—both to bolster her alibi and to ensure she didn't look tousled. She certainly *felt* tousled, and it was glorious.

Pressing a final kiss to his lips, she whispered, "I love you."

As she left the closet, she heard him say, "Not as much as I love you."

Chapter Sixteen

❧❧❧

Bring vengeance, dark justice, to evil men!
No woman should witness the darkness end.
What sin hath done to the good and the right,
Cruel retribution in dark Devil light.

-Beck's writings

As BECK STRODE into White's, the tension Lavinia had
driven away with her touch gripped him once more.
He'd been incredibly wound up before the ball, and he
knew his behavior had alarmed Lavinia as they'd
danced. And then Sir Martin had decided to be an ass,
and Beck had nearly plunged over the edge.

Sometimes anger took over, not as much as a need to
be alone, but when rage came upon him, it wasn't
always easy to let it go. And he supposed he hadn't.
He'd simply set it aside until he could fully inhabit it.
Now that he was here, he could.

He wasn't entirely certain where he might find
Haywood, but knew White's was the blackguard's
preferred club. Beck circulated through the main rooms
then situated himself in the morning room where he
could see the hall and watch as gentlemen arrived.

He sipped whiskey—slowly so as to keep his wits
about him—and waited.

Over an hour after he took his post, Haywood strode

into the hall. He didn't come into the morning room, but continued straight back to the main staircase. Beck waited a minute, then followed him up. He found his quarry in the coffee room seated at a table with another gentleman Beck barely recognized.

Gripping his whiskey, Beck made his way to the table. "Mind if I sit?"

Haywood looked up at him. "Didn't I just run into you this morning?"

"Indeed you did." Beck sat down and inclined his head toward the other gentleman.

"I was just telling Goodwin here about that debacle." Haywood shook his head. "Stupid chit. Ah well, she's the one who will bear the brunt of her mistake. Laurence will be just fine."

Goodwin, whom Beck vaguely recalled now, nodded. He was similar in age to Haywood—early forties at least and apparently of a similar mind. "She'll regret it, if she doesn't already."

Haywood snorted. "I'm sure she does. She may even be at my cousin's right now begging him to take her back."

The conversation was enough to make Beck want to pummel them both, but he had an objective and that wasn't it. He really hoped Goodwin would just go away. Alas, Beck had to suffer his presence for some time before he excused himself.

By then, Haywood was on his third glass of whiskey, while Beck was on his second—again nursing it slowly. Now he had his chance.

Beck moved his chair closer to Haywood and took a drink. "I wanted to ask you about something. You seem a man of a certain…expertise."

Haywood's brows arched, and his eyes lit with

curiosity behind the sheen of a whiskey-induced haze. "Expertise, eh?"

"You possessed a certain reputation before you wed, which is not all that different from mine."

He chuckled low in his throat. "You're a bit of a rakehell?" He lifted his glass in a toast. "The only way to survive."

Beck swallowed his disgust and lifted his mouth in a brief smile. "I find myself engaged as of this afternoon."

"Is that right? Hell, we should have been celebrating your fortune—or despairing of your impending shackle." He shouted with laughter before taking a drink. "Who's the lucky chit?"

Beck wanted to hit the man and tell him to never refer to his future wife that way, but he had to stay on task. He didn't really want to say her name in his presence, as if that alone would sully her. "Lady Lavinia Gillingham."

"Balcombe's gel? She's a bit odd, isn't she?" He winced and apologized, demonstrating that he maybe wasn't a complete dolt, though Beck wasn't sure he believed that. "Had a bit of whiskey tonight, and sometimes my tongue gets ahead of me!" Haywood laughed and took another drink, clearly not at all concerned that he was on his way to being drunk and perhaps having an even more negligent tongue. "I hope you'll be very happy together. As happy as one can be in matrimony." He gave Beck a stern look and a nod for good measure.

"The advice I seek is regarding that, actually. You see, I have a mistress and she's proving a bit difficult." He rolled his eyes and tried not to choke on the revolting tale. "She's threatened to reveal herself to my wife, which I just can't have."

"Have you tried paying her off? That's the easiest way to rid yourself of a clinging bitch."

God, he was awful. "Yes, but I'm not sure I can trust her to remain quiet."

"Have a contract drawn up. Hell, you can even write it yourself and say your solicitor did. That usually scares the cheek right out of them."

"You seem to have considerable experience."

Haywood shrugged. "You're the one who called me an expert." He laughed again, then finished his whiskey. His gaze roved until he spotted a footman, who inclined his head, indicating he'd fetch another glass.

Lowering his voice, Haywood leaned over the table and angled himself toward Beck. "If that course of action won't work, may I suggest pennyroyal? It's known to take care of unwanted babes, but if the bitch takes enough, you may be free of her entirely." His brows climbed toward his bald pate just before he narrowed his eyes with a knowing tip of his head.

The words sank into Beck's brain with a searing agony. Was that what he'd done to Helen? She'd been poisoned. Had she been with child? Beck nearly exploded in that moment.

But he held himself together. Instead, he feigned surprise. "Are you suggesting she could…die?"

Haywood flinched and waved his hand toward the floor because the footman had just arrived with his whiskey. The man swept up the empty glass and left before Haywood answered. "It can happen," he whispered. "I gave it to a gel once—years ago—and she took too much of it, not that I minded. She demanded I marry her. Because of a babe, of course.

But I'd no intention of doing that. Wasn't quite ready to settle." He stuck his lips out in an exaggerated pout. "Who was that?" The blackguard didn't even remember.

It had to be Helen. It *had* to be.

With a shrug, Haywood picked up his new glass. "In any case, it was very effective, and I've relied on it a few times since. Pennyroyal—you can get it from any apothecary."

Rage poured through Beck, almost paralyzing him. But he leaned close to Haywood as the man brought the tumbler to his lips. "Was her name Helen?" Beck whispered silkily. "Small, with dark hair, almost like a woodland fairy."

Haywood blinked at him, the glass arrested at his mouth. "Yes, that was her." Awareness crept over Haywood's features.

"She looked nothing like me, despite the fact that we shared a father." Beck snarled. "You murdered my sister, you son of a bitch." He shoved at Haywood, sending the whiskey sloshing into his face and him sprawling from his chair.

From an ungainly heap on the floor, Haywood wiped at his face. "She was your sister? Helen *Beckett*. Christ, I'd forgotten." His face went completely white. "I didn't murder her. We just wanted to get rid of the babe."

"'We,'" Beck spat. "There was no 'we,' just you exerting your control over a vulnerable young woman. Get up."

Haywood flinched. "Why?"

"So I can bloody challenge you."

The man went even paler, if that were possible, and it seemed it was. "No."

"Then I'll do it while you lie there like a coward." Everyone in the room had turned toward the commotion, and now Beck raised his voice to ensure they heard him. "I demand satisfaction. For the murder of my sister. Name your second. Mine is the Earl of Ware." Beck hadn't asked him, of course, but was certain Felix would agree. Hell, they couldn't duel tomorrow—it was Sunday. "Dawn on Monday. Hyde Park." He leaned down, baring his teeth. "And don't think to escape town tomorrow. I *will* find you."

Goodwin returned and helped Haywood to his feet. Haywood wiped ineffectually at his face.

Beck gave in to the fury. "You missed a spot." He sent his fist into the man's chin, splitting his lip. Haywood went down again as blood ran from the cut.

"Was that necessary?" Goodwin asked angrily.

"More than." Beck leaned over Haywood. "Send the name of your second to Ware by noon tomorrow along with your choice of weapon. I'm quite skilled with either pistol or sword."

With a final sneer, Beck turned and stalked from the room. On his way downstairs, he passed curious gentlemen eager to get up to the coffee room to see what was happening. News of the altercation had spread and would continue to do so.

He put it from his mind and strode from the club. He could hardly wait for Monday.

❧

BECK HAD ARRIVED for church just before the service began, barely stealing in to sit beside Lavinia. They didn't have a chance to speak, but she sent him a warm smile and brushed her hand over his. He flinched, his hand jerking slightly. Her smile faded, but he gave her fingers a quick, reassuring squeeze.

After the service, they walked out to the vestibule, where several people congratulated them on their upcoming nuptials. Lavinia was growing weary of all the attention, particularly since everyone felt it necessary to point out the brevity of their engagement, as if it were an oddity, which it wasn't. She began to regret not obtaining the special license. She and Beck could be married tomorrow instead of in a fortnight.

Lavinia's mother joined a small group of women in the corner while her father congregated with a handful of other gentlemen. As soon as she and Beck were without company, she took his hand. "Is something the matter with your hand?"

Before he could answer, her father strode toward them, his brow dark. He glared at Beck. "I think we should go outside. *Now.*"

Beck didn't look the least bit surprised at her father's tone or his expression of rage. Perhaps because Beck didn't realize that her father *never* looked like that.

"Yes, I suppose we should." Beck sounded resigned as he turned toward the exit.

Lavinia tightened her grip on his hand. "I'm coming with you."

Father glowered at her. "No. This isn't a conversation for young ladies."

"If it concerns Beck, it concerns me." She wasn't going to let him exclude her. Curling her hand around Beck's arm, she led them both outside.

They moved to the side of the door, and her father didn't waste a moment getting to his point. "What the devil are you about, challenging Haywood to a duel?"

Beck's muscles tensed beneath her fingertips just as

her muscles loosened, and she worried she was going to pitch over. "It was necessary." Beck's tone was clipped and coated in ice.

Lavinia turned and took her arm from his. Her legs were wobbly, but she refused to show any weakness. She stared at Beck, whose gaze was stoic, his mouth set in a hard line. She barely recognized this man. "You challenged Haywood to a duel?"

"He murdered my sister."

Now she wavered, and Beck's arms shot out to steady her. His face folded with concern. "Are you all right?"

"*No*. Your sister was murdered, and you're going to duel someone. How can I possibly be all right?"

"If he indeed had something to do with her death—I didn't even realize she'd been murdered." Her father blanched. "If he was involved, you must notify Bow Street."

"He admitted it to my face. I demanded satisfaction." Beck stared at her father with scorching heat. "You mean to tell me that if a man killed your sister and got away with it for sixteen years, you wouldn't want satisfaction?"

Father glanced away briefly before looking at Beck with pity. "I understand. However, without a father here to guide you, I hope you'll allow my counsel. This is not the way."

"No, it isn't," Lavinia said. She turned to her father, grateful for the care he was showing to her future husband. "Father, I'm going to have Beck drive me home in his phaeton." She wasn't asking permission. "I'll see you shortly." She went and kissed him on the cheek, eliciting a small grunt of surprise from him.

He looked at Beck. "Think about what I said."

Beck didn't respond as he offered his arm to Lavinia and escorted her to his vehicle. After he helped her inside, he said, "You're not going to change my mind."

"I must. We're to be married in a fortnight. I'd rather not have to bury you first." She was trying to inject a bit of levity but ended up feeling a stab of distress.

"You're not going to bury me. Haywood's a coward and probably a terrible shot."

"Then I don't want his death upsetting the start of our life together." She turned toward him as he drove the phaeton into the street. "Please, Beck, you can't do this."

"I can and I must. He killed my sister."

She could feel the fury coming off him in waves, as if he were a raging bonfire. Maybe she could calm him down a bit and find some reason. "What happened? Is this why you were acting strangely at the ball last night?"

It took him a moment to respond. He seemed to have difficulty finding words today, which was odd since words were so much a part of who he was. "I received a letter from my sister Margaret. She said Haywood was the man who'd given my sister hope for a union. Given his reputation, I wanted to know what happened, so I asked him for advice with my mistress."

She didn't think it was possible to feel any more distressed. "You have a mistress?"

"Of course not," he said in a rush. "I meant what I told you yesterday. I love *you*, Lavinia. There is only you."

And Haywood, apparently. Obviously, Beck didn't love him, but right now he was standing between her and the man she loved.

"He suggested I dispose of her with pennyroyal,

which is toxic in large amounts."

Lavinia had heard of that herb. "It's also used to get rid of unwanted babes." Her voice was low, disbelieving. "Was your sister...with child?" She watched as his hands clenched the reins and the muscles in his jaw tightened.

"Yes. And he didn't want to marry her, so he killed her." He swallowed. "I'm just glad my father isn't here. Actually, I hate that he went to his grave thinking Helen took her own life." His voice broke at the end.

Lavinia wanted to hold him, but she couldn't without causing an accident. She touched his arm as tears stung her eyes. "I'm so sorry. I can understand how you feel."

"I don't think you can. If you could, you'd know that I have to meet him tomorrow. My sister's honor is at stake. Do you know how awful it's been for my family to live with the knowledge that she killed herself and to keep that secret to protect her and our family?" His voice rose. "It's bloody torture, and it was all unnecessary. She *didn't* kill herself. Haywood killed her. And an innocent child."

Nausea swirled in Lavinia's gut. The anguish in his voice forced the tears from her eyes, and they tracked down her cheeks. "Which is why you can't kill him. He did wrong. *You* must not. If he admitted the crime, you can have him arrested. He'll be tried and hanged."

"Perhaps. Or perhaps the judge will show him mercy, and he'll only be transported or even less. He's a peer, and I doubt he'll hang. Lavinia, he deserves to die for what he did. Painfully."

The darkness and hatred in his voice frightened her. "Listen to yourself," she said softly. "You aren't the Beck I know, the man I fell in love with."

They rode in silence for several minutes, until he turned onto Park Street. "I am the same man. This is me, Lavinia. All of me. I...feel...deeply."

Of course he did. How else could he write such beautiful poetry or play such wondrous music? He drew the phaeton to a stop in front of her house, and she turned fully to him.

She wiped her cheeks with the back of her glove. "I know you do, and I love you so much for that. I know how much you must hate him, but if you kill him, you'll be wrecked. *Because* you feel so deeply."

"Lavinia, I can't let him walk away from this. I *can't.*"

"And I can't watch you do it. What if he kills you? What if *I* am with child, and I have to raise him or her without a father?"

His eyes widened slightly, and she felt a dash of hope that she'd finally broken through to him. "He won't. I'm going to kill Haywood tomorrow. It won't happen any other way." He climbed down and started around the phaeton, but she scrambled out by herself. She didn't want his help, not when he was behaving like a complete jackass.

He frowned at her. "I was going to help you down."

"I know. But I don't want your help right now. I'm not even sure I want to marry you right now. What sort of marriage are we to have if you won't listen to me?"

"*I* won't listen to *you*? It's as if you didn't even hear that *he killed my sister.*" His eyes blazed as he stared down at her.

"Yes, I heard you," she said sharply. "And the solution is to have him arrested, not risk your life. Or break the law. Dueling is illegal!"

"No one will fault me for this."

"I can see there's no talking sense into you. I can

only imagine what the next fifty years will be like."

"What are you saying?" His voice went dangerously low.

"I'm saying you're a stubborn toad, and now I'm going inside. If you don't cancel this duel, I—" She wasn't sure what. She loved him. So much. But this cloud around him was far more troubling than she'd realized. If he wouldn't listen to her, could she stand by and watch him drown in anger or despair?

"You'll what?" he asked softly.

"I don't know. And please don't make me find out." She turned and went inside, where, for the first time in her life, she went promptly and thoroughly to pieces.

Chapter Seventeen

❦

Sweet lady of science, you temper the fire,
And tame my wild heart that churns on the pyre.
Love lost in wonder where words and song dwell,
Don thy sweet brightness and break this black spell.
With warmth and passion, you bless this poor knave
My soul and future, you surely have saved.

-Beck's writings

BECK JUMPED FROM his phaeton, his mood darker than it had been before he'd gone to church, which he'd never imagined possible. The groom took charge of the vehicle as Beck stormed to the door, which Gage opened with considerable haste.

"You're in a hurry, my lord."

He grunted in response and hastened to his office, slamming the door behind him. Divesting himself of his hat, gloves, coat, cravat, and waistcoat, he picked up a guitar and began to play. Loudly. Discordantly. With vengeance and hatred and despair.

Then he did the unthinkable. He slammed the instrument into the hearth. Wood splintered—some flying and some falling into the coals. He held the ruined guitar and sank to the floor, where he sat for an indeterminate amount of time.

He tossed the guitar aside and lay down across the

carpet, stretching his legs out as he stared at the ceiling. Somewhere inside, a small piece of him worried she was right—that killing Haywood would wreck him. But he couldn't let it go.

He heard voices in the next room and sat up a moment before there was a knock on his door. "Come."

Gage stepped inside and closed the door behind him. "My lord, a Bow Street Runner is here to see you."

Fuck.

Gage offered his hand, which Beck clasped, and the butler pulled him to his feet. "He's in the sitting room."

Beck went looking for his discarded clothing, but Gage came up with the waistcoat and cravat first. His gaze drifted to the ruined guitar as Beck donned his waistcoat. "Was there a problem with your instrument?" Gage asked.

"No."

Taking the cravat, Beck wound it around his neck, not particularly caring if it was tied well. Gage stepped forward and took over, tying the silk with expert flicks of his fingers. When he was finished, he retrieved Beck's coat and brought it around for Beck to shrug into.

"Better," Gage said softly before opening the door.

Beck went into the sitting room, where a stocky fellow with a thick head of dark red hair was waiting near the window. He turned and bowed. "Good afternoon, my lord. I've come to speak with you about Lord Haywood."

There was no surprise, just severe disappointment. He wanted to ask who had turned Haywood in to Bow Street, but was certain he knew. Beck said nothing. He just stood and waited for the Runner to continue.

"Name's Mason," he said. "Do you mind if I sit?"

"No."

The Runner eyed the settee but rested his uncertain gaze on Beck and ultimately didn't move. "I understand Lord Haywood confessed a crime to you."

He couldn't deny it. Just as he couldn't kill the man—not now. "A murder."

"Yes." The Runner shifted uncomfortably, his neck coloring a bit. "Your sister, I gather. That must have been a shock. I can see why you didn't immediately come forward." It was an obvious fiction, and they both knew it. But the Runner couldn't mention the duel.

"How did you find out?" He hadn't meant to ask, but the question leapt from his mouth.

"Several people, actually. Lord Balcombe and his daughter paid a visit, as did Lord Ware."

Fucking *Felix* had gone behind his back? Beck worried he was going to break a second guitar when they were finished. No, he wouldn't do that.

"Can you provide testimony detailing what Lord Haywood said?"

"Yes." The thought of having to relive what that beast had done to Helen hollowed him from the inside. "When?"

"Now, if you're able."

"Fine." He finally sat, taking a chair near the hearth and sitting ramrod straight while he repeated precisely what Haywood had said. He finished by saying, "He should hang."

"And he may." The Runner had sat on the settee and now stood. "Thank you for your time, my lord. You'll hear from me very soon."

He strode from the room, and Beck collapsed back

against the chair.

A few moments later, Gage came in, his gait halting, his stature a bit…slumped. He stopped near the settee and looked over at Beck.

"I'm incredibly sorry for what happened to your sister."

Beck wasn't surprised to hear Gage had listened. He did that sometimes, and in every single case, it was something Beck hadn't wanted to repeat but didn't mind Gage knowing. "You've a gift for being exactly where I need you, when I need you."

"I do try."

"Sit." Beck inclined his head toward the settee. "If you want."

Gage lowered himself—slowly—onto the cushion. "I perceived you were in a particular state. Yesterday and then today with the guitar. It's strange enough that you became engaged without a hint of it, and then all this with your sister."

Beck pressed his lips together, thinking about Gage's perceptions. "You think my betrothal is somehow related to…this?"

"Not directly. But your emotions, which run very deep, as we know, are perhaps at an all-time fervor. High and low—your betrothal made you happy, did it not?"

"More than I've ever been. I love her beyond anything, Gage." As angry as he was at her right now, as betrayed as he felt, he loved her.

Gage's expression softened. "I suspected as much. And yet learning what happened to Miss Beckett has sent you to the opposite end of the spectrum."

"Yes." he barely croaked the word out, his mind tumbling into a ravine where sunlight spilled over the tangle of vines and branches that sought to pin him down. He looked up at the light. He *wanted* the light. Lavinia was his light.

"Perhaps there is a way for you to move to the other end. The end where Lady Lavinia resides. Rather, your feelings for her."

"I was just thinking that." Words formed and joined in his head. The shadows gave way to a warm glow, but not completely. It wasn't ever that easy.

Beck stood. "I need to write."

"Of course." Gage rose. "Shall I begin the transformation of this room into her ladyship's office?"

"Yes, and have the door cut," Beck said. He went toward the door and paused at the threshold, turning. "Thank you, Gage. I never say it enough, but without you, I fear I would have drowned in the abyss long ago."

"It is my pleasure to provide assistance. Of any kind. And may I say how pleased the staff is to hear of your engagement. If you are amenable, we should like to raise a toast to you this evening."

"I should like that very much, thank you." Beck turned and went to his office with a far lighter step than when he'd left.

Once again, he tore away his outer clothing, then he sat down and began to write.

◆℈•3◆

THIS HAD BEEN one of the longest days of Lavinia's life. She felt utterly drained and could barely make the effort to brush her hair. But since she'd sent Carrin off to bed, she supposed she must.

She picked up her brush and went to sit in front of

the windows. The candlelight from the table next to her bed cast a warm glow, and she was soon lulled into a semidazed state. It was the most serene she'd felt all day.

Except for those few moments in church when she'd sat beside Beck, his body lightly touching hers, his scent filling the air around her, her love for him filling her with joy.

She still loved him. Even if he hated her. Which he might after what she'd done that afternoon.

She'd escaped to her room to compose herself before her parents had arrived home, but a short time later, her father—*her father*—had come up to see her. She said she wanted to report Haywood's crime to Bow Street. Her father had been supportive and patient, and he'd insisted on accompanying her. Not just because he had to, but because he wanted to stand at her side. She'd appreciated it very much.

Afterward, they'd come home and spent a quiet afternoon and evening. They'd even played cards together after dinner. She didn't remember the last time she'd enjoyed their company so much. Her melancholy remained, however, as she wondered how Beck had reacted to Bow Street's visit.

The Runner had told her he would go and talk to him. They needed to hear his testimony about what Haywood had said. She expected he was furious with her. The question was how furious. Angry enough to call off the wedding?

Terrified she was making a mistake, she'd wondered if she should do the same. She barely understood his moods and emotions.

But the thought of not being with him made the melancholy worse. She recalled what he'd said, that he couldn't imagine a future without her. Well, she didn't want one without him.

The strains of a melody drifted to her, like an echo on the wind. She opened her eyes, not even aware she'd closed them, and set down her brush to listen.

The sound grew louder. Was it coming from outside?

She stood and went to the window, squinting down onto the street. There, standing in the light of the lamp, was Beck. Strumming his guitar.

She opened the sash and pushed at the window.

And he was singing.

His voice, as she'd suspected, was beautiful. A rich baritone that hummed across her skin and burrowed into her soul. The words were for her—of love and the future and a light so bright, it blinded him.

She turned to her bedside table and reached for her glasses. Sliding them onto her face, she returned to the window and leaned out to listen. He played and sang, and she fell in love with him all over again.

He finished, pausing for just a moment, then started again. Was he just going to play the song over and over? As much as she wanted to listen to it over and over, she wanted something else more.

She went to the armoire and found a dressing gown. Wrapping it tightly around herself and tying the sash, she raced down two flights of stairs and flew across the hall. The footman barely made it to the door to open it in time.

When she went outside, Beck was still playing. The night was cool and damp with the promise of rain.

She walked out to the pavement and leaned against the railing to listen to the song once more. This time when he finished, he lowered his guitar and came toward her.

"Should I keep playing?" he asked.

"Yes!" a neighbor from across the street called from her front door.

"Don't stop!" came another call from the house to their left.

Lavinia giggled. "I'm afraid you may be in trouble now that your secret's out."

"What secret is that?"

"Your talent with the guitar—and your voice." She mock-scowled at him. "You lied to me. You're a wonderful singer. You promised you wouldn't lie."

His brows arched. "And I didn't. Perception is everything. I think I'm a terrible singer, just as I think you in spectacles is the most beautiful thing I've ever seen. And just as I see that I was an ass." He tipped his head to the side and then righted it once more. "Rather, I see *your* perception that I was an ass. I still think I was maybe right."

She tensed, unsure of what that meant. "Are you angry with me?"

He shook his head. "I was. But I understand why you did it, and why it was the right thing to do. For everyone. Most of all for me. I think you were right that the darkness would claim me."

She moved toward him and touched his face, gently stroking her fingertips along his jaw, which was rough with the onset of his beard. "I wouldn't let it. I will never let it."

"Does that mean you're still going to marry me?"

"Of course. Assuming you still want me to."

He arched a brow. "My song didn't persuade you? Damn, I really am terrible."

She laughed. "You're wonderful. And you are *mine*. For all time."

A raindrop, fat and cold, landed on her nose. He leaned forward and licked it off, sending a shiver of delight along her flesh.

"I have to go," he said, his tone reluctant. "The rain isn't good for my guitar, and I can't afford to lose another one today."

"What happened?"

He winced. "That darkness crept in a little too far."

She pressed forward, and he held his guitar to the side so she could lean into his chest. "I'll buy you a new one."

"What a lovely wedding gift."

She wrapped her arms around him. "It's the least I can do since you gave me fossils."

"I'm also making the sitting room next to my office into your personal library and office. You'll have bookshelves with all manner of geological texts, fossils, and a door that leads directly to *my* office."

She grinned up at him. "I can't decide what I like best."

"Fortunately, you don't have to."

"You. You're the best part of all of it," she said softly. Then she stood on her toes and kissed him, her lips clinging to his as the rain began to fall in earnest. "Come inside!"

He glanced toward the house. "Your parents won't want me to."

"Nonsense, they'll be thrilled to know the wedding is still happening. My mother was on the verge of a nervous attack."

"It's late. I should go."

She took his hand and shook her head. "Come inside. I'm not taking no for an answer."

"I'm beginning to think you plan to win every

argument."

Laughing, she pulled him toward the house. "I do indeed."

He smiled, his gray-green eyes sparkling with love and desire. "And I may just let you."

Epilogue

❦

We walk in the garden, our hands entwined,
Surrounded by beauty, your love is mine.
We are one and the same, dear, you and I,
Naught shall part us, nor shall we say goodbye.

-The Marquess of Northam to his wife on their wedding day

Devon, August 1818

"ARE THEY BACK yet?" Beck's stepmother, Rachel, joined him in the garden.

He set his guitar down and leaned it against the bench where he'd been sitting. Rising, he looked toward the path that led to the beach a mile away. "No."

Lavinia and George had gone to look for fossils, one of their favorite pastimes on a beautiful summer day like today. That George preferred geology to learning to play guitar was just another example of a battle she'd won.

Beck smiled to himself. His wife was formidable and amazing.

"What are you smiling at?" Rachel asked.

"Just thinking of my wife," he said. "And George."

His stepmother peered at him from beneath the wide

brim of her bonnet. "You're quite changed since you wed. Lavinia has done you good."

"Was I beastly before?" he asked in mock offense.

She laughed softly. "Of course not. You just seem more…settled."

Yes, that was a good word to describe it. He still suffered from dark moods, but they were far less intrusive. He was working through them and finding his way back to the light. And yes, he credited Lavinia.

She'd guided him through the particularly horrid trial of Haywood, which had included the testimony of one of the other women he'd given pennyroyal—Lady Kipp-Landon. The woman had tearfully admitted that he'd gotten her with child and insisted she take the herb to dispose of it. She hadn't needed to because she'd ended up miscarrying, but her story had sealed the man's fate, and he was currently on his way to Australia. If he survived the voyage, he'd likely spend the rest of his life on the other side of the world.

Haywood had begged for mercy, and even Beck had been swayed. He'd seen the man's wife and children one day and had felt terrible for their loss. Lavinia had been so right when she'd said that killing Haywood would have wrecked him. Just knowing the villain would never see his family again had nearly done the same.

Following the trial, Lady Kipp-Landon had apologized to Beck for tormenting Helen. When Beck had asked her why she and Lady Abercrombie—who had retreated from Society for the remainder of the Season—had singled out Helen and why they'd suggested she kill herself, she'd broken down and said it was because of Haywood. Lady Kipp-Landon had been in love with him, and she'd wanted to push every other woman he paid attention to out of the way.

While Beck had wanted to know the truth, he couldn't say he was satisfied. The entire situation was just sad. Still, with Lavinia's help, he found the courage to let the darkness go.

Forgiveness, it seemed, wasn't something you granted to someone, but a gift you gave yourself. Once Beck had done that, he'd felt free.

"George likes her a great deal," Martha said, looking toward the path just as Lavinia and her son came into view. "Here they come." She turned to Beck. "I like her too."

How could they not? Lavinia was kind, generous, funny, and wickedly smart. In fact, she'd practically taken over George's studies in science. When he went off to school, he'd know more than most of his mates.

A few moments later, George and Lavinia strolled into the garden. George toted a basket, which contained today's treasures.

"Hungry for luncheon?" Rachel called.

"Famished!" George answered. He handed the basket to Lavinia, then veered toward the house and broke into a run.

Rachel laughed. "See you both inside."

Lavinia walked up to Beck and kissed him, her lips lingering on his.

"You taste like salt and wind," he said, inhaling her scent. "And you smell like perfection."

She wrinkled her nose. "What does that even smell like?"

Chuckling, he peered into the basket. "I'm going to have to build you a second library."

"Nonsense, Waverly Court's library is massive. I could collect fossils every day of my life and never fill it."

"Yes, but what if you add rocks from the Outer Hebrides?"

She looked up at him, her eyes widening. "Are we going?"

He nodded. "In a fortnight, if that meets with your approval."

She set the basket on the bench next to his guitar and threw her arms around his neck. "Oh yes!" She kissed the side of his face near his ear and whispered, "Thank you, Beck."

He encircled his arms around her and cupped her neck so he could kiss her. Time and space ceased to exist as he lost himself in her embrace, and it was some while before she lifted her lips from his. "We should go in to luncheon," she said.

"Or I could ravish you here."

"They can see from the house." Her voice held a smile.

"Have I ever told you that sometimes you're too sensible?"

"Often."

"After lunch, may I ravish you? I'll even let you choose the location."

"How can I refuse such a polite request? You're always so polite."

"Always? What about the time I tore your chemise? Or when I surprised you in the bath?"

"You still managed to make those occasions charming."

"Hmm, perhaps I shall write an ode to the sensible marchioness and her polite husband."

"Oh dear, they sound rather dull."

He looked down at her with a sultry smile. "I shall

make them exciting. Care to give me any ideas?"

"Oh yes. After lunch. In the library, I think." She lowered her lids in a seductive fashion. "You can help me put my new treasures away."

"Is that what we're calling it?"

She pressed another kiss to his lips then spun away from him, picking up the basket and starting toward the house. She looked over her shoulder. "Are you coming?"

"Not yet, but I will be after lunch." He picked up his guitar as she laughed at his double entendre.

When he caught up to her, she twined her arm through his and looked up at him. "I love you so, my mad but oh so polite poet."

He gazed at her beloved face, so full of emotion, he wondered how there ever could have been a void—but there had been. Until her. "And I love you my sensible, impatient scientist. For as long as the earth lives."

Her eyes shone with love. "And into eternity."

THE END

Thank You!

❦

Thank you so much for reading *The Duke of Seduction*. I hope you enjoyed it! Stay tuned for The Duke of Kisses featuring Fanny and The Duke of Mischief featuring Sarah and Felix! (A hero who's vowed never to love and his oldest friend's sister...what could go wrong?)

Would you like to know when my next book is available? You can sign up for my newsletter, follow me on Twitter at @darcyburke, or like my Facebook page at http://facebook.com/DarcyBurkeFans. I also have a reader group on Facebook called Darcy's Duchesses, which is a great place to hang out with other readers and chat with me. Find us at http://facebook.com/groups/DarcysDuchesses.

The Duke of Seduction is the tenth book in The Untouchables series. The next book in the series is *The Duke of Kisses*. Don't miss my other historical series: Secrets and Scandals and Legendary Rogues. If you like contemporary romance, I hope you'll check out my Ribbon Ridge series available from Avon Impulse and my latest series, which continues the lives and loves of Ribbon Ridge's denizens – So Hot.

I appreciate my readers so much. Thank you, thank you, *thank you*.

Acknowledgments

❊•❊•❊

When I decided I wanted to write poetry at the start of each chapter, I decided to take my husband up on one of his numerous offers to help. He's a guitarist and writes the occasional song (my daughter is a fantastic lyricist, but she was busy with things when I was writing this), so I asked if he could write some poetry in the style of Byron. He took the task very seriously and wrote all the poems. I think he did a fabulous job and you can check him out on the copyright page. Thank you, babe!

I also want to thank my amazing team: Jill, Kathy, Jenn, Sarah (and the rest of the fabulous folks at Social Butterfly!), Carrie, Elizabeth, Linda, and Toni. Huge thanks to Julie for all the plotting calls—we are insane but we wouldn't have it any other way!

I work a lot but try to always make time for the two most important people: my kids. On that note, I need to go watch a funny video with my son.

Books by Darcy Burke

Historical Romance

The Untouchables

The Forbidden Duke
The Duke of Daring
The Duke of Deception
The Duke of Desire
The Duke of Defiance
The Duke of Danger
The Duke of Ice
The Duke of Ruin
The Duke of Lies
The Duke of Seduction
The Duke of Kisses
The Duke of Mischief

Secrets and Scandals

Her Wicked Ways
His Wicked Heart
To Seduce a Scoundrel
To Love a Thief (a novella)
Never Love a Scoundrel
Scoundrel Ever After

Praise for Darcy Burke's
Secrets & Scandals Series

HER WICKED WAYS

"A bad girl heroine steals both the show and a highwayman's heart in Darcy Burke's deliciously wicked debut."

—Courtney Milan, *NYT* Bestselling Author

"…fast paced, very sexy, with engaging characters."

—Smexybooks

HIS WICKED HEART

"Intense and intriguing. Cinderella meets *Fight Club* in a historical romance packed with passion, action and secrets."

—Anna Campbell, *Seven Nights in a Rogue's Bed*

"A romance…to make you smile and sigh…a wonderful read!"

—Rogues Under the Covers

TO SEDUCE A SCOUNDREL

"Darcy Burke pulls no punches with this sexy, romantic page-turner. Sevrin and Philippa's story grabs you from the first scene and doesn't let go. To Seduce a Scoundrel is simply delicious!"

—Tessa Dare, *NYT* Bestselling Author

"I was captivated on the first page and didn't let go until this glorious book was finished!"

—Romancing the Book

TO LOVE A THIEF

"With refreshing circumstances surrounding both the hero and the heroine, a nice little mystery, and a touch of heat, this novella was a perfect way to pass the day."

–The Romanceaholic

"A refreshing read with a dash of danger and a little heat. For fans of honorable heroes and fun heroines who know what they want and take it."

-The Luv NV

NEVER LOVE A SCOUNDREL

"I loved the story of these two misfits thumbing their noses at society and finding love." Five stars.

–A Lust for Reading

"A nice mix of intrigue and passion...wonderfully complex characters, with flaws and quirks that will draw you in and steal your heart."

–BookTrib

SCOUNDREL EVER AFTER

"There is something so delicious about a bad boy, no matter what era he is from, and Ethan was definitely delicious."

-A Lust for Reading

"I loved the chemistry between the two main characters...Jagger/Ethan is not what he seems at all and neither is sweet society Miss Audrey. They are believably compatible."

-Confessions of a College Angel

Legendary Rogues Series
LADY of DESIRE

"A fast-paced mixture of adventure and romance, very much in the mould of *Romancing the Stone* or *Indiana Jones*."

-All About Romance

"...gave me such a book hangover! ...addictive...one of the most entertaining stories I've read this year!"

-Adria's Romance Reviews

ROMANCING the EARL

"Once again Darcy Burke takes an interesting story and...turns it into magic. An exceptionally well-written book."

-Bodice Rippers, Femme Fatale, and Fantasy

"...A fast paced story that was exciting and interesting. This is a definite must add to your book lists!"

-Kilts and Swords

LORD of FORTUNE

"I don't think I know enough superlatives to describe this book! It is wonderfully, magically delicious. It sucked me in from the very first sentence and didn't turn me loose—not even at the end ..."

-Flippin Pages

"If you love a deep, passionate romance with a bit of mystery, then this is the book for you!"

-Teatime and Books

The Untouchables Series
THE FORBIDDEN DUKE

"I LOVED this story!!" 5 Stars

-Historical Romance Lover

"This is a wonderful read and I can't wait to see what comes next in this amazing series..." 5 Stars

-Teatime and Books

THE DUKE of DARING

"You will not be able to put it down once you start. Such a good read."

-Books Need TLC

"An unconventional beauty set on life as a spinster meets the one man who might change her mind, only to find his painful past makes it impossible to love. A wonderfully emotional journey from attraction, to friendship, to a love that conquers all."

-Bronwen Evans, USA Today Bestselling Author

THE DUKE of DECEPTION

"...an enjoyable, well-paced story ... Ned and Aquilla are an engaging, well-matched couple — strong, caring and compassionate; and ...it's easy to believe that they will continue to be happy together long after the book is ended."

-All About Romance

"This is my favorite so far in the series! They had chemistry from the moment they met...their passion leaps off the pages."

-Sassy Book Lover

THE DUKE of DESIRE

"Masterfully written with great characterization...with a flourish toward characters, secrets, and romance... Must read addition to "The Untouchables" series!"

-My Book Addiction and More

"If you are looking for a truly endearing story about two people who take the path least travelled to find the other, with a side of 'YAH THAT'S HOT!' then this book is absolutely for you!"

-The Reading Cafe

THE DUKE of DEFIANCE

"This story was so beautifully written, and it hooked me from page one. I couldn't put the book down and just had to read it in one sitting even though it meant reading into the wee hours of the morning."

-Buried Under Romance

"I loved the Duke of Defiance! This is the kind of book you hate when it is over and I had to make myself stop reading just so I wouldn't have to leave the fun of Knighton's (aka Bran) and Joanna's story!"

-Behind Closed Doors Book Review

THE DUKE of DANGER

"The sparks fly between them right from the start... the HEA is certainly very hard-won, and well-deserved."

-All About Romance

"Another book hangover by Darcy! Every time I pick a favorite in this series, she tops it. The ending was perfect and made me want more."

-Sassy Book Lover

THE DUKE of ICE

"Each book gets better and better, and this novel was no exception. I think this one may be my fave yet! 5 out 5 for this reader!"

-Front Porch Romance

"An incredibly emotional story...I dare anyone to stop reading once the second half gets under way because this is intense!"

-Buried Under Romance

THE DUKE of RUIN

"This is a fast paced novel that held me until the last page."
-Guilty Pleasures Book Reviews

" ...everything I could ask for in a historical romance... impossible to stop reading."

-The Bookish Sisters

THE DUKE of LIES

"THE DUKE OF LIES is a work of genius! The characters are wonderfully complex, engaging; there is much mystery, and so many, many lies from so many people; I couldn't wait to see it all uncovered."

-Buried U

"..the epitome of romantic [with]...a bit of danger/action. The main characters are mature, fierce, passionate, and full of surprises. If you are a hopeless romantic and you love reading stories that'll leave you feeling like you're walking on clouds then you need to read this book or maybe even this entire series."

-The Bookish Sisters

Ribbon Ridge Series

A contemporary family saga featuring the Archer family of sextuplets who return to their small Oregon wine country town to confront tragedy and find love...

The "multilayered plot keeps readers invested in the story line, and the explicit sensuality adds to the excitement that will have readers craving the next Ribbon Ridge offering."
-Library Journal Starred Review on YOURS TO HOLD

"Darcy Burke writes a uniquely touching and heart-warming series about the love, pain, and joys of family as well as the love that feeds your soul when you meet "the one.""
-The Many Faces of Romance

I can't tell you how much I love this series. Each book gets better and better.
-Romancing the Readers

"Darcy Burke's Ribbon Ridge series is one of my all-time favorites. Fall in love with the Archer family, I know I did."
-Forever Book Lover

Ribbon Ridge: So Hot

SO GOOD

" ...worth the read with its well-written words, beautiful descriptions, and likeable characters...they are flirty, sexy and a match made in wine heaven."
-Harlequin Junkie Top Pick

"I absolutely love the characters in this book and the families. I honestly could not put it down and finished it in a day."

-Chin Up Mom

SO RIGHT

"This is another great story by Darcy Burke. Painting pictures with her words that make you want to sit and stare at them for hours. I love the banter between the characters and the general sense of fun and friendliness."

-The Ardent Reader

" ...the romance is emotional; the characters are spirited and passionate... "

-The Reading Café

SO WRONG

"As usual, Ms. Burke brings you fun characters and witty banter in this sweet hometown series. I loved the dance between Crystal and Jamie as they fought their attraction."

-The Many Faces of Romance

"I really love both this series and the Ribbon Ridge series from Darcy Burke. She has this way of taking your heart and ripping it right out of your chest one second and then the next you are laughing at something the characters are doing."

-Romancing the Readers

About the Author

◆⋅ε⋅϶⋅◆

Darcy Burke is the USA Today Bestselling Author of hot, action-packed historical and sexy, emotional contemporary romance. Darcy wrote her first book at age 11, a happily ever after about a swan addicted to magic and the female swan who loved him, with exceedingly poor illustrations.

A native Oregonian, Darcy lives on the edge of wine country with her guitar-strumming husband, their two hilarious kids who seem to have inherited the writing gene. They're a crazy cat family with two Bengal cats, a small, fame-seeking cat named after a fruit, and an older rescue Maine Coon who is the master of chill and five a.m. serenading. In her "spare" time Darcy is a serial volunteer enrolled in a 12-step program where one learns to say "no," but she keeps having to start over. Her happy places are Disneyland and Labor Day weekend at the Gorge. Visit Darcy online at http://www.darcyburke.com and sign up for her newsletter, follow her on Twitter at http://twitter.com/darcyburke, or like her Facebook page, http://www.facebook.com/darcyburkefans.

Made in the USA
Columbia, SC
29 August 2018